PRETTY IN PINK SLIP

JENNIFER SKULLY

Redwood Valley Publishing

ISBN: 978-1974099917

PRETTY IN PINK SLIP

After Office Hours, Book 3
By Jennifer Skully

She's a single mother. He's a brilliant CEO. And she's got something he wants. Badly.

Ivy Elliot dreams of being a stay-at-home mom, but in a career-oriented world, she's reluctant to admit it. Besides, she's a single mother and quitting work to homeschool her daughter just isn't an option. Asking for a raise, however, is an alternative. But when she works up the nerve, disaster strikes. Instead of a raise, Ivy gets the dreaded pink slip.

But Ivy is also handed the key to making her dream come true. If she sues the company for the terrible names her boss Rhonda called her when she asked for a raise... she might very well get millions.

Brett Baker has worked his whole life to be able to take a company of his own into the Fortune 500, and he's sitting on the cusp of his dream. Until Ivy could potentially ruin all his plans by suing the company for discrimination and harassment. He's got to use every weapon in his arsenal to make sure she doesn't do that.

Even if it means falling in love with her.

She gave her heart and soul to the wrong man once. Can she ever trust enough to give it all again?

Author Note: This book contains material intended for mature readers

Join Jasmine's newsletter for free books and updates on new releases, contests, freebies and exclusive content : http://bit.ly/SkullyNews

ACKNOWLEDGMENTS

Thank you to my special network of friends who support me, brainstorm with me, and encourage me: Bella Andre, Shelley Adina, Jenny Andersen, Jackie Yau, Ellen Higuchi, Kate Curran, Ava Bradley, Rosemary Gunn, Laurel Jacobson, and Lloyd Russell. Thank you to Rae Monet for such great covers! Thanks also to Nancy Warren and Linda McGinnis for all their input on the series. A special thank you to Nancy for the fabulous title, which, of course, drove the story! As always, my husband is the greatest, helping to make my writing career flourish and my life easier.

1

Brett Baker's smile was like something straight off a movie screen. It always made Ivy weak in the knees. Which was why she never failed to ask him if he had any new baby pictures of his granddaughter.

"Are you kidding?" Brett reached for the smart phone he kept in his suit pocket, dazzling Ivy with that gorgeous smile.

He was the sexiest grandfather she'd ever seen, obviously working out daily, his shoulders broad and his chest muscular beneath his white dress shirt. Sure she was partial to older men, but she liked his sense of humor, too. The entire company had celebrated his October birthday a couple of weeks ago in the cafeteria, and he'd enjoyed the joke as much as anyone when the fifty-two candles on the birthday cake set off the smoke alarm.

He leaned close over the sill of her office cubicle so he could show Ivy the picture and look at it himself, too. His aftershave was something subtle and tempting. Or maybe that was just his fresh morning-shower smell. "Will you look at that cutie?" He beamed at the picture. "She already knows how to smile."

The baby looked more like she was passing wind, but Ivy smiled and agreed right along with him. "So how old is she now?" Of course, she knew, but she liked to keep him talking.

He grinned, flipping to another picture. "My darling little Valerie was born on September twenty-third, so she's six weeks and six days old." He laughed, and Ivy felt the delicious vibration of it in the pit of her stomach. "My daughter's a math teacher," he explained, "and she actually adds in the hours and minutes, too. But I'll spare you that."

"Thank you so much."

She'd always thought of him as a workaholic because he was here before she arrived at eight and his car was still in the parking lot when she left at five. But though he was divorced, where his daughter and granddaughter were concerned, family was first. He'd even left a conference right in the middle when Megan went into labor. Sure he'd had two of his best executives, Parker Hunt and Gloria King, to take over for him, but his rush to his daughter's side had endeared him to Ivy. Made him more than *just* a CEO.

Of course, he wouldn't even know who she was if she didn't sit right between Grady's and Rhonda's offices.

The light on her console went out. "Grady's off the phone now."

"You can just wait," Brett called out to Grady. "We're looking at baby pictures."

She was pretty sure Grady did an eye roll. Since falling for Ivy's friend, Jordana Davis, Grady Masterson was a new man. He'd always been a great boss, but now he laughed more, smiled more.

"All right," Brett said to her softly. "Duty calls. And I know you're bored with all the pictures."

"I most definitely am not." Nothing about Brett Baker could ever bore her. "Please, drop by any time to show me more."

He laughed, turned the phone dark, and strolled into Grady's office.

Her pulse was racing. She'd actually sounded forward, even flirty. He was the CEO. She was just a lowly admin. He'd never notice her. Even if he did, it wasn't like anything would *ever* happen. And she didn't want it either. She'd gotten herself into one dicey relationship, and once was way more than enough. The only reason she didn't regret it was her six-year-old daughter Joy. She could never regret having Joy.

"Ivy."

Rhonda Clark's voice snapped through the open door of her office. Speaking of bosses...

Ivy had more than one, since Jordana had been promoted from Human Resources Admin to HR Manager. Now Ivy was admin for both Grady *and* Rhonda. But working for Rhonda wasn't supposed to take up more than half her time.

It should have been easy, and Ivy had wanted the additional duties for the extra money. But the raise she'd been hoping for hadn't materialized. Rhonda said she was still in training, and since she didn't have a college degree... Rhonda always punctuated that with a shrug of her shoulders.

Not finishing her degree was the biggest regret of Ivy's life.

"I want that report on my desk first thing in the morning, Ivy." Rhonda stood in her open office door.

Rhonda always wanted things *first thing* in the morning. "I'll have it done," Ivy told her. Although it wasn't past ten in the morning, she already knew she'd have to work on the report tonight. Since she had to pick up Joy at five thirty, she'd never been able to stay late—which Rhonda knew—and she finished a lot of work after Joy went to bed. Of course, then, because she couldn't prove she'd been working, she didn't get paid for the overtime. In Rhonda's mind, she should be able to finish all these projects and reports *before* she left for the day.

"You'd get more work done if you did less fraternizing." Rhonda kept her voice low so it didn't carry into Grady's office.

"It wasn't fraternizing. It was just baby pictures." And it was Brett. How was Ivy supposed to say no to the CEO?

Because of her daughter, Ivy didn't date. She didn't want Joy to get attached only to have the guy leave. So Ivy's few relationships were conducted clandestinely, away from home. God, they weren't even relationships. They were more like... well, *not* relationships. And she hadn't had a *non*-relationship in over six months.

Therefore she deserved the few minutes she got up close and personal with Brett Baker and his baby pictures. The few heady minutes next to his body heat, with the smell of his aftershave swirling around her. She deserved them because she knew nothing would ever come of them.

"Well, I don't expect to see any overtime on this," Rhonda sniped at her. "You should be able to finish it before you leave."

Rhonda had no clue how long things took. She underestimated the effort required, usually by half.

Maybe it was time for a new job. Except that Ivy loved working for Grady. She'd even followed him here from his last position since they worked so well together. Plus she'd made good friends, especially Jordana and Gloria. She didn't want to leave. She didn't want to start over somewhere else with all the upheaval and uncertainty of a new job.

But whatever she did, she was *not* giving up any so-called fraternization with Brett Baker and his granddaughter's pictures.

"WEST COAST MANUFACTURES THIN FILM," GRADY WAS saying. "It would be perfect for our application. See here?"

Grady had a schematic up on his computer screen, but Brett wasn't concentrating. Standing next to the desk, looking over Grady's shoulder, Brett could see right into Ivy Elliot's cubicle between the two offices.

She typed away, then stopped, biting her lip, thinking as she pushed a silky lock of short dark hair behind her ear.

"Yeah. Let's bring their sales people in, see what they can offer," he told Grady. "And send me the website link, too."

But his gaze was on Ivy. He'd taken stock of her skirmish with Rhonda, though he hadn't been able to hear what it was about. Rhonda was both his blessing and his curse. Her knowledge in the Human Relations field was invaluable, often averting disasters before they happened, and her instincts about new hires were spot on. But she had favorites, and just as quickly held grudges.

He had a feeling she'd taken a dislike to Ivy Elliot.

That situation—and Ivy, especially Ivy—would bear watching.

"SHE'S DRIVING ME CRAZY," IVY TOLD JORDANA AND Gloria over a small bowl of chili for lunch. She was on a budget and brown-bagged it most days, but once a week they all went out, usually on Friday. Despite the fact that it was only Thursday, after the morning she'd had with Rhonda, she'd needed a good talk with friends who understood.

Both Jordana and Gloria had their run-ins with Rhonda. And those battles seemed to be increasing to outright warfare.

"You can't let her walk all over you," Jordana said. They'd

chosen a diner for lunch, and Jordana had ordered the grilled ham and cheese while Gloria had the Chinese chicken salad.

Ivy's mouth watered for a taste of both. And some French Fries. Maybe she'd make Joy grilled cheese sandwiches for dinner. Comfort food.

Gloria snorted. "No one can *stop* Rhonda walking all over them, Jordana, and you know it."

Jordana hung her head, wagging it sadly, her long brunette hair barely missing the blotch of ketchup on her plate. "Yes, I know. But I've got Grady to stick up for me, and you've got Parker. Poor Ivy doesn't have anyone."

Poor Ivy. Neither of them needed someone else to fight their battles. They both handled their clashes with Rhonda so much better than Ivy did. She didn't seem to have what it took to stand up to Rhonda the way she knew she should.

Not that she was going to admit that to her friends.

"Girls, girls," she jumped in. "I can totally handle it. But only because I've got you guys to whine to."

"We need a better strategy." Gloria speared a mandarin and chewed thoughtfully. She was beautiful—and Ivy would *not* add *for her age* to that. At forty-eight—she'd had a birthday just a few weeks ago but her candles hadn't set off the smoke alarm—Gloria was the kind of sophisticated, elegant woman Ivy strove to be: self-controlled, smart, confident, articulate. Which were all the reasons Parker Hunt had fallen for her.

Ivy equally admired Jordana, who was only thirty. Yes, she was four years younger than Ivy, but she was already a manager, a position for which she'd had to go up against Rhonda. And she'd won. She was totally together. Plus she'd completely wowed Grady.

Ivy suddenly wondered if she were jealous. Jordana had Grady. And though Gloria and Parker had been together officially for only a month, they were meant for each other. For her friends, it was more than just having someone to back them against Rhonda. It was having someone to share everything else with. A man to go home to.

But Ivy had Joy. That was more than enough for her.

Except sometimes, late at night, alone in her bed. But really, been there done that, got the T-shirt and the heartache to prove it. If she could find the *perfect* man, maybe. But after Parker and Grady, how many more perfect men could there be?

An image of Brett Baker, gorgeous smile and toned body, jumped into her mind.

No. No, no, no. He wasn't even a fantasy. He was the CEO.

"Earth to Ivy." Jordana nudged her. "We need a strategy."

Ivy smiled big. "I totally love that you guys use the royal *we*."

"The three musketeers," Gloria said sweetly and honestly, tucking her blond hair behind her ear. "We're going to do everything we can for you."

Ivy let her spoon plop into her chili. "You're right. I *am* letting her walk all over me."

Her mother had called her a doormat. Joy's father had left Ivy high and dry when he found out she was pregnant. After treating her like a doormat for years. He hadn't married her, and he'd even claimed Joy wasn't his child.

So Ivy had to admit she had a history of allowing people to take advantage. If she thought about it too much, she felt like a failure. Especially since she hadn't finished her college degree either.

"I didn't mean anything negative," Jordana said. "Just that—"

Ivy flapped her hand. "I know what you meant. You guys have been telling me all along. And I keep telling you I can handle it, but I don't. Honestly, I know you want to just step in and *do* something," she stressed. "But really, we're all waiting for *me* to do *something*." Why couldn't she be as strong as Jordana or Gloria?

"You work for Grady, too, you know. Rhonda's monopolizing your time."

"Actually, she's not. I take it home with me."

Jordana shook her finger at her. "But you don't get paid for it. That's just wrong. And it's illegal. You can't expect hourly employees to work off the clock and not pay them."

Ivy tipped her head. "Do you believe I'm inefficient?" She stopped Gloria when she opened her mouth to protest. "I'm serious. Rhonda claims I work hard, but I don't work smart."

"She's crazy," Jordana retorted, her teeth grinding.

"How did she ever get into Human Resources when she actually hates people?" Gloria asked. It was rhetorical because no one had answers about Rhonda.

But maybe Rhonda had a point. Ivy had worked hard in college. But she'd never graduated. Instead, she'd fallen in love with her professor. Who had eventually become Joy's father. And he'd left her.

She wasn't doing *something* right. Except for raising Joy. Her daughter was her only success. What Ivy really wanted was to stay home with Joy, homeschool her, help her get the absolute best start in life. Instead, Joy went to a *decent* school in a *decent* neighborhood because that's all Ivy could afford. She wanted more than *decent* for Joy. She wanted exceptional.

But now, even when they were together, she was giving her daughter short shrift because she worked in the evenings. And didn't get paid for it.

"No," she said, as if the girls had said something. "I'm doing a good job."

"A *great* job. Grady certainly knows it," Jordana reinforced.

Ivy continued to bolster herself. "If the work can't get done during office hours, then the expectations are way too high."

"Of course they are." Gloria leaned forward in earnest agreement. "You're right, we do want to step in and make it all better for you. Strangling Rhonda would be the best idea."

"But you might get arrested," Jordana observed with total solemnity.

Gloria grinned evilly. "Not if you both cover for me."

Just like Grady, after Parker had come back into her life, Gloria had started smiling more, laughing more. Making more jokes. But Ivy was deadly serious right now. "I really appreciate the support—" Jordana and Gloria had become her rocks over the past couple of months. "—but I'm not a little girl with a booboo you can fix. I can't go to the HR Manager and say my boss is mistreating me. I can't go to my other boss and say that either. This problem is mine to solve."

She had to tackle Rhonda, to prove to herself that she was strong enough. She would force Rhonda to acknowledge that there needed to be compensation for the constant underestimating of her time. "If she can't assess the job properly, I'll just have to make her pay for my overtime."

Both Gloria and Jordana raised their hands. "You go, girl."

They all high-fived in the center of the table.

"But let me ask you this," Gloria said, her head tipped to the side. "What do you *really* want to do? What I mean is that you're sort of falling into Human Resources."

"Or," Jordana added, "we're pushing you into it."

The chili suddenly seemed way too spicy and Ivy's cheeks heated. She wasn't sure she wanted to answer these questions. "Of course you're not pushing. I want to move up. I need the money for Joy."

"Yes, but," Gloria persisted, "sometimes we get locked

into jobs we don't really like. Especially if it's just about the money."

Ivy's chili was definitely too hot, burning her throat a little. It wasn't about the questions. It was about her failures. About the dreams she would never realize. And about wanting to do something that would be frowned on in a career-oriented world.

"Come on, spill," Jordana urged. "I can see it written all over you."

"It's really not possible," she said softly.

"Everything's possible." Gloria's voice was just as soft, encouraging Ivy's confidences.

For Gloria, everything was possible because she was at the top of her field. She hadn't dropped out of college. She hadn't had a baby she couldn't afford to raise. She'd made good choices.

"We'd really love to know."

Ivy didn't have friends. At least not until these two women had taken her under their wings. She hadn't confided things in years, except to her mother, who'd never been the most sympathetic ear. She'd even forgotten what it was like to have someone to share your feelings with. To talk with about your dreams, as silly as they might seem. "It sounds dumb, but what I'd like to do more than anything is homeschool Joy." She'd even love to have more children, homeschool them all, be a full-time mom. But then she'd need a husband.

"Wow," Jordana said. "That's amazing. I could never do that, but it sounds fabulous."

"That's perfect," Gloria said, setting down her fork, her eyes narrowed. "Maybe you could make a business out of it by starting a day care."

Ivy groaned. "Yeah, but then I'd have to deal with other people's issues all the time. And believe me, I see how badly some of those moms can behave."

Jordana licked crumbs off her finger and thumb. "Don't kids who get homeschooled become sort of isolated and maybe even antisocial? Because they're never around other kids?"

"It's not like that at all. There are online communities of homeschoolers. The kids get together for outings and projects, sports, all sorts of activities."

Jordana blinked, then smiled. "Learn something new every day."

"It sounds like you've really looked into this." Gloria gave her a thoughtful, considering gaze.

"It's just a pipedream. And really, after the women's movement, aren't we all supposed to be out there earning more money and making our way in a man's world?" Right, which was why she was still a secretary. And embarrassed about a silly dream, especially with two friends who were climbing the corporate ladder.

"The essence of feminism," Gloria said, "is the freedom to do what you want, whether it's being President of the United States or a stay-at-home mom."

"That's beautiful," Jordana said, awe in her voice.

Ivy felt the same awe. But there was also reality. "You still have to support your kid. And without a partner to help..." She shrugged with the impossibility of it.

"But maybe you could think of a way to have both," Gloria suggested, staring across the room, as if she were already devising a plan. "Some way of making a career out of homeschooling."

"Like homeschooling other people's kids?" Jordana asked.

Gloria shrugged and nodded. "Maybe."

"Or," Ivy said, pausing, thinking, "doing something with outside programs and activities for homeschoolers." It was just an idea, encouraged by friends who thought outside the box. It would probably never come to anything. And yet it was nice to dream.

Before considering anything else, however, she needed to tackle Rhonda.

Ivy could never be strong enough to create her own specialized business if she couldn't even handle a difficult boss.

2

Overnight Ivy had been too busy with her plan of attack to give any more thought to Gloria's suggestion about changing career paths. Instead she'd looked up regulations in some online manuals—in addition to finishing Rhonda's project.

She had a right to a raise, and she had extremely good reasons to back up her request. There was no way Rhonda could beat her down. Especially since before finally going to bed, she'd emailed the report Rhonda had requested.

Thank God it was Friday, which was always good for tackling unpleasant tasks so you didn't have to obsess about them over the weekend. She'd wanted to get the confrontation out of the way first thing—to quote Rhonda—but Rhonda had been in with Brett for a while, both speaking intensely. Then Grady had required her attention, and it was almost eleven before she got a chance.

When the opportunity finally came, she stepped up to Rhonda's door with confidence. She would make this work. She could be strong like Gloria and Jordana. "Have you got a minute?"

Rhonda looked up from a folder on her tidy desk. The office was orderly, with filing cabinets, a credenza, a small conference table, but no plants or personal pictures. After being asked, most people would say *Sure* or *Of course*, but Rhonda just gazed at her unblinkingly. Ivy took the look for an invitation. She closed the door behind her, glad that Rhonda's second door at the front of the office was also closed.

"I hope the report was satisfactory." Ivy started with an ice breaker. Rhonda was like a frozen block that needed chipping away.

"Thanks. It was well done."

A compliment. Would miracles never cease. "I wanted to talk to you about that. I had to work on it at home last night."

Rhonda's nostrils flared. She was a matronly woman whose face had a tendency to turn blotchy red when she was irritated. And blotches of red had suddenly bloomed on her cheeks. "We've already discussed that, Ivy. You should be able to complete these tasks during your normal working hours. I'm not asking for too much."

Trust Rhonda to shoot her down before she'd even asked for anything. But she *wasn't* going to be put off so easily. "I had no trouble accomplishing all my tasks when I worked for Grady," she said firmly. "But I've got double the work now." She launched into her explanation. "Because I have to pick up my daughter, I can't stay late most days, and I'm taking home many of the projects you give me, where I don't get paid for it. And on the days when you've *insisted* I stay after five—" She used the word purposely and watched Rhonda's eyes narrow, but it was a calculated risk. "—I've had to pay a premium at the day care for my daughter."

She was surprised Rhonda had said nothing, just let her go on, but Ivy took advantage of it. "I have more responsibility dealing with employees as well. Plus there's juggling both yours and Grady's scheduling."

Finally, Rhonda broke in. "So, you want a promotion." Her tone was soft and hard.

Ivy got a bad feeling. "No. Not a promotion. But I've proven—" She was very careful not to add the word *think* in there. She didn't *think* she'd proven herself, she *had.* "—that I'm a valuable asset to the HR Department, more than just the admin I was for Grady."

Rhonda stood, her chair rolling back slowly. She pivoted, her hands clasped behind her, and ambled out from the desk. She reminded Ivy of an old movie about a prisoner and a female Nazi commandant wearing sensible pumps and a knee-length skirt.

"So you want a raise," Rhonda said, her voice suspiciously mild as she sauntered closer.

Ivy had to stop herself from taking an instinctual step backward, like the prisoner from the commandant. Or prey from its predator. But her voice was solid when she spoke. "Yes. In the beginning we discussed a probationary period." Sort of. "And two months is sufficient." She again avoided that word *think.* She didn't *think* it was sufficient, it simply was.

"So tell me, did Jordana and Gloria put you up to this? I noticed you had lunch with them yesterday."

Ivy saw things going south. "Actually we didn't discuss a raise." That had been her idea. Jordana and Gloria had told her not to let Rhonda treat her like a doormat she could wipe her feet all over. "But Jordana and Gloria have nothing to do with this. This is about fairness and getting paid appropriately for the work I do."

"Appropriately?" Rhonda's chest rose and fell rapidly beneath her high-collared blouse. "Just like it was *appropriate*

—" Her voice snapped on the word and her pupils dilated. "—for Jordana to blackmail me into promoting her and for Grady to stick up for her because she was sleeping with him?" Her voice rose, not in volume but in pitch until she was hitting a high note. "And that Gloria King, who thinks she's better than everyone but all the while she's screwing the VP of Marketing? Who do you people think you are? You all want to force me out. Well, let me tell you, it's not happening. I can see right through what you're all doing."

Backing toward the door, Ivy wished fervently she hadn't closed it. Rhonda sounded a little crazy and paranoid, like Jordana and Gloria were trying to steal her power base. Like this was a coup they were planning together.

"So who are you sleeping with that you think you can come in here demanding a raise?"

This was ridiculous. She actually wondered if Rhonda was having a nervous breakdown. But she wasn't letting her walk all over her. "No one put me up to it. I deserve a raise."

"You deserve it." Spittle bubbled on Rhonda's lips. "You're nothing but a money-grubbing whore trying to blackmail me into giving you a raise because you think I can't run this department without you. Well, you can't hold this company hostage. You can't hold *me* hostage."

Ivy's anger flared. "Now wait one minute—"

"You're just some single mother who thinks that because you opened your legs for a man without benefit of marriage and produced a *child*, you don't have to work for anything. It's all about the children." Rhonda air-quoted, and the blotchy redness traveled from her cheeks down to her neck. "All you women, wearing your single motherhood like a badge, when all it really means is that you're a loser."

She could handle being called a whore and a blackmailer. But Ivy's stomach suddenly rolled at being a loser. Not just *called* a loser, but actually being one.

Rhonda went on relentlessly. "You don't know how to work hard. You just want a handout." She put her face an inch inside Ivy's personal space and muttered. "Being a single mother just spells failure."

All sorts of comebacks flew through her head. Rhonda was being unfair. She was vicious. Her attack was totally uncalled for. And completely over-the-top, even ridiculous. But those words. *Failure. Loser.* It was like looking at the last ten years of her life and seeing all the mistakes she'd made, falling for the wrong man, her professor no less, quitting school before she'd gotten her degree, failing to demand child support for her baby. Failing to give her daughter a better life. So many failures.

The only thing that made it through her strained vocal cords was, "All you really had to do was say no."

"No." Rhonda's eyes flared. "All I really had to say was that you're fired. I can easily find someone to do your job. Just like *that*." She snapped her fingers. "Because you're completely replaceable. So pack up your little kit bag and get out."

It was crazy. Like she'd stepped into the Tardis time machine with Dr. Who. Or fallen into Munchkinland with the wicked witch shaking her broomstick.

This couldn't be real. Rhonda couldn't actually fire her.

"Yes, I *can* fire you," Rhonda said as if she could read Ivy's thoughts. "Would you like me to point out the regulation which allows me to fire someone who tries to extort a raise or promotion?" She stomped past Ivy to her bookcase and grabbed a three-ring binder crammed with employee regulations.

Ivy summoned whatever dignity she could. "That won't be necessary." It would be mortifying to hear Rhonda quote a regulation.

She backed up, wary of taking her eyes off Rhonda. She

could straighten this out. She could fix it. She could quit working for a monster and go back to Grady full time. Couldn't she?

Or could Rhonda actually do this?

She opened the door, and across the way, Grady's office was empty.

Rhonda was suddenly right behind her, her voice low. "You can't run to him. And don't even think of running to Jordana either. *I* own this department, not her. Just get your stuff and get out. I'll send your final paycheck."

Her fingers were numb. She even felt faintly dizzy. She was sure she was in shock. Especially with the humiliating prick of tears at her eyes.

"I'll be watching you every second to make sure you don't steal any personnel files."

She absolutely would not cry in front of Rhonda. So Ivy did the only thing she could at that moment, she grabbed her purse, her photos of Joy, and the small cardboard box of snacks and sundries she kept in her drawer.

And walked away.

It was wrong on so many levels. Yet the words that chased her out were *loser*, *failure*, and *You're fired.*

Ivy didn't look into Jordana's office as she headed out to the second-floor landing. She thought only of escaping to a place where she could regroup. She pushed through, intent only on getting out.

And almost smacked the door into Brett Baker.

Oh no. No, no, no.

"Ivy?"

"Sorry. Just going out." She rushed past him, not caring how bad it looked.

Rhonda's voice hounded her. *Loser. Failure.*

She wasn't a loser because she was a single mother. She

was a loser for all the choices she'd made before Joy was ever born. If she hadn't quit college to be with a man, she'd have a career right now, one in which she could have supported Joy. But she *hadn't* gotten her degree, and she'd let her bastard boyfriend take advantage of her then kick her out. Now she lived paycheck to paycheck, barely making enough to live in a decent neighborhood with decent schools. And good Lord, what about medical insurance if she didn't have a job?

She'd even failed at this, a simple request for a modest raise.

She bounded down the stairs even as Brett called after her, afraid she would spontaneously combust into tears. Jordana wouldn't cry. Gloria certainly never would. They weren't failures. They were strong women.

Shoving open the front lobby door, she hit the parking lot pavement close to a dash, then slowed, not wanting to be caught running like a maniac. She just needed to think. She could fix this. She could stand up to Rhonda and say how wrong she was.

But would Rhonda listen to her?

Would anyone?

"Ivy."

The voice was louder, stronger, and finally penetrated the fog enveloping her head. She'd almost made it to her car.

But Brett Baker was suddenly standing in her way.

"Ivy. Stop. Talk to me."

It was the last thing on earth she wanted to do.

What if he realized she was about to burst into mortifying tears?

"SOMETHING'S WRONG, IVY. WHAT'S GOING ON?"

Brett looked down at the small box in Ivy's trembling hands. Snacks, a bottle of lotion, a lipstick. And all the photos of her daughter. "You look like you're leaving for good."

"Just lunch," she said softly, not looking up at him.

"That's not lunch. That's everything out of your cubicle." She wasn't the kind of woman to have a lot of clutter, but she'd always had a few adorable pictures of her daughter that she changed out regularly.

"I really need to get going."

Beyond a handshake or a clap on the back, he didn't normally touch employees. But he put a finger beneath Ivy's chin and forced her to look at him.

Her dark eyes were blurred by a sheen of moisture, the rims slightly red, her cheeks pale. Then she sniffed lightly.

She looked devastated... by something.

His heart lurched. "Is your daughter okay?"

She nodded. "Yeah. She's fine."

So something else. Something that had occurred on the job.

"Let's go for a walk. I'm a good listener. My daughter always tells me that."

"I really don't need to talk." She sidestepped him to her car, beeped the remote, and set her box of personal items on the passenger seat.

A box of personal items that you'd take if you were quitting your job.

Rhonda had probably pushed her too far, and she'd handed in her resignation. Damn. He'd have to talk her out of it. Ivy was a good employee, personable, and she'd been working out well in the part-time HR spot.

"Ivy," he said again. "Give me a chance to make whatever it is right."

He should probably leave it to Grady since he was actually her boss, but there was something about the devastated look on her face that tugged at Brett.

"Please." He wasn't used to asking. He usually just told people what to do. But his daughter had taught him taking command didn't always work outside the office building.

Ivy's acquiescence was in the closing of her car door and the remote's beep to lock it.

"Thank you," he said softly, like a man gentling a frightened animal. "Why don't we head out to the park?" It was a short stroll to Shoreline Park, which ran along the southern edge of the bay. Runners and walkers frequented the paths at lunchtime, and in the spring, the geese loved it, too. It was a favorite breeding ground. "There have been occasions when I've just wanted to clear my mind, and I've grabbed a sandwich to eat out there." He kept it conversational as they strolled.

"I've done that, too," she finally said after a long silent moment. "I've often thought I should start walking out there at lunch every day."

"There's a locker room with showers over in the Manufacturing building. I'm sure no one would mind if you used it."

"Thank you," she said politely. She'd laughed so much at all his pictures of Valerie, yet now it seemed impossible to coax a smile out of her.

"Are you okay in those shoes?" He hadn't thought about walking in high heels, though hers weren't spiked.

"If you don't mind, I'd rather take them off." She put a hand on his arm to steady herself as she removed first one, then the other.

A tingle of awareness shot through him at the light touch.

"I'm better in bare feet," she told him.

And bare legs. Shapely bare legs. Her toes were painted

bright red, in contrast to the clear polish on her fingernails. As if she had hidden depths.

He would have called himself a leg man, but he'd never have said he was a foot man—that sounded like a fetish—but Ivy's bare feet sent another wave of awareness shimmying across his skin.

He'd always thought her to be a lovely woman with a pretty smile and a sweet laugh. But seeing her bare feet, her bare legs, things shifted inside. Tilted until she was no longer merely Grady's admin. No longer just an employee.

He only realized he'd been looking far too long when she said, "Rhonda doesn't like it when women don't wear pantyhose, but the weather has been so lovely for that past few days. Especially for November, and I know the rain will be starting soon, then I'll have to wear boots all the time." She talked fast, almost as if she were nervous.

They turned down the main path from the office complexes into the park. She'd given him the perfect opening by using Rhonda's name. "Did you have a run-in with Rhonda? Is that what upset you?"

He'd already had a talk with Rhonda today, about playing nice with the other VPs, especially Gloria.

But Ivy didn't jump into the opening, keeping her mouth shut as a runner passed them.

"It's okay, Ivy. This is purely confidential. I just don't like seeing—" He didn't like seeing *her* upset. It did something to him. She was only a few years older than Megan, who was twenty-eight, but the feeling was nothing fatherly. It was... protective. More than protective. It had something to do with her pretty bare feet and her toned, tanned legs. And that shift he'd felt deep inside. "I don't like anything upsetting my employees." It seemed the safest thing to say.

"I'm okay," she said. "It was really nothing. I can handle it."

The sheen was gone from her eyes now, a good thing. But that hadn't been *nothing.* "I'm sure you can handle it, but sometimes talking gives a little perspective. Gives you a different view of it. It might help."

She swallowed and squinted to watch a bird fly overhead. Then finally she said, "Rhonda fired me."

"What the f—" He stopped the expletive just in time. "Why would she do that?"

What the hell was going on? First of all, Rhonda didn't have the right to fire Ivy. Grady was her boss. And second, Rhonda was supposed to use Ivy only 25 percent of the time, at least that's what the budget said. But even he was aware she monopolized Ivy. He'd assumed it was fine, because Grady said Ivy wanted the experience. But *firing* her?

Ivy winced as she stepped on a pebble.

"You okay?" He touched her arm, steadied her. And found he liked touching her way too much. Jesus, he'd even liked it when she'd held his arm as she took off her shoes.

"I'm fine. My feet are pretty tough. My daughter and I go barefoot all the time."

He wondered if she'd winced to avoid his question. Or to give herself time to think.

He didn't let up. Not after that bombshell. "So, Rhonda fired you because?" he trailed off in a question.

"I asked her for a raise." She clamped her lips a moment, then added, "And that offended her."

It was crazy. What the hell was Rhonda thinking? "You can't fire someone for asking."

"No." She said it slowly, thoughtfully. "But she seems to think there's some sort of conspiracy against her."

He actually laughed. "That's absurd."

Then he glanced at Ivy's face. He remembered the moisture he'd seen at the corners of her eyes. And he recalled his conversation with Rhonda this morning. He didn't like discord in the ranks, and Rhonda had gone off on Gloria in a meeting yesterday afternoon about an issue he couldn't actually make sense of. He'd have a talk with Rhonda. She wasn't being professional, acting more like a spoiled child.

But this? Firing Ivy simply because she'd asked for a raise? "What exactly did you say?"

This time she stopped, looked up at him, her dark eyes sparking. "I told her that I had to take work home and didn't get paid for it, and I have to pay a premium at day care when she makes me stay late. And that I felt I should be compensated properly for it."

He held up a hand. "I didn't mean that as a criticism or as if anything is your fault. I'm just trying to figure out Rhonda's state of mind." Rhonda's actions had suddenly become a huge problem. Something he'd said this morning might very well have set her off, and she'd taken it out on Ivy. "I'm sorry this happened. But I need to know everything so I can deal with Rhonda properly."

"All right. You want to know?" Her eyes were blazing now, as if she were shooting with both barrels. "She called me a money-grubbing whore and a blackmailer. She said that single mothers who have never been married are just losers who expect something for nothing." She waved her hand. "Or something like that. Single mothers are losers and failures. Then she asked me who I was sleeping with in the company. Just like Jordana got the promotion because she was sleeping with Grady and Gloria was safe because she was screwing Parker, so someone had to be protecting me, too. *That's* what she said. Then she fired me."

He was stunned, then just as quickly, he was close to laughing hysterically. Because it was preposterous. Like some evil queen bee destroying lives in a fifties B movie. It didn't even seem real. Yet it was. "What the hell was she thinking?"

"I don't know. You tell me. She works for you."

He focused on Ivy again. "I apologize profusely for her behavior." He'd had no clue Rhonda was so out of control. Difficult yes, but this? No, he hadn't realized. And that his fault. "You are definitely not fired. And I agree with your reasons for a raise. I'll talk to Grady and we'll get that in the works." But he was still reeling. Just yesterday he'd been thinking of Rhonda as his blessing and his curse. But now he saw the real truth: She was no blessing, only a curse. "And I'll talk to Rhonda. What she did is beyond that pale. I *will* fix this."

"I don't need you to fix it." Then she stomped her foot despite the fact that it was bare. "Dammit, yes, I do need you to fix it. Because it's your responsibility. Rhonda can't talk to people that way. It's not right. I am not a—" She stopped, looking at him as if she were suddenly afraid she'd said too much. "What I mean is—"

He put his finger on her lips, cut her off in the middle, and shocked himself with the action. With the softness of her mouth. With the charge that leaped between them. With the heat that rushed to his core.

He dropped his hand, but what he had to say was too important to stop now. "It *is* my responsibility. And I promise you I will take care of it."

She blinked, then stared at him, her lips slightly parted, until finally she said, "Thank you."

"I want you to take the rest of the afternoon off while I deal with this."

"But—"

Everything in him wanted to touch her again, but he overrode the start of her sentence with just a look. "She's a monster I helped create, and I will neutralize her. Her reaction was unconscionable. This is *not* your problem."

Rhonda was an executive. He expected her to act like one,

not like a child of eight who couldn't get along with the other kids on the playground.

"I hope you'll accept my apology." This time he allowed himself to touch Ivy's arm. Just a gesture of comfort. He wasn't supposed to feel anything.

But he did.

3

It was the strangest feeling to be home in the middle of a Friday afternoon. It was... a total luxury. She should have used the time to catch up on laundry. Or make meals ahead to put in the freezer. Or even think about how she could turn homeschooling into a paying proposition. Anything but sit in front of the TV.

But Ivy didn't care. She'd plopped down on the sofa to watch one of her favorite movies, *Jane Eyre*. She'd seen just about every version made, from 1943 with Orson Welles and Joan Fontaine to the latest with Judi Dench as Mrs. Fairfax. By far the best was the one with Timothy Dalton from the early eighties. He was to die for as Mr. Rochester.

He reminded her a bit of Brett Baker.

Or maybe she just had Brett on the brain after their lunchtime walk. After he'd touched his finger to her lips and sparks had detonated on her skin.

She'd ignored the sparks. They didn't mean anything—even if she could still feel them. It had been truly embarrassing to be caught after that debacle with Rhonda. But

Brett took the problem right out of her hands, dealing with everything. She'd even told him to.

But had she done the right thing?

On the TV, Mr. Rochester was declaring his love for Jane. Ivy had skipped all the school years and gotten right into the romance.

There was just something about a commanding man. A man who knew what he wanted. A man who was decisive.

Like Brett.

She'd told herself she could have handled the situation. Just like Gloria and Jordana would have. When she'd calmed down. When Rhonda had calmed down. But the reality was that as much as Ivy wanted to take care of the issue, if Rhonda didn't back down, she would still need to go to someone and say, *She can't do this to me.* It was either Grady or Jordana.

Or Brett Baker.

Deep inside her, there was a Jane Eyre who was drawn to the big commanding CEO offering to take charge.

Not that she'd actually want a man to take over her life again. She was pretty much done with men, at least for anything other than a very short stint. Most of them weren't Mr. Rochester. You couldn't count on them.

Ah, the kiss. Her favorite part. Ivy melted just watching it. She was such a sucker for these old gothic romances. And when she closed her eyes, she could feel Brett's hand on her arm as he apologized and told her *he* was responsible for the monster he'd created in Rhonda.

She could feel the spark of his finger on her lips.

She'd believed him. Brett Baker was that kind of man, running the company like it was his ship to command. Rhonda was the first mate who'd just keelhauled a sailor behind the captain's back. Brett wouldn't let anyone get away with something like that.

Her phone rang and her heart actually started to beat faster. Brett had said he was going to call, and she was filled with the most ridiculous fluttery feeling. As if she were interested in him as a man.

Which she most certainly couldn't be. He was just a fantasy.

She answered with a simple, "Hello," not even looking at the caller ID.

"Hi hon." Not Brett. Her mother instead. A dash of disappointment peppered her mood. "I wondered if you'd seen my jade necklace," her mother said. Ivy had given her the necklace for her birthday a few years ago. "I've looked everywhere and I can't find it."

"Did you check in your swim bag?"

Her mother did water exercises at the YWCA three days a week.

"It's not there. I think someone stole it while I was swimming."

"Why were you wearing it to go swimming? And no one stole it. It's somewhere in your house." Leonora Elliot was notorious for misplacing things. She also had a distinct lack of trust in people since Ivy's father had run away with his secretary. Ivy had been Joy's age at the time. Her mother never got over it.

She'd made sure Ivy didn't get over it either.

That, however, hadn't stopped Ivy from falling for Rupert the professor.

"What's that noise?" her mother asked. "It sounds like a TV."

Ivy leaned forward for the remote to pause Jane and Rochester's wedding. She didn't want to miss the part where even Mr. Rochester turned out to be a cad. Despite the fact that he had a good reason.

"It was the TV. But there, I've paused it."

"What on earth are you doing home in the middle of the day? Did you get yourself fired?"

Ivy frowned, both at her mother's tone and her phrasing, as if Ivy were responsible for her own firing. Honestly, why would that be her mother's first thought, over worrying that Ivy might be sick? The answer was plain enough. Her mother thought she was a failure just like Rhonda did. "No, I didn't get *myself* fired. My boss had a bug up her—" She caught herself just in time, because she unequivocally refused to justify what happened as if somehow it were her fault. "You want the whole story? All right, here it is." She didn't spare a single detail, not from the moment she walked into Rhonda's office to the names Rhonda called her, every single demeaning word.

"Oh my *Gawd*." Mom practically squealed, then gasped, and almost sounded like she was hyperventilating before she sucked in a deep breath of air and said so softly Ivy almost couldn't hear, "Are you joking?"

"Would I joke about a thing like that?"

"It's like mana from heaven," her mother said, her voice deep with reverence.

"I got fired, Mom. It's not mana from anything. But I think—"

Her mother wasn't listening. "Do you realize what you've got here? You can sue the pants off them. You could set yourself up for life. Or at least enough years to finish college so you can get a decent job."

At her age, she'd probably need a master's degree before an employer would even look at her, despite her work experience. "I'm not going to sue Rhonda."

"Not your boss. The *company*. They've got deep pockets. Tell 'em to take it out of there."

"Mom," she said, hoping that would be enough to stop her mother.

It wasn't. "Don't 'Mom' me. You wouldn't sue that good-for-nothing professor for child support. Though you had every right to."

It was true she hadn't forced the issue with Rupert. They weren't married, only living together. She'd gotten pregnant. He'd said the child wasn't his, that he'd had a vasectomy years ago. In addition, he'd accused her of cheating on him and kicked her out. But she hadn't had a cent with which to sue him. She'd been too devastated to even think about it. Instead, she'd moved in with her mom. Who simply would not let up on the palimony/child support thing, harping until Ivy thought she might tear her hair out.

It hadn't been just about the money. It was also about Rupert and his mercurial mind, that if she won against him, someday, he'd change his mind and try to take the baby away from her because she'd forced him to acknowledge the child.

But God, it had been hard in those early years.

"Mom, please." Ivy could hear the pleading in her voice.

"I said don't 'Mom' me. I'm not going to let you do this again. You dropped out of college for that man. You spent five years cooking, cleaning, taking care of him, doing whatever the hell he wanted you to do. And look what he did to you in the end. Pretty much called you a cheating whore. Just like your *boss* did."

Ivy winced. Rupert hadn't used that word. But it didn't matter because that was still the gist of it.

"Why the hell did you drop out of college anyway? That was the dumbest thing you ever did." Then the sound of her mother slapping her own forehead. "Oh wait, I forgot. The dumbest thing was getting pregnant out of wedlock."

"You can stop now," Ivy said, masking the hurt with a bored tone in her voice. "I've heard the refrain more times than I can count. I should never have fallen for Rupert," she started for her mother. "I should never have—"

But Mom cut her off. "The mistake wasn't falling in love with your professor. It was leaving school to traipse across the globe with him while he wrote his masterpiece. The one he never even published."

Yet those two years had been such a glorious time. She'd seen Europe and Asia at Rupert's side, places she never would have gone on her own, Paris, Berlin, Holland, the northern lights in Norway, Stonehenge, the Great Wall of China, the pyramids of Egypt, the temples of Angkor Wat in Cambodia. There was nothing like seeing the world with love as your guide.

The mistake had been coming home with all her savings depleted. She'd been working since she was thirteen, babysitting, then fast food joints, scrimping for college. She'd managed to get a small scholarship, too. But everything was gone when she returned, and she didn't have the money to finish her degree. So she'd moved in with Rupert and gotten a job as a receptionist.

"You should have made him marry you when you got back here. Especially after everything you gave up for him." Mom had only ever seen the bad, which was the world view she'd learned through her own marriage, abandonment, and divorce. With a six-year-old child she had to support on her own.

"Getting married never helped you." Ivy didn't say it to be mean. It was simply fact.

"Touché," her mother said. "But while I had to cook for your father, clean for him, wash his dirty underwear, and scream at him every time he blew his nose in the shower, at least I didn't have to work outside the home as well."

True enough. Ivy'd had to work all day, then cook and clean, as well as pay her half of the expenses. Which meant her savings hadn't grown at all. But she'd loved Rupert. She hadn't minded. He'd had a bad divorce, and he wasn't ready for marriage again. There were all sorts of excuses. But all along, she was dreaming of the day he'd be ready for marriage. The day he'd want to start a family with her.

Then she'd gotten pregnant.

Instead of a dream come true, he'd kicked her out. Six weeks later, he was with another of his students.

Ivy had known in her heart the affair had been going on long before that, and she'd simply ignored the warning signs because she couldn't bear the heartache, couldn't bear for life to change all over again. She could even admit now—if only to herself—that she'd been afraid he'd never marry her, that she'd been trying to cook and clean her way into his heart as much as anything else. Stupid, stupid, stupid. She was ashamed she'd gone on that way for so long.

"You know, Mom, you're totally depressing me. I'd like to get back to Jane and Mr. Rochester."

Her mother laughed, not exactly with humor, more like disgust. "Just like you and Rupert, older man, younger woman. Except that I never liked Rupert."

But Ivy was free of him now. As hard as it had been, she was glad he would never have a claim on Joy. "Yes, I know you've told me 'I told you so.'"

"Well, don't make me say it all again. Sue the company. Collect a million dollars. And I won't ever have to let you move in with me again."

"I moved out five years ago, Mom, and I've never asked you for any money." Since her mother was retired, she'd taken care of Joy that first year, but Ivy had managed on her own ever since. She'd done well enough as an administrative aide to pay for anything Joy needed. Except private school. Or the cute clothes little girls wanted. Or the fashionably expensive toys.

"Sue them. Take whatever you can get. But I know you never listen to your mother."

Ivy sighed. "I forget why you called in the first place, Mom. Did you actually need something?"

"My jade necklace. But I found it while I've been talking to you."

"Where was it?"

"I was wearing it, but it was underneath my blouse, so I didn't see it."

Ivy laughed.

Her mother laughed, too, before turning serious again. "You know I only say all this for your sake. I just want life to be easier for you." Easier than it had been for Mom, who'd worked two jobs while Ivy was growing up, cleaning houses by day and office buildings in the evenings.

"I know, Mom. But everything's going to be okay. I'll get my job sorted out."

"You'd get a lot more than sorted out if you sued them. Emotional distress. Discrimination against single mothers. Not to mention the awful names she called you. Just don't be too hasty in deciding not to sue. And don't burn any bridges by signing something that says you won't sue them later. Keep your options open." Then her mother made a zipping sound. "But that's the last word I'll say about it."

It wouldn't be.

Long after her mother hung up, Ivy stared at the TV screen with Jane's devastated face and Rochester's angry visage.

Did she actually have a case?

The bigger question was whether she would do that to the company. To Jordana, Gloria, Grady. To Brett Baker.

Because it wasn't just about Rhonda. It would be all of them. It could very well devastate the chances the company had of getting the investment from that venture capital firm in Des Moines, The Nelson Group.

Everyone was counting on the financing. Most especially Brett.

BRETT WANTED TO RAM HIS FIST THROUGH RHONDA'S door. Or shout at her until his anger was cleansed away.

Or cup Ivy Elliot's face in his hands and kiss her. Long and slow and sweet.

Yesterday, she'd been a pretty young woman, a hard worker, a good employee, admiring pictures of his granddaughter. Today, she'd suddenly become something else. Like turning the dial on an old radio where there was static one minute and in the next, the room was filled with music so beautiful you had to close your eyes and savor it.

He honestly couldn't tell whether he was furious with Rhonda for what she'd done. Or because she'd done it to Ivy.

With any employee who'd suffered that kind of abuse, he'd have read the manager the riot act. But right now, his blood had reached its boiling point, and he wanted to fire Rhonda's ass, kick her out the door, and throw her stuff out the window.

He was well aware he should wait to talk to her, but he marched up the stairs, threw open the door into the Accounting quadrant of the building. The low hum of keyboards, voices, and phones filtered out from the warren of cubicles as he stalked into Rhonda's office.

The urge to slam the door was irresistible. But he did resist. Her second door, the one leading out to Ivy's cubicle and with a view into Grady's office, was thankfully closed.

"Brett." Seated behind her desk, she said his name so pleasantly, with a smile, as if she didn't have a clue why he was here. But the color in her face was high, her skin mottled shades of red.

You're fired. Get the hell out.

He didn't say it. He simply pulled a chair from her small conference table, turned it, and sat facing her across the desk. "I understand you had an altercation with Ivy earlier." He sounded calm, something which took a monumental effort.

Rhonda's nostrils flared, but just like him, she kept a civil tone. "I wouldn't call it an altercation. It was more like a difference of opinion." But her face turned a deeper shade of crimson.

"A difference of opinion and you fired her?"

"Did she tell you that?" she snapped like a giant turtle. Then tried to compose herself with a deep breath. "I did feel that her demands were a little over the top."

"Rhonda, she asked for a raise since we doubled her responsibilities without any compensation. That sounds pretty reasonable to me."

She sniffed, as if she had a meatloaf sandwich going bad in her desk drawer. "Yes, well, it was the way she asked."

This was Rhonda's genius. She could describe a situation with such diplomacy that suddenly everything sounded perfectly normal. He'd always admired how she came up with just the right words to soothe an employee's fractured temper. She managed to rephrase an incomprehensible regulation and make it completely understandable. So what had happened to her? Not just today, but over the past few months.

While he still simmered over the abominable way she'd treated Ivy, he found his ire subsiding slightly. He needed to understand what the hell was going on.

"Let me get this straight," he said, hitching one pant leg and crossing his legs casually. "You didn't like the way she asked for a raise, so you called her a whore, a blackmailer, and demeaned her status as a single mother."

"Oh, I never said it like that," she scoffed. "Ivy's sensitive.

She took it all the wrong way. I just wanted her to see the mistake she was making."

"So you're saying she lied to me."

She tut-tutted. "I wouldn't put it like that exactly." But her hand had started to shake and she clasped both in her lap.

"How would you put it?"

"Well..." She swallowed, drew in a sharp breath. "I simply wanted her to know that I saw through her motivations."

He held up a hand. "Let's stop playing games. Did you call her a whore?"

He heard her fingers drumming on her thighs beneath the desk. "I might have in a moment of..." She paused, actually biting her lip. "Well, yes, I might have," she admitted.

"*Might* have?" he stressed.

This time she shot out her breath like a burst of air from a horse's nostrils. "All right, yes, I did." Then it all came rushing out. "She wants to blackmail us, Brett, coming in here, demanding a raise, saying she's been doing overtime without getting paid for it, when the truth is that she'd only taken work home because she's inefficient when she's here. She's always talking on the phone, gabbing at everyone. Talk, talk, talk." She mimicked with her fingers. "And if I ask her to stay one moment late, she's demanding that I pay for her child care. Good Lord, I'm not the one whose child doesn't have a father. When you take a job, you make a commitment. But she's all about money, money, money. As if the invaluable experience I'm giving her means nothing. You know, I did several summer internships and didn't get paid a dime. It was for the *experience*." She air-quoted.

He let her go on as she damned herself with every word.

"She's just a secretary, for God's sake. She answers the phone and takes messages." Spots of spittle collected along her lower lip.

He had to break in then. "So you haven't asked her to take over any of Jordana's duties or given her special projects?"

"Of course I gave her some of Jordana's duties. That's what we all agreed to. And I had a few special projects."

When Jordana had first been promoted to HR manager a few months ago, Grady had agreed to share Ivy part time with Rhonda. It had made perfect sense. Even Ivy admitted she felt underutilized. But it wasn't supposed to be more than 25 percent of the time. It wasn't supposed to require overtime or working from home.

"I told you it's because she's slow," Rhonda almost shouted, remembering herself only at the last moment, her breath puffing with the effort to sound calm when she was the furthest thing from it.

The further off the rails she went, the calmer Brett became. "What's really going on here, Rhonda?"

Her mouth worked, the muscles of her neck tensed, and finally she let loose. "You want to know what's going on? All right, I'll tell you. It's a conspiracy. The three of them go out to lunch yesterday, then they're all eyeing me the rest of the afternoon, like they're plotting behind my back. And then bam, Ivy comes in here at the first opportunity and starts demanding. She wants this, she deserves that. And I know they put her up to it. They've had it out for me from day one."

"Who has it out for you?" he asked softly. Because this was goddamned strange.

"Them. Jordana. Gloria." Her eyes narrowed, throwing daggers at the walls as if her nemeses were standing there. "And don't forget Grady and Parker. Because they're sleeping with them, of course they support whatever they do."

Her fight with Gloria yesterday afternoon suddenly made sense. "Rhonda."

For her, he was no longer in the room. "They planned all

this to humiliate me. They probably even coached her on how to goad me into losing my temper and saying all those things." She spread her hands, her face animated, her words coming fast, spittle on her lip. "So that she could sue me. Sue the company. Because the company has the deep pockets. She could claim discrimination and harassment, and everything else in the book. She'd ask for damages and get millions. I can see it all, how they planned everything, and I just fell for it."

He hadn't thought of lawyers or courts and could have smacked himself for not considering it. But all he'd really been thinking about was Ivy and the devastation staining her pretty face.

"Rhonda," he said loudly, putting the brakes on her runaway train.

She looked at him as if she'd truly forgotten he was there until his voice broke through.

"There is no conspiracy against you," he said. "No one is suing the company. But you need a rest. A few weeks off. Time to take stock of things."

He'd walked in here needing to fire her. Even to crush her.

But now he simply felt a deep sadness for her. Maybe she was having a breakdown.

"Time off," she said, her tone bewildered, her gaze slightly unfocused.

"A leave of absence."

Her lips parted. She stared at him. "I don't need a leave of absence." She blinked rapidly, and cheeks that had once been reddened with emotion now turned a stark white. "I admit that I got a little carried away with Ivy. I'll talk to her. I'll apologize. I'll explain. It won't happen again. I'm really sorry, Brett."

"No one's out to get you, Rhonda. You need to take some time off," he reiterated unequivocally. She needed help.

And he needed time to clean up her mess.

Because he couldn't let Ivy sue the company. The Nelson Group was coming within the next few weeks to perform due diligence before making a decision on investing. As a relative start-up, the company would be shipping its first product at the beginning of the year, and Brett was counting on that investment to fund R&D to broaden their product line. He couldn't allow even the hint of scandal to jeopardize this deal.

He wanted growth, he wanted to take this company public, *his* company. He wanted to be one of the Fortune 500.

So right now he had to do whatever was necessary to fix Rhonda's screw-up.

4

Brett spent the afternoon on the Rhonda problem. Jordana had to draw up the leave-of-absence paperwork. Rather than bring in a temporary HR person, they decided to hire a temp to handle Ivy's duties for Grady so that she could work full time assisting Jordana—if Ivy was willing after what she'd been through. It was a bold move, letting Jordana take over HR, but Brett believed she could handle it. So did Grady, who, though he might be biased, was fully behind her.

What Brett didn't want was for Rhonda's absence to look anything but mutually agreed upon and temporary.

He also had Jordana put through the paperwork for Ivy's raise. She deserved it, especially if she agreed to be the full-time HR assistant.

Lastly, he called Larry Price, their corporate lawyer, and apprised him of the situation.

"Holy Hell. She's HR!" Larry's voice was more than just capital letters. "You didn't fire her, did you?"

"No. But why not?"

"It might be construed as an admission of guilt that Miss

Elliot could use. You can also open yourself up to a wrongful termination suit from Rhonda."

Brett spun in his chair to look out the window. His office was on the second floor in the back corner, with a view of the employee picnic tables, a row of trees, and beyond that, Shoreline Park and the bay. "That's freaking ridiculous. She was definitely in the wrong."

"I've got stories that will turn your hair completely white."

Brett figured his was getting there, so what the heck.

"The things employers will try to get away with. And employees. It's crazy out there. Sure there are totally legit suits, but there's also a bunch of scam artists who try to provoke something they can make bank on."

"Look, I believe Rhonda needs some psychological help."

Larry choked on the other end of the line. "You didn't say that, did you?"

"No."

A loud exhale spelled Larry's relief. "Thank God."

"I said she needed time to take stock of things and put her on LOA."

"What about Miss Elliot?"

"I'm giving her a raise."

Larry groaned. "Is this a bribe?"

"Of course not. She deserves it. Plus I'm asking her to take on extra duties while Rhonda's gone." He was not being talked out of the raise.

"Okay, okay. That could actually work in our favor. If it doesn't blow up in our faces later. Do whatever you can to make sure she doesn't call a lawyer."

"My intention is to make sure she's treated fairly." But yes, he also needed to make sure she didn't bring a lawyer into the mess. He didn't believe she'd even thought of it. Yet.

"On the plus side, with the raise, she won't be able to prove any damages. I mean, she didn't actually get fired. The problem with lawyers is that they think up devious ways to screw you."

"Larry, you're a lawyer."

"And I'm devious. So be very glad I'm on your side. See, what you have to worry about is that some lawyer tries to say you encouraged a hostile work environment because of Rhonda's crap. They could argue that you knew you had a problem and didn't do anything about it."

Jesus. He'd known Rhonda was difficult, but he'd always used the excuse that she knew her stuff. And she did. She'd been invaluable on any number of occasions.

But you couldn't let someone get away with over-the-top bad behavior just because they had knowledge you needed.

This thing had been heating up, and he hadn't done anything to put out the flames.

"All I can say is," Larry continued dispensing advice, "appease Miss Elliot at all costs. Just don't do it with a cash payout. We don't want anything recorded on the books."

Especially not something The Nelson Group auditors would find. Nothing could quash this deal faster than the hint of a large lawsuit in the wings.

He would have to make sure Ivy was happy.

The idea appealed to him far more than it should.

THE NEXT CALL, AT CLOSE TO FOUR O'CLOCK, WAS FROM Jordana, and Ivy knew the proverbial cat was out of the bag.

"Are you okay?" was the first thing Jordana asked, her voice just above a whisper as if she were afraid of being overheard by the entire office.

It was nice to have someone checking on her. "I'm fine. It

was just shocking." She wondered exactly how much Brett had told Jordana.

Her friend's soft, "Bitch," floated over the airwaves. "She had no right." Obviously Brett had revealed enough. "But I can't say much more than that because it's all confidential. And for now, no one else but Grady knows. Not even Gloria. Anyway, my main concern is you."

"Honestly, I'm okay. Don't worry." Then Ivy thought of her mother's insistence on calling a lawyer. If she told Jordana she was fine, wouldn't the company lawyers use that against her? *If* she decided to sue. But this was Jordana. This was between friends. Not HR and employee. What she said to Jordana was strictly between them. Right?

Anger at Rhonda flashed through her all over again for making Ivy doubt her friend.

"I'm so glad you called me," she said, her gratitude heartfelt. Since having Joy, she hadn't let many people into her life, and none that had stayed. "I feel a bit isolated at home."

"Hey, what are friends for."

They were for exactly this, ensuring that you were okay, just being there for you. Ivy shoved away any doubt. "Thanks."

"We'll talk on Monday, okay? But if you start feeling weirded out, call me. Anytime."

"I will. That means a lot."

She sat for a few moments, phone in her hand, after Jordana rang off. It *did* mean a lot. Her mother was always pushing, always questioning. They talked, but Ivy always felt on the defensive. But Jordana and Gloria? They were support. They were shoulders to cry on.

They were friends she was grateful for.

She had a feeling she was going to need friends after that fight with Rhonda.

And after her walk in the park with Brett Baker.

IVY WORE AN OVERSIZED DUSTY PINK SWEATER THAT JUST covered her rear end and tight purple leggings that showcased her legs.

It was enough to make Brett's heart start a marathon, especially with the sight of her bare feet. Her delicate toes. Her smooth skin.

She was ultra-sexy in the intimacy of her apartment.

"Thank you for inviting me for dinner." He at least managed a little courtesy despite his thoughts.

She hadn't actually made an invitation, but Brett had called after his conversation with Larry and asked if he could come over during the evening. Dinner was on the table when he arrived, and she'd had no choice but to set another place. They'd silently and mutually agreed to talk about Rhonda after dinner, when Ivy's daughter was out of the room.

"My name's Joy." The little girl jumped down from the table and stuck out her hand.

Brett shook solemnly. "It's nice to meet you."

"This is Mr. Baker," Ivy said. "He's my big boss."

"Wow!" Joy exclaimed. She was utterly adorable, with hair dark like her mother's, though full of bouncing curls unlike her mom's short, straight, silky, and very touchable locks.

"Please, sit." Ivy pointed to a chair at the small round table. There were only three chairs, not four, as if she didn't want anything in the apartment that might not get used.

The seats were vinyl, the table Formica-topped, the placemats set with mismatched dishes. Vintage, root beer-colored appliances crowded the narrow kitchen. The small dining area was attached to a larger living room. The worn sculptured carpet had been cleaned recently, the lines of the steam cleaner still marking it. The place was old, no doubt about it, but it was spotless. Joy's toys and games and dolls packed a large plastic tub by the side of the sofa. Crayons and a coloring book lay open on the coffee table. The TV was the smallest flat screen available at Costco, and sat on a trolley that could be rolled into the center of the room for a better view.

And the dinner was meatloaf.

It all reminded him of his youth. Meatloaf was a staple in his household, as were the avocado appliances. His mother had refused to get rid of the ancient stove because it had both a warming oven and a griddle. He'd finally convinced her five years ago, when he'd had her kitchen remodeled for her, that paying eight hundred dollars to fix the thermostat—for the second time—didn't make sense when he could buy her a brand new stove for the same amount.

"I like your apartment," he said, meaning every word.

Ivy eyed him, skepticism written in her pressed lips. "The neighborhood's okay and the schools are decent."

The apartment building was in the hills with a good view all the way down to the Peninsula and the bay. A great location with the elementary school right across the street, he was sure the rent wasn't cheap, despite the ancient appliances and worn carpet.

"This place reminds me of home when I was a kid. We had avocado instead of root beer."

Joy tipped her head. "But you drink root beer and you eat avocado. So I don't get it."

Brett laughed. The little girl made him realize how old he was. Even Ivy probably didn't know what he was talking about. He suspected she was more that fifteen years younger than him. "The appliances," he explained. "Everyone had colors like avocado, root beer, or harvest gold."

"In the fifties, I think they were robin's egg blue. Or pink," Ivy offered up.

Joy screwed up her face. "Pink. Yuk. Like Pepto Bismol."

She was a precocious child, reminding him of his own daughter. Megan was twenty-eight now, a mother herself, but she'd been curious about everything as a child.

"Don't worry, sweetheart, we're going to stick with root beer." Ivy began dishing out the meatloaf.

It was simple fare yet delicious with both flavor and childhood memories. "Very tasty," he said, his smile wide.

Ivy gave him a sarcastic eye roll. "It's hamburger," she said dryly. "But if you want the lower fat cut, it costs almost as much as steak unless you get it on sale."

He was sure Ivy shopped on sale. He knew what they'd been paying her, and he knew what rents were like in the Bay Area.

"You make it taste like gourmet," he said.

"Mommy, may I have more green beans, please?" Joy held up her plate.

As Ivy served another helping, Brett said, "I thought little girls don't like green beans. My daughter hated anything green."

"I like them," Joy said wisely, "because they squeak on my teeth when I eat them."

"They squeak?"

Joy nodded sagely, spearing a few on her fork. "Okay, you have to be really quiet while you chew." She waited while Brett stabbed several as well. "Okay, now try it."

The room was silent as they all chewed the green beans. Sure enough, there was a tiny squeak from inside his mouth. "You're a genius. I never would have known."

Joy beamed. "Mommy says I'm way ahead of the other kids in reading. That's 'cause she read to me when I was in the wooomb." She elongated the word.

"Wow. That's really cool."

Ivy was smiling, gazing at her daughter with so much love that her face glowed.

Together they made him remember those idyllic days of Megan's childhood, when she looked at him like he was Superman. Before the divorce. Before her parents started to fight too much because he worked too much. Megan was ten when the marriage ended. He'd done his damndest after that to be there every weekend that he had her, never shunting her off unless it was completely beyond his control. He might actually have been a better father after he'd lost everything.

"Someday I would like a real house with a real yard," Joy was saying. "Then we can have a puppy."

"You know we can't have a puppy, Joy," Ivy said sternly.

Joy ignored her. "Little kids should have puppies so they can learn responsibility, don't you think, Mr. Baker?"

God, he wanted to laugh out loud. She was indeed smart and precocious, working on her mother right there in front of him. "Puppies are a handful. Especially when you're not home with them all day."

Ivy gave him an encouraging smile. "They dig under fences."

"They pull up the sprinklers," he added.

"They bark and disturb the neighbors."

Joy squeaked more green beans in her mouth. "Maybe we should get a cat then. Cats can use litterboxes and they sleep all day so they don't need you to be around all the time." She smiled up at Brett. "Do you have a cat, Mr. Baker?"

"No." He shook his head. "I travel too much." Then he winked at Joy. "But I adore my daughter's cat."

"Is your little girl as old as me?"

He actually guffawed at that. "My daughter is old enough to be your mother. And she's got a daughter of her own now. Would you like to see a picture of the baby?"

"Yes, please."

She was so polite, her mother's doing. Brett tapped his phone and brought up the latest picture of Valerie.

Joy pretended that she was suitably impressed, then launched into another soliloquy. "I'd like to have a brother or sister, but Mommy says I can't because she's not married. And she'll never get married. But my friend Susie at school doesn't have a daddy and isn't married, but she's got a little brother. So don't you think I should get one, Mr. Baker?"

Ivy slapped her hands lightly on the table. "It's time for you to start your homework, Ivy." The child's plate was clean. "You can have some fruit for dessert when you're done."

"But Mommy—"

"Homework," her mother said. "Mr. Baker and I have business to discuss." Ivy stood and carried plates into the kitchen. Brett brought the meatloaf platter while Joy scampered off through the living room and down the short hall which presumably led to her bedroom.

"Do six-year-olds even have homework?"

"The teachers start them early." She began running water over the dirty dishes. "And," she said exaggeratedly, "someone teaches them that having a dog breeds responsibility. She's really angling for a pet." Ivy rolled her eyes dramatically, and he saw the resemblance to her daughter. "Not just a hamster or a gerbil, but something that can sleep on her bed at night. Thank God she doesn't know where our lease is, or she'd be looking up whether we can actually have pets."

He smiled at the child's precociousness. He believed she'd do it, too. "What does the lease say?"

Ivy lowered her voice to a whisper. "We're allowed small dogs and cats. It's a secret."

He zipped his lips. "I won't say a word. But I suppose pets do teach responsibility."

"Children also have to learn when you shouldn't have them. Like you, because you travel too much."

"I'd have a cat if I could."

She shook her finger at him. "You're as bad as she is.

Don't play devil's advocate with me."

"But a sweet little kitty," he purred at her, liking the way she smiled back.

"She's too young to start getting attached to a pet we might have to get rid of if our circumstances change. I had a dog when I was a kid, and it was devastating to have to give her away when we moved after my dad left us."

He stopped her then as she rinsed another dish, putting a finger beneath her chin. "I'm not letting your circumstances change." He felt the pain of the little girl she'd been, losing her father and her dog all at once.

She swallowed hard, looking at him a moment. Her eyes were the deepest chocolate, like melted cocoa, and he found himself falling into them.

"You can't control *all* my circumstances," she said, then whispered, "Shit happens." She pulled away, took a deep breath. "You can sit in the living room. I'll only be a minute."

"I can help."

He liked the way she smelled, sweet and fruity. He liked the heat of her body as he stood close to her in the tiny kitchen.

He liked way too many things about her.

"Honestly, I can handle the dishes." She shooed him off. "You sit."

She was trying to get rid of him, but he moved infinitesimally closer, taking a plate from her hand. Holding it a moment longer, his thigh pressed against her, then he released her, backed off, and opened the dishwasher to fill it with the dirties.

During his marriage, his wife had complained that he went to his office to work while she cleaned up, even though she'd done all the cooking. He'd thought of it as division of labor, he worked outside the home—and in his home office—and she worked inside.

She'd never seen it that way. All she'd remembered was that he was gone one to two weeks out of the month on business trips.

In hindsight, he'd had to admit she was right. After the divorce, he'd stayed married to his career instead of another woman.

But look at Ivy, who was doing it all on her own. Working, cooking, cleaning, raising her daughter.

He almost gave a snort of disgust with the memory of what Rhonda had said to her, that single mothers were failures. Ridiculous.

"Why don't you sit down and rest?" he offered. "I can put these in the dishwasher."

"That's not necessary."

"Do you have any wine?"

Her eyes went wide. "Well, yes."

"I'll pour you a glass, and you go take a load off while I finish up here. Then I'll tell you about my talk with Rhonda. Sound good?"

"Are you sending me out of my own kitchen?"

"Yes. Just tell me where the wineglasses are and the plastic wrap so I can cover up the leftover meatloaf."

After one more moment spent staring at him as if he were a genie out of a bottle, she pointed. "The wrap is in the second drawer down, the glasses are in the cupboard over the stove, and there's an open bottle of wine in the fridge."

"Then let me take care of everything for you."

Finally, she backed out of the kitchen, her gaze still on him as if she were afraid he might disappear when she turned her back.

Or maybe she was hoping he would. It was hard to tell.

But he wasn't going anywhere. He was going to take care of the problem he'd created.

He was going to take care of *her*.

5

God, it was good having someone take care of her for a little while, even if it was something as small as doing the dishes and pouring her a glass of wine. Ivy melted into the couch.

Rupert had been old-fashioned, expecting his dinner on the table when he got home from a hard day of teaching college students. He liked his drink ready—gin and tonic in the summer, rye and ginger in the winter—plus a bowl of nuts or cheese or some small snack. After dinner, he settled in to watch the news while she did the dishes. She washed his laundry, cleaned his house, made his meals, warmed his bed. Until he threw her out. And kept the cat, a Persian that *he'd* paid for.

She'd missed the Persian more than him at that point. Just as she'd missed the dog her mother had given away when they'd moved after Ivy's father left. Sherry had been such a sweet dog. But her mom had said they didn't have the room or the money for food and vet bills.

She wasn't going to think about that now. Instead she'd

listen to the pad of Brett's footsteps as he moved around her kitchen.

She shouldn't get used to it, but she'd sure enjoy it for the moment.

"Here you go." He entered with the white wine.

She liked a glass in the evening once in a while. "Aren't you having any?"

"I have to drive." He settled on the couch beside her. A tad too close, a slight invasion of her space. His proximity should have made her nervous. He was the CEO, for God's sake.

Yet she'd fed him meatloaf, green beans, and mashed potatoes while Joy chattered on about everything from brothers and sisters to puppies and pets. He'd noted the worn carpet, the outdated appliances, the mismatched dishes and cutlery, the ancient furniture, and the lumpy sofa.

And she just felt... comfortable. With him. With the way his scent of the outdoors and man settled around her. With his big body right next to hers and the dip in the couch making her roll toward him.

She'd loved how he was with Joy, interested, involved. Not condescending or bored.

Tonight she could forget he was the CEO. He was just a man who'd complimented her cooking, done her dishes, and poured her wine.

"Thank you for letting me enjoy dinner with your daughter. That was special. I hope in a few years I can have dinner just like that with my granddaughter and talk about puppies and reading in the womb."

She laughed. "I really did read to her when she was in the wooomb." She *zooomed* it just like Joy had.

"There's scientific evidence that it works. My daughter swears by it."

That's what she liked best about him. He was a proud father and grandfather. There was also the small fact that he was totally gorgeous even at his age. What did they call men like him? A silver fox.

Then he ruined it all. "We need to talk about Rhonda."

She'd been trying to forget. "All that really matters is whether I still have a job."

"Of course you do."

She closed her eyes briefly in relief. Though she hadn't expected anything different with Brett in charge.

"What Rhonda did was unconscionable. I apologize for the whole company. She's on leave of absence until I decide what to do with her. And I'd like you to come back on Monday, if you're willing, to help cover for her."

She rolled her head on the couch to look at him. "How can I cover for Rhonda?"

"Between you and Jordana, I have confidence that everything in HR will be taken care of. Until we find a more permanent solution. Are you willing?"

She couldn't say anything for a moment. He'd taken her side. Even after talking with Rhonda.

"Grady is willing to give you full time to Jordana. We'll get a temp to cover your duties for him. And we've worked out an equitable salary since you'll be taking on more. Plus there will be a promotion since your job will be far more than admin work. Obviously we'll make sure it doesn't interfere with your childcare."

She gulped her wine. It was everything she could have hoped for. It was totally crazy. She was never this lucky. "Thank you."

"Rhonda stepped completely out of bounds, but I'd like to keep the resolution in-house, if at all possible."

She finished for him. "In other words, don't bring in a lawyer."

He cracked a very slight smile. “I would prefer that you didn’t. I’d like you to give me the chance to make this right.”

She parted her lips, the words on the tip of her tongue to say that she had no intention of suing. That just because one person had wronged her didn’t mean she had to make everyone pay.

That she didn’t blame him.

But there was her mother’s voice in her head. *Don’t be too hasty. Don’t burn your bridges. Keep your options open.*

Ivy studied her wine, letting him wait. Everything that happened with Rupert at the end had moved so fast. She hadn’t taken any time to think. The moment he said he’d had a vasectomy, accused her of having an affair, and refused to help with child support, she’d cut him out of her life, denying him any opportunity to get a foothold with her child. Not that he’d ever tried.

She did *not* regret that decision, even as hard as things had been.

But she didn’t want to be lulled—or bullied—into accepting whatever Brett offered. She needed to see that he acted rather than simply talked. He needed to demonstrate that things would change.

“Here’s what I can promise. I won’t call a lawyer over the weekend.” Then she got bold. “But I do want to see some changes. You can’t let one person terrorize the whole company.”

“Terrorize?”

She looked at him, his face earnest and concerned. Though he might also be a very good actor. He might have been acting all night. And this afternoon, too. “Not *you*. But her employees. She liked to use people as pawns in her little wars with other VPs.” She pressed her lips together a moment, then started up again before he could answer. “Are you going to let her come back?”

His answer would say a lot about whether he was just blowing smoke to get her to shut up about what had happened.

"I don't know." He leaned his elbow on the back of the sofa, looked down at her, and the moment suddenly felt intimate. "Is she worth a second chance? Is she too much of a pain in the ass? I don't know."

"I thought CEOs knew everything."

He shrugged, and the couch moved beneath them. Ivy let herself slide closer.

"If I knew everything," he said, "this whole mess never would have happened in the first place. But if she does come back, there will be major changes. I'm not willing to accept anyone's crap anymore just because they have a skill I need."

She'd always seen him as perfectly in control. But somehow his answer made him more human.

"I can assure you there will be no terrorizing on my watch again. Will you come back on Monday?"

He didn't ask again if she'd refrain from suing him. And she didn't tell him she wouldn't.

But she would force him to make an offer. "How much is the raise you're giving me for taking on the extra duties?"

He named a number that made her breath catch. It wouldn't get her out of this apartment or put Joy in a private school. But good Lord, she could at least start saving some money instead of living paycheck to paycheck.

"All right, I'll be there Monday."

"Thank you." Then he smiled.

Her heart flip-flopped as if she'd agreed to something deliciously sexual.

BRETT SAT IN HIS CAR WITHOUT STARTING THE ENGINE.

She was utterly enchanting. Like a beautiful, multicolored butterfly.

He'd wanted to put his mouth to hers, taste the sweet wine on her lips, close his eyes and breathe in her fruity scent.

The sad thing was that between all of them, him, the lawyers, Rhonda, they were about to tear the gossamer wings off her body.

If she decided to sue him.

Because he would have to fight. He couldn't let the company go down.

Maybe he just needed to fire Rhonda. But he'd never in his life given up on anyone completely. Not even his wife, until the day she'd asked him to leave and not come back.

If he could salvage Rhonda, salvage the situation.

And do right by Ivy at the same time.

He could do it. He would do it.

Everything depended on him.

"DON'T FALL FOR IT," HER MOTHER ADMONISHED. "HE'S just trying to buy you off, being nice, making promises."

Joy had gone to bed still talking about how nice Mr. Baker was. Ivy poured herself another glass of wine and turned out all the lights in the living room to sit in the dark and look out over the city below her.

She could still feel his warmth on the couch and detect his male scent. She'd wanted to savor it a little while longer.

Until her mother called.

"I'm not falling for anything, Mom."

"Men are scum. They'll say anything to get what they want." Her mother had blamed every man for what Ivy's father had done.

The lesson Ivy learned from her childhood—and from her time with Rupert—was that she could depend only on herself. She'd never depended on a man to keep her and Joy safe. Yes, she'd lived with her mother for a year after Joy was born, but she'd moved on as soon as she could. She didn't depend on anyone else's income that could suddenly be ripped away when they decided they were tired of you.

Was taking the raise Brett offered in the same realm?

"Here's what you need to do." Her mother went on and on. "Talk to a lawyer. You don't have to sue the company. But you do need to protect yourself. What if this big CEO decides to fire you later on down the road so you can't make trouble? You need him to sign some sort of agreement. And what the hell is this business with him *maybe* taking that bitch back after what she did to you?" Mom was definitely a plain speaker.

"He didn't say he was taking her back. He just said he wasn't firing her yet."

But really, what did that mean? And *if* he brought her back, would Rhonda find a way to punish her for telling Brett? And what about her promotion? Would that vanish?

"Anyway, Mom, it doesn't matter right now. I'm getting a new job title, a higher salary, and if he fires me, I'll be able to take that experience to an even better job." She was determined to think about the here and now, not what may or may not happen.

Her mother snorted. "Give me a break. He'll blackball you. He won't give you a good reference."

"Jordana, Gloria, and Grady will."

"I didn't raise a stupid girl, but you are being stupid. You have a daughter to protect. Don't screw this up."

Her mother had never pulled her punches. And she always managed a direct hit.

What was the right thing to do? The best thing for Joy?

She could go to a lawyer and *maybe* get a lot of money. Then again, she might not get anything. She could take the raise and the new job and gain some really good experience. She could even go back to night school and add that to her resume as well.

Or Brett could bring back Rhonda and fire Ivy instead.

"You know, Mom, I don't know what's going to happen. But I want to learn everything I can from Jordana. This is an opportunity. And I want to try."

"Fine. Try. But at least see a lawyer and learn what he can do for you. It's your responsibility to your child to find out."

The apartment was blessedly silent after her mother hung up. The lights below were so pretty. Ivy curled into the corner of the sofa, smoothing out the lumpy cushion beneath her bottom. Then she sipped the wine.

What *was* her responsibility to Joy? Was it to make Rhonda and the company pay?

Or was it to learn a new skill, get a promotion, more money, and keep moving her way up? Somehow that seemed to be the lesson she wanted to teach Joy.

Rather than teaching her that all men were liars and scum.

IVY'S CELL PHONE RANG AT A LITTLE AFTER EIGHT ON Saturday morning. Joy was eating cereal at the table and playing on Ivy's iPad.

"Hey, it's me."

Her heart did a funky pitter-patter. Brett's low tone and his words were so casual. So sweet. So intimate in her ear.

"It's a sunny day. Probably the last nice weekend since the weatherman is forecasting a week of rain starting Monday. I wondered if you and Joy would like to go to the zoo."

She almost pulled the phone away to look at the screen,

to make sure she actually knew the person on the other end. She'd expected him to call to see if she'd changed her mind about contacting a lawyer. Or even to see if she was still upset after all the things Rhonda had said.

But the zoo?

"I... well... the zoo?" She sounded inane.

He gave her an out. "Unless you have other plans."

"The zoo?" Joy piped up, suddenly *not* so absorbed in the iPad.

Ivy had big plans for the day. There was laundry, changing the sheets, the shopping, paying bills, fixing meals that she could stick in the freezer for the following week.

Joy barreled into the kitchen, hanging on Ivy's pant leg and mouthed, *The zoo*, her eyes wide and bright as copper pennies.

"Um, which zoo?" Another inane comment, because it didn't matter which zoo he took them to. But it gave her time to think. It gave her time to listen to her mother's voice again.

To her mother's warnings.

"San Francisco. I love the lemurs." He said it without inflection, but she swore she heard a smile in there somewhere. "They're little rascals."

Joy tugged on her pant leg again, and Ivy clenched the phone tighter. "It's such short notice."

But God help her, she wanted to go. As much as Joy did. She wanted to ignore her mother's words.

"The idea came to me out of the blue when I was out for my run this morning," he explained. "It was so damn pretty with all that sun."

The man certainly knew how to entice. With that voice, he could get a woman to do just about anything.

Especially when she *wanted* to say yes.

"Please," her daughter pleaded.

Ivy put a hand over the phone. "You don't even know who it is."

"But it's the *zoo*."

She had the urge to growl at Joy.

"You should know," Brett said, "that I asked my daughter first, but she said the baby's too young. I don't think so, but I couldn't get her to budge."

"So you're saying we're second choice." She laughed softly.

"Not second choice. But I do have to maintain my status as the best grandpa ever. Not that I'll let Valerie call me Grandpa. I'm going to be Pops to her. When she can talk."

This time she gave a full-throated laugh. He was crazy about being a grandfather. She couldn't help liking him for that.

"Joy is pulling on my leg and begging me to let her go."

"Not just her, I want you to, too."

I want you. It was all she really heard.

Even though she knew what she should say, "Yes, we'd love it," was what came out of her mouth.

"Great. Can you both be ready by nine? The park opens at ten. I'm sure Joy won't want to miss a moment."

Joy was ready now, leaping around the kitchen at the idea of an outing to the zoo. "We'll be ready," Ivy told him. "And thank you," she added. "It's a very nice offer."

But what exactly did he want from her?

Yesterday he was her CEO, the sum total of their conversations being about work and his granddaughter. Then suddenly everything was turned upside down, and they were taking walks in the park, he came over for dinner, did her dishes, poured her wine, and took them out to the zoo.

He had to want *something*.

Of course he did. He wanted to make sure she didn't sue.

He was attempting to turn her into a friend so that she'd feel too guilty to call a lawyer.

At least that's what her mother would say. Ivy didn't want to listen.

She'd rather go to the zoo.

6

It had been an insane idea, but once it popped into Brett's head, he couldn't get rid of it. Megan thought two months old was too young for the zoo. But six years old was perfect.

It was like doing the things he'd missed out on when Megan was young. He'd always been too busy for a trip to the zoo with his wife and daughter.

Of course he should have been at the office preparing for the audit by The Nelson Group. But that was the beauty of being CEO. You could delegate. And make the executive decision that you'd rather go to the zoo with a pretty woman and her adorably precocious child.

They'd been waiting at the curb for him when he pulled up, dressed in layers in case San Francisco was much colder than the Peninsula. Which it often was if the fog rolled in.

Joy had chattered the whole way, about her friends at school, her favorite books, her favorite movies, her favorite songs, her favorite games.

Ivy was silent most of the drive, smiling at her daughter in the backseat, answering a question when she had to, but quiet. She'd been far more enthusiastic at work when he'd shown her pictures of Valerie.

She was wary. He couldn't blame her.

But he couldn't help his awareness of every move she made, the shifting of her legs in her skinny jeans, her bare ankles above her sneakers, the long column of her throat. Her sweet, citrusy scent. The deep plum of her lipstick.

And the irreverent thought that he wanted plum lipstick stains all over him.

He felt twenty-two instead of fifty-two, lusting after the girl in the front row of his college statistics class.

The parking lot was only half full, but there were folks unloading, lots of strollers, and gaggles of kids with parents. When Ivy reached into her purse as they entered the ticket line, he stilled her with a hand on her arm. She hadn't put on her jacket and her skin was warm in the thin shirt she'd worn.

"My treat," he said.

"We can't let you—"

He put a finger to her lips, the touch electric, like a current running through them both. "I invited you. So I'm paying."

She didn't move, didn't speak, as if she were afraid that opening her mouth might seem like an invitation to something.

Something equally electric.

Their eyes held. Then Joy raced back to them from the entrance through which she'd been gazing longingly. He dropped his hand.

Ivy whispered, "Thank you," as if she didn't have more voice than that sexy murmur.

He understood then why he'd brought her. It wasn't about reliving his past or fixing his mistakes or making sure she didn't sue for the things Rhonda had said.

It was about her. Spending time with her. Looking at her.

Being close to her. Shutting his eyes and scenting her next to him. Sneaking in a touch when he could find an excuse.

Joy was a bonus.

All it had taken was that first sighting of Ivy's bare feet. Completely crazy, but her bare feet had turned his pilot light to On.

Joy tugged on her mother's hand. "Can we go in the store, Mommy?"

It was filled with stuffed animals and pictures, postcards and books, trinkets and stamp pads. All things animal. Joy hugged a tiger to her. Then a bear. Then a lion, and next a monkey as she raced down the aisle of fluffy stuffed toys. "Look, this monkey's fifty percent off. And look how big he is."

Ivy winced beside him. He'd never thought in terms of bargain prices. He saw something he wanted, he bought it. But Ivy had taught her daughter to be thrifty.

He sensed Ivy's embarrassment, as if watching expenses was something she had to be ashamed of. He wanted to buy the monkey, but he appreciated the faux pas that would be.

"That's a sloth, sweetie, not a monkey." Ivy didn't say the girl couldn't have it.

Joy held out the big brown animal. "He's cute."

"Yes, he is. Come on, we've got lots of stuff to see." Ivy held out her hand.

Joy stowed the sloth back on the shelf without an argument and slipped her hand into her mother's. Then she held out her other hand to him as she skipped outside.

It was so damn sweet, and his heart flipped in his chest. "What do you want to see first?" he asked the little sweetheart, his gaze on Ivy.

A puff of wind lifted her hair, blowing it across her cheek. His heart hammered with the need to reach out, smooth it down for her. Touch the soft skin of her cheek.

"You said you loved the lemurs." Then she bent slightly to Joy. "What do you think? The lemurs first? Mr. Baker says they're rascals."

Joy began to bounce on her toes between them. "The lemurs, the lemurs." Together, they lifted her, swinging her between them.

She could only be held back so long, then she was racing ahead, bounding up to hug the railing outside the lemur habitat. "I don't see them."

Brett caught up with her. "You have to look up in the trees."

There were reds and browns and ring-tails, and ones whose eyes looked like raccoons. Joy capered back and forth, pointing out every one she could find.

"I'd really like to be Brett instead of Mr. Baker," he said as Ivy stood at his side. "If that's okay with you. It's just for today."

She held her breath, then finally let it out. "Okay. Just for today. I like her to respect formality with adults."

He understood. But it was a way to keep their distance from him.

"Can we see the monkeys, too?" Joy's curls bobbed as she jumped from foot to foot with excitement and anticipation.

She wanted to see everything, and Brett and Ivy were just along for the ride. He adored the exuberance of children, the way they said whatever was in their heads

"The baboons have funny butts," she whispered. And like all children, she wanted to know the *why* of everything.

Why did the baboons have such colorful faces? "They look like they're painted on."

When a couple walked by, two children in tow, chattering in a foreign language, Joy had to know. "What are you speaking?"

"Norwegian," the blond woman told her.

"It sounds very pretty," Joy said, before dashing off to another adventure.

She clung to the gorilla cage, willing them to approach over. "The silverback. I want him to say hi. How come they don't move?"

He took pictures of Ivy and Joy, then he took selfies of all of them together.

They watched the giraffe feeding, then Joy dragged them to the sea lions as they performed for their lunch.

She carried a spiral notebook with her and laboriously wrote down the name of every animal she saw, asking Brett to help her spell. She screamed with delight when the hippo rose up and shot out a great spout of water. She wanted to eat in the Leaping Lemur Café because she loved the name of it, then shrieked her amazement at all the flamingos close by as they ate. She rode the steam train over and over, seeing something new every time.

Everything was spectacular to her, and Brett felt renewed watching her delight as he stood beside Ivy, their shoulders brushing, the backs of their hands sliding against each other, setting off sparks inside him.

"Oh my God, my feet are getting tired," Ivy whispered to him, her scent enveloping him as she laughed softly. "Was I ever that young with that much energy?"

"Just watching her makes me feel young again." Just as his reaction to Ivy suffused him with heat and tingled along his skin. Like he was a teenager anticipating his first kiss, his first touch.

"You're crazy. And just wait, she's going to zonk out like a light on the way home." Her unrestrained laughter reached deep inside him.

But Joy was a wind-up doll that never wound down. She raced to view the anteaters and the rhinos and lamented the absence of elephants. She was fascinated by the kangaroos and adored the cuddly koalas. She grumbled when Ivy made her stop long enough to put her jacket on as the city's legendary fog rolled in off the ocean, which was just across the highway. Then they had to stop at the sloth exhibit because Joy absolutely needed to see what a real sloth looked like after holding the stuffed toy in her arms.

"They're so cute. And so slow," she said with a hint of amazement.

Outside the polar bear habitat, Brett picked up Ivy's hand, raising it to his lips to brush a kiss over her knuckles, electricity zipping through him. Resistance was futile; he'd wanted to touch her all day. "Thank you for letting me bring her here. I hope Valerie is just as excited, but watching Joy has given me a glimpse of what it will be like."

He'd expected her to pull away, but instead Ivy squeezed his hand. "We're the ones who have to thank you. For the tickets, lunch, the ice cream, for driving us. I really didn't expect you to pay for all this."

She'd argued over every purchase, but he'd won in the end. "I wouldn't have missed a minute." His gaze fell to her mouth and some extraordinary force compelled him closer, closer—

Joy tugged on his jacket. "Why don't the polar bears have ice and snow? Don't they need it to live on? When I see them on TV, they're always in the snow."

Brett squatted in front of her. "That's why they have water to play in. It makes them feel like home."

Joy pouted prettily. "But I want to see snow. I've never seen snow."

He gave her a wide-eyed stare of amazement. "Never?"

She shook her head. "Uh-uh."

"No snowballs or snowmen?"

Her lower lip jutted out as she shook her head vigorously.

"What about ice skating?"

She shook again, her curls flying.

"So see, if you can live without snowmen and snowballs and ice skating, so can the polar bears."

She frowned, thinking. "I guess so. Plus they have people to give them food so they don't have to hunt."

She was truly adorable. He'd always believed that animals were better off in the wild. But little kids needed zoos.

They stayed until the very last moment before closing, Joy sneaking in one more fascinated minute with a docent holding a cockatoo.

"I don't think she's missed a darn thing." Ivy tucked her hair behind her ear.

He had the strangest urge to lick her right there, along the shell, biting lightly on her lobe. He wanted to watch her eyes widen with the carnal nature of it.

"Come on, sweetie," Ivy called, holding out her hand. "We're going to get locked in if you don't hurry."

"That's okay," but the little girl came running, grabbing both their hands at once.

"Let's use the restroom one more time before we leave. It's a long drive." Ivy steered them in the right direction, giving him a laughing smile over her shoulder.

The restrooms were across from the gift shop, which offered one more thing he couldn't resist.

He exited the store just as Ivy and Joy left the women's room. He met them halfway.

When Ivy opened her mouth to protest the sloth under his arm, he said, "Don't say a word. Just let me do this. Please."

She huffed once. "It's too much."

"It was fifty percent off."

Joy was bug-eyed, her little hands quivering to grab the sloth, but she was too polite to rush him.

Ivy eyed him, pursed her lips, then finally smiled a smile to knock him sideways. "All right. Thank you."

"Is that for me?" Joy whispered with awe.

"For you." He held out the sloth.

She put her hand over her mouth with a gasp of wonder.

"What do you say, sweetie?" Ivy urged.

"Thank you." Then she hugged the big furry brown toy tightly to her. "He's beautiful."

He realized then how much he missed spoiling a little girl.

How much he missed spoiling a special woman.

And these two deserved all the spoiling he could give them.

JOY HAD FALLEN ASLEEP, THE SLOTH AS HER PILLOW, ALMOST as soon as they'd merged onto the freeway. When they got home, Brett carried the sleeping child up the stairs, inside, and straight down the hall to her bedroom, which was obvious with the stars and clouds painted on the walls, the pink comforter on the twin bed, and the mountain of stuffed animals.

"Thank you." Ivy had said thank you way too many times. Overkill. But she still felt guilty accepting everything like the day had been some sort of date.

Now she wasn't sure how to get rid of Brett once he was inside her apartment.

Worse, she didn't want to get rid of him.

The day had been glorious. He hadn't fussed that Joy had to see ab-so-lutely *everything*. He'd been engaged, listening raptly to her childish chatter. He'd answered a million questions, silly and otherwise, and not one complaint.

By one o'clock, Ivy decided he was trying to get to her through her daughter. By three o'clock, she didn't care. She'd enjoyed every moment, delighted in his nearness as much as Joy delighted in the animals. She found herself caught up in watching him, the way he smiled, the sound of his laughter, his concentration over Joy's every question.

He was getting to her, oh boy, was he ever getting to her.

But what did he really want?

"I just took off her shoes and pulled a blanket over her." He filled up the kitchen with his presence just the way he filled up a boardroom.

It wasn't obligation that made her say, "There's some leftover meatloaf and potatoes if you're hungry." They hadn't stopped along the way for dinner since Joy had been asleep.

A long moment of silence lay between them, as if they were both weighing the options—and the consequences—of a dinner of leftovers. Alone in the apartment while Joy slept.

Leftovers won. "That would be great. Thanks."

Or maybe Ivy had lost her mind. "It's the least I can do after all you did today." The day had been so good, so easy, yet suddenly she sounded stilted and nervous. She flapped a hand at the table. "Have a seat. It'll be ready in a jiffy."

"Let me get you a glass of wine while you cook?" He put his hand on the fridge door.

"Only if you have one with me." Which meant he'd have to stay longer for any alcohol effects to wear off. Not that one glass in a big man would impair him.

"That sounds great," he agreed and opened the fridge to hand her the leftovers.

They drank wine and ate on the sofa. For some strange reason, warmed-up meatloaf had never tasted so good.

No man had ever smelled so good.

Even when they'd finished, she wasn't ready for him to leave. It might crazy, even wrong on so many levels, but she shucked her shoes and curled her bare feet up on the embarrassingly lumpy couch.

"I haven't seen Joy so excited in—" She shrugged. "—probably forever. Thank you for that."

He relaxed deeper into the sofa. "I wasn't around for my family as much as I should have been when my daughter was a kid."

"Working too much?"

He smiled, a hint of sadness in his eyes. "My ex-wife called me a workaholic. And I could never deny that. I was always pushing to get ahead, taking on stuff that pulled me away from the family." He'd turned inward, but suddenly came back. "That's why I admire your insistence on leaving work on time to be with Joy."

Ivy huffed a laugh. "That's nothing noble. It's about not having to pay the day care premium if I'm late."

"Don't sell yourself short." He touched her arm, shooting a zing along her nerve endings. "Rhonda was a fool for saying the things she did. Being a single mother without any help from the father is one of the hardest jobs I know. But rewarding, I'm sure."

"Yes, it's rewarding." And incredibly difficult. "I wouldn't trade Joy in for anything."

He nodded, understanding completely. "Watching her today fed my soul. It made me resolve that I'm not going to miss out on those times with my granddaughter."

She admired him. "Do you have other kids?" He'd never talked about any.

"Just Megan. My wife couldn't have any more after our daughter was born."

She wanted to ask so many questions, exactly when he'd gotten divorced, did he date, why he'd never remarried—though that was obvious, the workaholic syndrome.

But none of it was her business. She didn't want to get tangled up in his life—he was the CEO, after all. Besides, she didn't need a man around telling her what to do or disapproving of her decisions or expecting her to wait on him or correcting her.

So why had she invited him to finish her leftovers? Especially now that she couldn't get rid of him until he was ready to go.

If only it didn't feel so right and comfortable to have him filling up her living room. If only his body so close to hers didn't feel divine.

If only she'd woken up Joy in the car instead of letting Brett carry her daughter to bed.

She jumped up then, fearing she'd do something she'd regret later if she didn't get away from him.

"More wine," she explained as she dashed to the kitchen. Thank God her wineglasses were small; there was just enough left in the bottle to fill them both halfway. It was a cheap brand, and she felt ashamed, but whatever, he knew it now. Her whole existence was about money and how much things cost. She blushed, remembering Joy's comment about the stuffed animal being 50 percent off, like she was teaching her daughter to be cheap. But really it was about not being wasteful.

Why did having him in her house make her feel like she needed to justify herself? Why did it make her feel like she was *less than*?

The onslaught of negativity marched her back into the living room, the wine bottle in her hand. He was still sitting there, larger than life, in *her* living room, big, bold, and beautiful, making her breath catch. Making her *want*. "I have to ask this. Because I don't understand. What do you really want from me? To promise I'm not going to sue? That I'm not going to screw up the deal with The Nelson Group? That I'll keep everyone's secret about how badly Rhonda treats people?"

He rose, slowly, until she felt as if he towered over her, and padded across the carpet like a stealthy predator sneaking up on her, stopping only inches away so that his scent invaded her thoughts, took over her mind.

"What I really want," he said so softly it was little more than a sexy whisper she felt across her skin, "is to taste every inch of your body."

The wine bottle slipped from her numb fingers, landing unbroken on the carpet and rolling a few inches.

There wasn't a breath left in her lungs, and she was suddenly lightheaded, swaying into him.

He reached out, so very slowly, giving her time to stop him if she wanted to, if she could. But she didn't have the will to budge a muscle.

His big hand slid beneath her hair, wrapped around her nape, pulled her close until she had to tip her head back to see him. He took her lips with a gentleness that set her blood humming in her veins and her skin buzzing. He tasted of sweet of wine and sizzling male. She opened her mouth to him without thought, without fight. With need and desire. With carnal loneliness.

God, he was so good. So perfect. Taking and giving, sliding his tongue over hers, setting her on fire and melting her down. There was just his hand holding her, his mouth drawing her in, and his scent draping her like a sensual curtain. He didn't touch her anywhere else, didn't press his hard body against hers.

What I really want is to taste every inch of your body.

Now he owned every inch of her.

When he backed off, her lips and body followed him as if they had all the will and she had none. She opened her eyes, realizing only then that she'd closed them.

He regarded her with a steel-gray gaze. "Whatever you decide to do about Rhonda isn't going to make any difference to how much I want to drag you down onto the carpet right this very minute." A flame blazed to life in his eyes. "But I'm not going to do that no matter how badly I want it. I won't bother you again this weekend. You need time to think. Time to separate *this*—" He pulled her in for one more devastating taste of his mouth. "—and work."

He bent down, swiping the wine bottle off the carpet and reaching around her to set it on the kitchen table. "No matter what you decide, today was the best day I've had in a long, long time." He grinned suddenly, like a little boy. "Right up there with the day Valerie was born."

Then he was gone. Leaving behind only the heady scent of big, hot male.

HIS BODY WAS VIBRATING IN TIME WITH CAR'S ENGINE AS he drove away from Ivy. More than anything in this universe, he'd wanted to stay, to lock out the rest of the world out and make love to her all night long.

With his mouth on hers, he hadn't cared about the company, about the investors, about Rhonda.

There was only Ivy's softness against his lips and her sweet taste in his mouth.

Since his divorce, he'd had only sophisticated affairs with sophisticated women who didn't expect more than 20 percent of his attention. They weren't bothered by broken dinner engagements because they did their share of the breaking. Business came first for them as much as it did for him.

But everything was different with Ivy. He wanted to give her so much more than 20 percent.

The problem was how long he could separate business and pleasure.

Because in the end, Ivy still held the key to the company's future as much as he did.

7

True to his word, Brett hadn't bothered her again the entire weekend. That would have been a good thing if Ivy hadn't relived that stupendous, delicious kiss over and over. She'd fallen asleep to the taste of him in her mouth and woken thinking she was sleeping in his arms.

Only to realize it was a dream.

His deep voice replayed in her head, saying the words that turned her inside out. *What I really want is to taste every inch of your body*.

Still, she'd managed to do the cleaning, laundry, shopping, and cooking. Sunday was usually her day with Joy, doing something different and special, but they'd had Saturday together.

Joy had helped her with the chores, chattering endlessly about Brett and the zoo. And the sloth—she'd named him Rolf because it sort of rhymed with sloth—went everywhere with her.

Monday morning at the office, Ivy's whole body tingled just waiting to see Brett. Yet she was mortified, too. She'd actually kissed the CEO.

"Ivy." Grady gestured her into his office, bursting her thought bubble.

He closed the door behind her. "I need to apologize for putting you in that position with Rhonda."

Tall, handsome, fit, he really was pretty darn sweet for a boss. She understood exactly why Jordana had fallen for him like a rock off a cliff. "It wasn't your fault, Grady."

"I wish you'd come to me first. I could have prevented that disaster."

Coming to Grady would have been like admitting she couldn't handle her own problems. Of course, she *hadn't* handled it. "Thanks, but it happened just the way it was supposed to."

"I mean I'm your boss, not Rhonda. That discussion should have taken place with me."

Her stomach sank. He was chiding her. And he had a point she couldn't deny. "I'm sorry. I didn't think."

"At least you exposed Rhonda for the petty tyrant she is."

Wow. Grady was usually so diplomatic.

He waved a hand, dismissing Rhonda's specter. "Jordana's got all your new paperwork. If something doesn't work for you, let me know. I'd appreciate it if you'd interview the temps they send as your replacement. You know best how I like things done."

"Yes. Of course." She was glad for the added responsibility—and the compliment—but the guilt remained over not going to him first. She should have. The whole mess could have been avoided.

Except that Grady would have waged the battle with Rhonda and Ivy believed the confrontation needed to be hers.

Even Gloria and Jordana thought so.

No wait, they'd simply said she had to stop letting

Rhonda walk all over her, not that she should ask Rhonda for a raise.

Her head was spinning by the time she entered Jordana's office.

"Hey." Jordana brushed her long dark hair off her shoulders where it had fallen as she'd hunched too close to her computer screen. "Let me look at you." She signaled for Ivy to twirl. "Okay. I don't see any bruises or broken bones. Thank God. Close the door and take a seat."

Taking the chair opposite Jordana, Ivy crossed her legs. She'd worn a shorter skirt today than the usual she'd chosen since working for Rhonda. Her heels were taller and her neckline lower. *Take that, Rhonda Clark.* But she hadn't been thinking about Rhonda when she dressed this morning.

She'd been floating in a haze of Brett Baker thoughts.

"No internal damage either," she said to follow along with Jordana's quip.

"Fabulous." Jordana pushed a folder across the desk. "Okay, this is confidential. I mean about why Rhonda isn't here. I'm not allowed to talk about it. Grady's not allowed to either." She leaned close and dropped her voice. "Except that we harped on it for hours over the weekend, and I explained concisely what a petty little tyrant she is."

Ivy laughed. "Grady seemed to think he came up with that description all on his own."

Jordana slapped her chest. "No way. That was me. Anyway, I haven't even told Gloria."

A chill tiptoed up Ivy's spine. "Did Brett tell you we can't talk to anyone?"

"No, no." Jordana's hair flew with a negative shake of her head. "I'm not saying *you* can't talk to whoever you want, just that *I* can't. Employee confidentiality and all. It's really for your protection. I can't discuss anything that I learn in the process of doing my job."

It still felt to Ivy as if she were being told to shut up. By Brett.

"But here's what I really want to say. Because we're friends." The smile on Jordana's face shone bright. "I'm so proud of you for standing up to Rhonda like that."

"Grady said I should have come to him because he's actually my boss."

Jordana made a face and flapped her hand. "Sure, whatever. He's got a technical point. But my point is you did great. I'm just sorry she was such a bitch to you. All that stuff she said is crap."

Ivy blushed. Yes, Brett had definitely revealed all, which wasn't surprising since it would have to be documented for both her and Rhonda's files. But it was like fluttering her intimate lingerie on the clothes line for the whole neighborhood to see. Even if it was Jordana, she hated her friend knowing that Rhonda had called her a failure for being a single mother.

Jordana tapped the folder. "So here it is. If you can look it over and sign the paperwork, then I can enter it into the system. You've got a new title, too, HR Supervisor."

"Supervisor?" Ivy blurted. "But I'm not supervising anyone."

"I didn't manage anyone either, but employees like it better if they're talking with someone who's got some authority."

Combined with the salary he'd mentioned, this appeared more and more like Brett was bribing her to keep her mouth shut.

"I already called the temp agency," Jordana went on briskly. "They're sending over a few resumes to see if you like any of them."

To see if *she* liked them. Grady had said it was because she knew how he wanted things done. Was it just another bribe?

Make her feel important so she doesn't go running to a lawyer.

But this was Jordana, her friend. Would Jordana really mouth the party line to get Ivy to go along?

She suddenly felt stifled, by the job, the raise, the promotion, by her own thoughts. She grabbed the folder and the list of temps Jordana had laid on top of it. "Sounds great. I'll look over everything, and I'll talk to the temps. Phone interviews should be fine to make the decision."

"Hey," Jordana said when Ivy stood. "You want to do lunch with Gloria?"

"No. Better not today. Too much going on. Besides, I brought my workout stuff to go for a walk out in the park today. But thanks." It would be great to get someone else's opinion besides her mother's. Or Brett's. But she didn't want to be in the middle between them, deciding what she should and shouldn't say in front of Gloria. Or putting Jordana in the middle between Ivy and the company.

And she needed to think.

Ivy hugged the folder to her chest. "I'll get the paperwork back to you."

Then she yanked the door open and marched past Rhonda's empty office, which yawned like a giant cave hiding a monster.

She turned the corner, her head down, and nearly collided with Brett.

"Hey." He steadied her with his hands on her shoulders.

She wanted to ask if there was a nondisclosure agreement inside the folder she was clutching. If there was some small paragraph hidden in all the other words that said she couldn't sue if she signed.

But there was also a huge, terrible part of her that wanted to throw herself into his arms and finish that kiss they'd started last night.

SHE FELT SO DAMN GOOD BENEATH HIS HANDS. THIS CLOSE, her body heat damn near singed him. Brett wanted last night's kiss all over again. It was insane how involved his emotions had become after only a weekend. After only one glorious day with her. After one perfect kiss.

Brett forced his hands back to his sides. He didn't trust himself not to touch more of her. Every inch of her.

"You okay?" he asked.

She flapped a folder at him. "Just work, work, work. Gotta run." She pushed past him.

Last night's kiss had embarrassed her. Or she was afraid someone would see them together and misconstrue. Or... there were any number of reasons she would run away from him.

Right now he had the staff meeting to deal with. Duty called. Much as he would have preferred to follow her back to her desk and ask what was wrong. Or gaze at her legs in that short skirt and her feet in heels tall enough to punch up his blood pressure.

He'd given her the weekend to think. Maybe she needed more time.

Fifteen minutes later, he sat at the head of the conference table. "As most of you will have noticed, Jordana is joining us in Rhonda's stead." He smiled at her, noticing that she'd chosen the opposite end of the table from Grady. Just as Gloria and Parker kept a professional distance. It was common knowledge that the four had melted down into couples.

"Where's Rhonda?" Knox Turner asked. He and Rhonda saw eye to eye on just about nothing.

"Rhonda is taking a leave of absence."

There was a heightened buzz of low conversation.

"Jesus," Court Stevens spouted. "For how long? Is she coming back?" There was definitely a hopeful glint in his eye. As VP of Manufacturing and controlling the largest headcount in the company, he had weekly dealings with Rhonda, not all of them easy or pleasant.

"The leave is indefinite and the reasons are confidential. And that's what you're going to tell your people when they ask." They would all speculate on everything from a power play by Jordana to firing to a fatal illness. And some tall tales he couldn't possibly imagine. "In the meantime, Jordana will be taking over for her. I have full confidence in her abilities. Ivy Elliot will become her aide as HR Supervisor." A strange kick jump-started his heart as he said her name.

Business versus pleasure.

Right now, there was only business.

"I've also got a definite start date for The Nelson Group from Des Moines. They're bringing their auditors in for due diligence on the Monday after Thanksgiving. You can expect them here for at least a week, maybe two."

"How's that going to affect the holiday?" Knox asked.

"It shouldn't have an impact. Their auditors will be working mostly with Gloria's group, and she's totally prepared. Parker, give Hannah a heads up, they're going to want to see the orders." Hannah Fall was their Customer Service manager, and since they would start shipping product the beginning of the new year, orders would also be a high priority for the Nelson auditors. "Lucy, they'll want to examine our systems to make sure we don't have any data holes."

"All systems are solid." Lucy Perez was VP of MIS. "Bring 'em on."

"Have no fear, there will be something for everyone." Manufacturing would be all about inventory levels and quality control. "Finn, they're going to hit R&D hard since that's where we want to use any capital they give us."

Their R&D head, Finn Rafferty, nodded. "I'm ready for anything they throw at us."

"That's two weeks to prepare, people. Mitch Redmond said they'd have a list of everything they'll want to examine by Wednesday. But be prepared for anything."

The rest of the meeting was the norm. Parker Hunt stayed behind as the rest of them filed out. "Is Mitch coming, too?"

"Sure." It was Mitch's gig, after all.

Parker slapped his hand to his forehead in mock terror. "Do not leave him alone with Gloria."

Brett laughed. "You don't have a thing to worry about. She already chose you."

"But that guy's slick and sly."

"You just have to be slicker and slyer." Brett cocked his head. "Why does that sound revolting?"

Parker laughed and clapped him on the back. "Because that guy is."

"Your jealousy's showing."

"Damn right. I'm nuts for that woman."

Parker went away whistling a tune Brett thought might be "On the Street Where you Live" from *My Fair Lady.* Or something equally romantic.

He hadn't felt like that about a woman in a long, long time.

Until now, when anticipating his next encounter with Ivy quickened his heart.

IVY HADN'T LIED ABOUT WALKING DURING HER LUNCH hour. Sometimes in the evening she did Jazzercise to a video while Joy finished her homework, but often she was too tired or there was too much to do. In the last couple of months since she'd started working for Rhonda, she was feeling out of shape. After walking out there with Brett and his suggestion about changing in the Manufacturing locker room, it sounded like a great way to ensure she exercised every day.

Of course, it didn't have anything to do with wanting to be in shape for Brett.

Just like wearing the short skirt, high heels, and low-cut shirt had nothing to do with him.

Right.

She was putting on her socks when Hannah Fall slammed through the door and darn near shrieked. "Oh my God, you scared me." She put a hand to her chest. "There's never anyone in here." Manufacturing was predominantly male.

"Sorry. I heard you run out at the park, and it sounded like a fabulous idea."

Hannah threw her bag on the bench. "I don't run. Bad for my knees." It didn't show. Around forty or so, Hannah was in great shape. "I do a fast walk. Really fast. Does that work for you?" She tipped to one side, yanking off a high heel, her strawberry hair falling over her shoulders. Her hair was the lightest shade of red and her skin a matching pale. A tube of sunblock peeked out of her gym bag.

"I don't want to get in the way of your exercise."

Hannah flapped a hand, then began unzipping her dress without a care. "The company will be nice. When I'm by myself, I think about work the whole time. The point is to clear your mind. Besides—" She waggled her eyebrows as she stripped off her pantyhose. "I'm going to pump you for information about Rhonda Clark. Everyone's dying to know if Brett fired her and he's just not letting the cat out of the bag yet."

"I really can't talk about that." She hadn't decided how much she wanted to tell.

Hannah didn't seem to mind being shut down. "And hey, congrats on the promotion."

"You have really heard everything." News traveled the grapevine way too fast, especially when she was the subject of it.

Tapping the side of her head, Hannah said, "Ears to the ground, gotta hear everything. In Customer Service, we get the best of all worlds, everything that's going on over in Manufacturing *and* with all the big bosses in the Admin building."

After dressing quickly, Hannah slathered on the sunblock—despite the fact that it was cloudy—and they were off after a few stretches outside the building.

Hannah set a good pace that quickly had Ivy's pulse rate up. She'd been right about *really fast*. "So what's the speculation about Rhonda?" Ivy shouldn't ask, since she was the reason Rhonda was gone. But she justified it by telling herself that as the new HR Supervisor, she needed to know what people were saying.

"Scuttlebutt is that Brett and Rhonda were having an affair and she got too serious."

Ivy actually felt her jaw drop. "That's a joke, right?" she finally managed to ask.

"No." Hannah held up three fingers. "Scout's honor. There's also the one about Knox Turner and Rhonda doing the do. You know, because they're always fighting. Opposites attract and all that." Hannah shuddered. "Actually, I find both images horrifying."

So did Ivy, especially the one about Brett. "But why would Rhonda go on leave if she was having an affair with Knox? Wouldn't Brett just fire them both?"

Hannah snorted. "He didn't fire Parker Hunt or Gloria

King. And he even gave Jordana Davis a promotion for sleeping with Grady Masterson."

The hairs on Ivy's arms rose with indignation. "She didn't get a promotion for *that*. She deserved the promotion because she did most of Rhonda's work."

"Really?" Hannah's eyes brightened despite the fact that dark clouds were starting to roll in over them.

Ivy realized how easy it was to let confidential stuff slip out, especially in defense of your friends. "What I mean is—"

"Oh come on. I know the real reason they promoted Jordana. Everyone knows it. Whenever, absolutely *whenever* you went to Rhonda for something, she sent you to Jordana. In fact, I stopped going to Rhonda altogether. The only time she did anything was if upper management got involved. Only the high profile stuff." Then she shrugged. "But people like to make up really good stories. Gossip needs to be salacious or no one's interested."

Runners and walkers dotted the park as they reached the path along the shoreline, but there were very few people having lunch out today as the sky darkened overhead.

Ivy glanced at her companion when they hit their stride and decided to keep her mouth shut. *She* didn't want to be salacious gossip.

"But here's the thing," Hannah went on, barely out of breath, "there's always a nugget of truth in some of the stuff you hear. I don't mean the sexy stuff, because honestly, I can't *ever* picture Knox Turner and Rhonda. I'm talking about the small things, like who's going for this promotion or who's shafting their buddy. Or departments suddenly combining and jobs becoming redundant. Knowledge is power when you're a female manager."

"And you're pumping me for knowledge right now?"

Hannah smiled wide. "Of course." Then she pointed a

finger. "But I also know how to keep secrets." She zipped her lips. "The thing is to gather intel, not give it away."

"So you're saying I can tell you everything I know and you won't tell a soul."

"Absolutely I won't tell. But if I were you I also wouldn't reveal something you don't want anyone else in the company to know. Not even to me." She dropped her voice. "Rhonda has spies everywhere." Then Hannah sprinted ahead. "Come on. We better pick up the pace or we'll get drenched."

Ivy realized Hannah was warning her.

Rhonda might be gone. But she was still watching.

8

After the staff meeting, Brett, along with Knox Turner, had headed over to the weekly production meeting. It ran well into the lunch hour.

Knox had just reached for the side door out of Manufacturing when it was wrenched open and two drenched runners in jogging gear came barreling through.

Their laughter turned into giggles as they shook water off themselves like wet dogs.

"Sorry." Hannah Fall put her hand over her mouth to stifle her laughter.

But Ivy was all Brett could focus on. Her short dark hair was stuck to her head, her T-shirt and tight leggings molded to her body.

"You know it's raining out there," Knox said with mock seriousness. "You could get wet. And I bet neither of you brought umbrellas over from the Admin building, did you?"

"No, sir, we didn't." Hannah said, raising her hand in a salute, her eyes sparkling. She always seemed ready to find the joke in anything. "It looks like you didn't either."

Knox snorted. "Brett drove the half block. I only have to

run across to Engineering." The two buildings were so close they were almost one with only a small driveway between. "I don't think it'll muss my do too much." He patted his hair.

Hannah laughed at him. "God forbid you should muss your do, sir." A very mocking *sir*.

"I can wait for you two and drive you back," Brett offered.

Ivy jumped in then. "No, that's okay. Thanks. The rain's letting up now. We'll be fine."

Hannah Fall looked at her. So did Knox. She'd sounded a little desperate. Like getting into Brett's car for a short ride back to the Admin building would suddenly make the gossip rounds, morphing from getting out of the rain to a full-blown affair. Even if Hannah Fall was in the car.

All because of that kiss on Saturday night. He had her running scared.

"We'll be a while anyway," Hannah said, as if she had to justify Ivy's rejection. "Have to shower and all that."

Knox watched Hannah as if he were shocked she'd talk in front of them about taking a shower.

Brett experienced a sudden visceral image of Ivy, water cascading over her body, her head thrown back as she rinsed her hair, the long column of her throat inviting his kiss, his lips, his tongue.

"Well, all right then." His voice seemed to crack in the middle like an adolescent.

With smiles, Hannah's broad and Ivy's hesitant, they dashed down the hall to the women's locker room.

"Well," Knox said, "That was charming."

It was so much more than charming. It was a picture Brett would carry into his dreams tonight.

Just what the hell was a CEO supposed to do when he was lusting for someone who worked for him?

"I'M SORRY, DAD, BUT DANIEL NEEDS TO GET UP TO Oregon to see his father. This bout with pneumonia has really taken its toll on Jim, and he's not getting any younger."

Brett was stretched out in the easy chair Tuesday evening, the TV on mute. When Megan called, his thoughts had been all Ivy and nothing but Ivy. She hadn't signed the promotion paperwork on Monday, and not today either. She hadn't said she wouldn't call a lawyer. But it was the kiss Brett couldn't get out of his head, the taste of her, the sweet scent surrounding her.

And the sight of her wet T-shirt.

Only Megan's call had managed to drag him back to reality. "I understand totally, honey. Daniel needs to be with his family."

"It's just that Jim can't travel right now."

"No explanations necessary," he assured her. For the past five years, Brett had rented a three-bedroom condo in Tahoe for the Thanksgiving holiday. Megan and Daniel came, and Daniel's parents drove down from Bend, Oregon. But Jim was in his late seventies, and this past year had been hard on him. "Give Jim and Evelyn my best."

"I will. But I hate to leave you alone. Can you get the money back on the condo?"

"Not a problem, honey." Actually, he'd needed to cancel two weeks in advance, which was last Wednesday, so the money was lost. But he wasn't about to heap any guilt on Megan. "Besides, we've got a big audit starting the week after Thanksgiving, so I would have had to spend a lot of time working anyway. This way I can go into the office." He'd have his prep work done before the holiday, but the white lie would make his daughter feel better.

"Gosh, Dad, I hate to think of you working over the holiday."

"Don't give it a second thought. Jim and Evelyn need you.

Plus they haven't even seen Valerie yet." Jim hadn't been well enough to travel, and Daniel had taken a couple of quick flights up on his own.

"Yeah, Evelyn's chomping at the bit to see her."

"Do you need me to take Archie?" Since he wouldn't be traveling over the holiday, he could handle Megan's cat. In fact, he'd enjoy having an animal around. Archie—short for Archimedes—was a lap cat.

Megan groaned. "I don't know what I'm going to do about her, Dad. Daniel and I are at our wits' end."

"She's still climbing into Valerie's crib?"

"Yes. It's *so* weird, especially that maniacal kneading thing she does on Valerie's blanket. And I'm pretty sure the noise she makes when I try to take her out of the crib is a growl. I'm afraid she's going to hurt the baby."

"She's probably just being protective."

"I don't know." Megan's sighed hissed through the phone. "But, well, I've come to a decision. I love her to death, but Valerie comes first. Do you know of a good home I can give her to?" *Hint, hint, Dad, will you take her?*

"Honey, is it that bad? You've had her since she was a kitten, fourteen years." Half of Megan's life.

"I know. It's killing me. But yeah, I really think it's that bad. I don't like to close Valerie's door, but if I don't, Archie is right up there again. A couple of times she's almost been sitting right on the baby. It's like she's gone psycho. Daniel calls her PC now, for Psycho Cat."

Brett felt like the cat was his, too. He couldn't stand seeing her go. "I can't take her for good, I travel too much. But I don't have any trips planned for the next four weeks because of this audit, so I can put her up for at least a month. In the meantime, we can both look for a home." He knew the cat would end up with him. He sure as hell wasn't taking her to the pound.

Maybe he could find someone at work.

He glanced at his watch. It was after nine. "It's too late to come tonight. I'll drop by on my way home from work tomorrow. Sound okay?"

"Thanks, Dad. You're a doll. I love you."

"Ditto, Kiddo." He'd been using the phrase since Megan could say *I love you*.

He left the TV on mute after she hung up. Who the hell could he hit up at work?

His mind turned immediately to Ivy. Everything always came back to Ivy. And Joy. A little girl who was dying for a pet. Maybe he could convince Ivy. Both an animal and a child in need. Maybe Ivy was in need herself. After all, wasn't there a little girl inside her who'd lost a beloved pet long ago?

All right, it was a stretch. But he wanted to give it a chance. He wouldn't talk about the cat in front of Joy—that was undo pressure. But he could give Ivy the option.

That would also give him a pretext to drop by after work tomorrow. Of course, he already had a pretext: today's phone call he'd made to Rhonda. He'd given Rhonda one month, until the auditors had gone, to think about the error of her ways. And how she was going to correct her behavior. Except that the ultimatum wasn't something he could readily discuss with Ivy due to its confidential nature.

But here he was manufacturing reasons to spend time with Ivy. It was beyond the lawsuit she could hit him with or the monkey wrench she could throw in his expansion plans for the capital from The Nelson Group. It was beyond how he handled Rhonda.

It was into the realm of desire and need.

Then, of course, he had a flash of even greater brilliance. He had a condo in Tahoe for the holiday break. And no one to spend that holiday with. Ivy had a daughter who had never seen snow, never ice skated, never tobogganed.

It was a ridiculous plan. She'd never agree. He couldn't even say why he suddenly wanted it so badly. But he did. He couldn't think of a single damaging consequence. There were three bedrooms. Ivy wouldn't be forced to share his. It would be a chance for both Ivy and Joy to get to know him better. Besides, after the holiday, the office would be a madhouse with the auditors there. They both needed time to relax before they entered the pandemonium.

He was manufacturing reasons again. And he recognized the craziness of it.

He just didn't care.

WEDNESDAY, JUST BEFORE FIVE, IVY STILL HAD THE promotion paperwork in the briefcase she carried home with her each night.

The word was out everywhere about Rhonda, and the rumors were worse than even Hannah had imagined, though thankfully there had been nothing about Ivy's involvement. On Tuesday, Gloria had called Ivy into her office to make sure she was okay. So someone—it had to be Jordana, or perhaps Grady—had told her the true facts, not the party line Brett had put out in the staff meeting.

Ivy was once again grateful to have friends.

But she hadn't discussed the paperwork in her briefcase though she'd had it for two days.

And then *he* called right before she got ready to leave. Her cubicle was flanked on either side by Grady's office—he was in a meeting somewhere—and Rhonda's empty office. Opposite her was the warren of accounting cubicles. They couldn't see her, but she knew they could hear because she was totally aware of them, clacking on their keyboards, on the phone, talking in low voices.

She was acutely conscious of Hannah's warning about spies. Not that she really believed anyone was spying on her, but speculation on Rhonda's leave of absence—and Ivy's promotion—was rampant.

She did *not* want that speculation to include anything salacious about her and Brett.

Yet here he was calling her and fanning the flames of the gossip mill.

"Yes," she said brightly. Nothing to hide here, her tone shouted.

"I'd like to drop by tonight, if that's all right." He was ever so polite. Nor did he need to say why. He was coming over because she hadn't signed the paperwork yet.

Which meant she hadn't decided to take his bribe even though she was doing the job. Of course, she couldn't leave Jordana to handle everything. The temp would be starting tomorrow, taking over the cubicle right next to Ivy's now that she'd taken over Jordana's old cubicle space. There would be ears everywhere.

Dammit, what did she have to hide? Rhonda had said those things. Rhonda was asked to leave.

But Brett had kissed her.

"Yeah, sure, fine," she said too abruptly, with a hint of sarcasm. She couldn't stop him.

Maybe she needed to have it out with him.

"Thank you, Ivy. I'll see you then." His voice was so smooth, so confident. Of course it was. He was the CEO. She was just the secretary.

The worst was that she resented him for coming to her house to discuss business. Instead of coming just to see *her*. It was crazy but it was how she felt. Especially after the zoo.

After that kiss.

At home, she actually held dinner for him, putting the lasagna into the oven over an hour later than she normally would. Joy usually did her homework after dinner, but tonight Ivy had her working on it now.

This was nuts. Waiting on a man. She hadn't done that since Rupert. She'd sworn she never would again. But one little kiss, and here she was... waiting.

When the doorbell rang, she called to Joy, telling her to finish her homework.

"Where's Joy?" was the first thing Brett asked.

"In her room doing homework."

Brett held up his hand, speaking softly, obviously so Joy wouldn't hear. "Just hear me out before you say no."

He was covered in the delicious scent of fresh rain that weakened her knees. "No to what?"

"Here's the story. My daughter's cat has gone a little psycho with the baby. She climbs into the crib and starts kneading maniacally."

"All cats knead."

"Yes, but Archimedes won't stop."

"Archimedes?"

"Megan's a math teacher, what can I say?" He shrugged. "Anyway, when Megan tries to get her out of the crib, the cat makes a weird noise. And Megan's afraid she might scratch the baby, or accidentally smother her, and she's finally decided she needs to get rid of the cat." He didn't even pause a beat when he added, "I thought perhaps she could stay with Joy."

She'd expected pressure on signing the paperwork. But pressuring her about a cat? He never stopped taking her by surprise. "What if she scratches Joy?"

"She's never done anything like this before. It's just with the baby for whatever weird reason. She's fourteen so she's perfectly trained, doesn't scratch the furniture, uses the cat box. I'm sure she's just feeling protective of the baby."

"Or jealous."

He nodded agreement. "Joy could be really good for the cat."

She crossed her arms over her chest. "We can't have a cat."

"Ivy."

"Mr. Baker," she started deliberately. "You know our situation." What if they had to move? What if they had to leave the cat behind after Joy had gotten attached? What if the cat died? After all, it was fourteen. She knew what it was like to lose something you loved dearly, and she couldn't put Joy through that.

"If it doesn't work out, I'll make other arrangements."

"That's my whole point. Joy will become attached even if things don't work out," Ivy repeated harshly. "She'll be crushed. Why are you doing this?"

Brett stared at her.

He could feel his heartbeat racing just being close to her. He could feel himself willing her to say yes, wanting her to fully invite him in. Simply wanting her.

Why *was* he doing this? Sure, Megan had said she needed to get rid of the cat, the baby came first, and all that. But why had he decided to bring Archimedes here?

Why was he pushing Ivy? Especially when this was a surefire method of pushing her away.

"I want *you* to have the cat. Not just Joy. To replace the dog you couldn't keep when you were a kid."

Ivy stared back at him. "You remember about the dog?" Her voice was so soft. As if she couldn't believe he'd stored every fact she'd told him about herself.

"Of course." Then he seduced her. "I believe deep down you really want a cat. They're cute and they lay on you and give you unconditional love."

He felt her twitching with nervous energy. With the need to say no and the desire to say yes.

She narrowed her eyes at him. "I should be really pissed at you for putting me in this position. If I don't take this cat, Joy's going to be so disappointed."

"She's in her bedroom. She can't hear. You can say no without consequences. I'll find another place for Archimedes."

She smirked. "Except then I'll feel guilty if you dump her at the pound."

"I won't do that. I promise. So you can say no without worrying." But he wanted her to say yes. He wanted this for her. For Joy. Even though he realized how totally nuts it was.

"Where's the cat now?" she asked.

"In the car."

She smiled, came close to a laugh. "You dirty rotten..." Pursing her lips, her arms folded over her chest, that smile flirting with her mouth, she finally said, "All right, bring her in. Do you have the cat box, too?"

"And the cat tree."

"Oh my God, a tree?"

He was laughing as he bounded down the stairs to his car. His heart hadn't felt this light in years.

9

The joy on her daughter's face brought Ivy to tears, and she was suddenly a child again, watching her mother take away Sherry, her little dog. Nothing had ever hurt so much, not Rupert, not even the day her dad had walked out. Probably because she hadn't understood what that meant. But she'd understood that Sherry was never coming back.

Now, since she'd decided to let the cat in, no matter what happened, Ivy would make sure Joy never had to give up Archimedes.

"Arc-a-me... what?" Joy asked after stumbling over the name.

"Archimedes. But my daughter calls her Archie," Brett told her, squatting down on the carpet beside Joy as the cat stuck its head out of the carrier.

"Isn't that a boy's name?" Joy said with childlike seriousness.

"Yes. But cats don't really mind what you call them. I once had a girl cat named Gort, after a robot in a movie I liked as a kid."

Brett was so good with Joy. He didn't talk down to her, didn't treat her like an annoying gnat he had to swat away. Somehow, between the zoo and the cat, they were bonding.

It was amazing. And scary.

How would it affect Joy when he didn't come around anymore?

That was the biggest reason she hadn't pushed paternity with Rupert. She'd been afraid he'd try to take the child away. Or that he'd come around only to lose interest. And Joy would suffer. It was also the reason Ivy didn't bring her dates home, so Joy wouldn't get attached to men who would never want to be permanent fixtures.

But Brett was here right now. And Joy was ecstatic. Over the cat. Over him. Ivy couldn't deny her.

"Would you like to stay for dinner?" Ivy asked. "It's just lasagna."

He glanced up, making her his sole focus. It was enough to take her breath away. "I love lasagna. You make all the perfect comfort food. Thanks."

What would he think if he knew she'd waited for him?

They put the cat box in the front hall closet, leaving the door ajar. The cat tree—which Brett had reassembled in a matter of minutes—towered by the sliding glass door that led out to the balcony. Archie ran first to the cat box, then to the tree, scratching furiously. And finally she ran back to Joy, flopping over onto Joy's feet and rolling around.

Her daughter's laughter was music.

"Cat bowls, cat food," Brett said, entering the kitchen with a big bag. "Thank you for taking Archie. She's up to date on all her shots, and she's been fixed, too. So no worries she'll go into heat."

Ivy suddenly thought of Brett's kiss and blushed, then quickly bent down to the oven, using the warmth to excuse her reddened cheeks. "It's ready."

"Smells good." He rubbed his stomach. "Megan's got Archie's food set up on autoship. She's just changing the address to yours."

"But what about the bills? I should give her my charge card."

He waved a hand like a magician. "Archie is her responsibility, and Megan feeds her a special grain-free food which is pretty expensive. She'll take care of the vet bills, too. She's just very grateful to have a good home for her."

"Well, that's generous. Tell her thank you." She felt a twinge of guilt in her belly, but at the same time, vets were expensive. She hated to think how much gourmet grain-free food cost.

In the living room, Joy squealed as Archie jumped at a cat toy on a string.

Brett glanced around the corner. "Even at fourteen, that cat still likes playtime."

He transported the hot lasagna plate for Ivy. She carried the salad and dressings.

Her heart wrenched at how amazingly good dinnertime felt. Joy chattered, the cat roamed around sniffing all the new scents, and finally curled up on the back of the couch, watching them as they ate, no psycho-cat tendencies in evidence. Brett told funny stories about Archie's antics. Dinner had always been... just dinner. Brett made it special.

Joy wasn't the only one who might get too attached.

"Have you finished your homework?" Ivy asked when the meal was done and she'd cleared the dishes.

"Almost," Joy said in a high, sweet voice. "I can finish it before I go to bed."

"You know the rules."

Her daughter pouted prettily. "But Mommy."

Ivy wasn't moved, and all she did was raise an eyebrow.

Like a typical kid, Joy huffed and puffed, then jumped down from the chair. "Come on, Archie."

In a stunning move, the cat jumped down off the back of the sofa and followed Joy.

Ivy stared after them. "Did I just see that?"

Brett nodded, his smile big. "Archie's like a dog. I bet you could even put a leash on her and take her for a walk."

"Wow. She's certainly settling in quickly."

"She's a love-the-one-she's-with kind of cat." Then he waved a hand at Ivy. "Come. Sit. We need to talk."

This was the real reason he was here: Why hadn't she signed the paperwork?

She sat at the table again. It was time they got it over with.

He put it out there. "Are you satisfied with the adjustments we've made, the promotion, the salary, Rhonda's leave? I want you to be happy with the solution."

"It's okay on paper, but what about when she returns?"

"She'll have conditions for returning. *If* she returns, she'll be coming back a changed woman. It won't happen otherwise."

"And what about me? If she comes back, she won't need a supervisor."

"Rhonda has clearly proven she needs the help."

But was that a guarantee? It was, however, the least of the things preying on her mind. Ivy clasped her hands beneath the table. "All right, here's my real problem. I feel like the promotion and the raise are bribes so I won't call a lawyer."

Additionally, she felt uncomfortable about what Hannah had said, too, that everyone was seeing the whole thing as some sex scandal.

"It's not a bribe," he said gently enough that she felt like a frightened cat he had to calm, a stroke of his voice as if it were his hand. "We were wrong for asking you to take on extra duties without compensation."

She'd heard that phrasing somewhere before. Maybe from Jordana. "But everyone's wondering why I got the promotion," she insisted, balling her hands into fists where he couldn't see. "They all know it has something to do with Rhonda's leave of absence. I don't like all this speculation."

"Most people believe she's got a medical issue. They aren't connecting the two episodes."

Right. That's what *he* thought. The underground gossip was completely different. All right, sure, so far they weren't saying *she* was involved with Rhonda's leave.

"The promotion and raise have nothing to do with what Rhonda did to you. She was the catalyst, but that's all. It's not a bribe. Did you see anything in the paperwork that said you couldn't sue Rhonda and the company if you took the promotion?"

"No." And she had scoured the wording. "But it just seems wrong that people don't get to know how badly Rhonda treats people. That she gets away with it."

He held her gaze. "I have no way of stopping you from telling people. If that's what you want. But she isn't getting away with anything. I promise you I am not bringing her back if she doesn't change her behavior. She knows that."

But she has spies. Ivy felt the need to speak like a cold sweat breaking out on her skin. Yet the words sounded paranoid. And childish. Besides, did she actually know if Rhonda had spies? And what difference did that make anyway?

"Look." He reached out a hand to her, but she kept hers firmly in her lap. She couldn't risk letting him sidetrack her with a touch. "You deserve this raise, Ivy. You deserve this promotion. Over the last two months, you've proven to Grady and Jordana that you can do the job. That's good enough for me. So take the promotion. It doesn't eliminate your ability to sue. I'm hoping you won't, but I'm not making that a condition."

She wanted what he offered. She enjoyed the work she did with Jordana. She enjoyed interfacing with employees. As much as she liked Grady, being his admin wasn't exactly fulfilling.

She stood then, grabbed her briefcase from the corner by the kitchen counter where she had a small phone table. Pulling out the folder, she flopped it open. And signed.

"Thank you," he said. "I apologize that it took Rhonda's mistreatment of you to get this done."

She was about to hand him the file, but held back suddenly. "I'll turn it into Jordana tomorrow since she'll be my new boss." She didn't want anyone wondering why Brett had it.

"Fine. Now I've got something else I'd like to talk with you about."

"Sure." She felt that cold sweat again and was afraid she might need a glass of wine to get through whatever he had to say.

"I have a Tahoe resort that I always rent at Thanksgiving. I take Megan and her husband along with his parents. But this year, Daniel's dad is recovering from pneumonia and they're driving up to Oregon to see him. The suite is nonrefundable, but I don't feel like going on my own." He hesitated just a moment before adding, "I wondered if you and Joy would like to go with me."

For the second time in just a few days, her jaw dropped. Flies could actually swoop into the gaping cavern of her mouth. The man was unbelievable.

"We hardly know you."

He shrugged. "This will help you get to know me better." She was sure that was a wicked smile on his lips.

She felt an answering wicked pull deep inside. One she

had to fight. "I am not going on some vacation and sleeping with you."

His delicious smile didn't falter. "There are three bedrooms. You and Joy will have your own room and adjoining bathroom."

She needed more excuses. Lots of them. Because part of her wanted to say yes, yes, yes until she was breathless. An insane, totally nutzoid part of her. "I can't leave my mother alone for Thanksgiving. She doesn't have anyone."

"Three bedrooms," he repeated. "She can have her own room, too. And adjoining bathroom."

Her breath seemed to come as fast as all the excuses racing through her mind—and the desire making her blood run hot. "You're inviting my *mother*?" She couldn't believe this.

He nodded.

"What about the cat? Your daughter will be gone, too."

"This place takes pets. We always bring Archie."

She got up, leaving the dinner table to pace the length of the living room. "Why do you want us to go?" Did he think a raise and a promotion weren't enough, that he had to seduce her so she wouldn't sue?

He rose, walked slowly to her. A panther stalking her. Just like he had the other night.

"Because I'm waiting for the day you'll trust me to make you feel better than you ever have in your life."

Trust.

She didn't have any. There was just the fever of desire burning her up inside. That wasn't enough. It just couldn't be—

Then his lips were on hers, and all her objections were swallowed up by his sweet taste on her lips. He hauled her tight against him, opened his mouth, and plundered her. It was like a battle, sweet and hot and overwhelming her defenses. He was all tough muscle and taut skin, surrounding her, invading her.

God, how she wanted to be invaded. She wanted him to take away her will, to the point where she'd beg for anything.

She wanted to simply melt into him.

His kiss was powerful, his embrace all-encompassing. Her resistance floated away, and he filled her up with desire and need. She curled her fingers into his shirt, held him close and tight, rose up on her toes to allow his kiss to take her deeper.

He let her go only when she was gasping, a moan crawling its way up her throat.

"Trust me," he whispered.

The word snapped her out of the sensual haze he'd drawn over them. She absolutely couldn't allow herself to get carried away. "If we go, I'm not sleeping with you."

"I promise I won't try sweet-talking or enticing you."

He was already enticing her. "I—" She didn't know what she wanted to say. What she actually wanted. He confused her. He made her desire him. He made her want a man again. To want *him*.

"Joy has never seen snow. Her first snowfall, I'd like to give her that."

"That's a low, dirty trick," she whispered.

He grinned. "Yeah. But Tahoe is supposed to get a nice dumping of snow with this storm and another coming over the weekend." His voice softened, even as the grin widened. "Come with me. Have pity on an old man who has to spend Thanksgiving alone."

She couldn't help the laugh. He was the furthest thing from an old man. "You're playing on my sympathy."

All he did was smile. It weakened her knees.

She thought of Joy and how much she'd love it. Thought of all the things she couldn't give her daughter.

But Brett could provide this one thing for her.

She narrowed her eyes and pointed a finger at him. "But I'm not sleeping with you."

He grabbed her finger, reeled her, but stopped short of kissing her again. "Whatever you want."

She held her breath, then blurted out, "All right. We'll go." With a laugh, she added, "Only because I feel sorry for an old man who has to spend Thanksgiving on his own."

But she was afraid that once she got to his three-bedroom suite, she'd change her mind and do some much more than sleep with him.

It didn't make any sense why she was saying yes. In fact, it felt like dropping out of school to fly off to Europe with Rupert.

It was probably a huge mistake, just like the last time. She could hear her mother's voice saying, *Don't you ever learn?*

But it was a risk she couldn't resist.

"I'M TELLING YOU, IVY, THAT MAN WANTS SOMETHING," her mother warned.

Well, of course, he did. He wanted to sleep with her. Ivy wasn't an idiot. Which is why she didn't say that to her mother. "His daughter can't go on the trip, and the rental is nonrefundable."

"Right," Mom drawled. "So you invite your secretary, plus her daughter and mother to go with you?"

Brett had left an hour ago, after reviewing the whole plan with her once she'd agreed to go. He'd even shown her the online layout of the condo resort. It was definitely five-star accommodations.

There had been no more kisses, and she'd told herself that was a good thing. She seemed to lose all common sense when he touched her. Actually, she lost her mind.

Now the hall was darkened, and Joy's lights were out. She had to be asleep because Archimedes had sauntered out fifteen minutes ago and crawled into Ivy's lap. If Joy had been awake, she'd have come for the cat.

The tabby was a sweet little thing, shades of gray, with patches of salmon and white. It purred, kneading her belly gently. Nothing psycho. And it really hadn't taken any time to adjust, settling in right away.

"I'm not *his* secretary," she told her mother. "I work for HR now. I report to the HR manager."

Mom gave a disgusted grunt. "So he gives you a promotion, a raise, *and* a trip to Tahoe. And he doesn't want anything," she said, her voice oozing sarcasm.

"I'm fully aware that he doesn't want me to sue him. But he hasn't put any conditions on the promotion. Or the raise. He didn't make me sign any papers saying I wouldn't sue the company."

"He's lulling you into submission. Trying to melt your heart." Mom's voice started out singsong, then dipped to a harsh note. "And when your statute of limitations runs out, he'll drop you like a hot potato."

Or shunt her off somewhere when she became inconvenient like Archie the cat.

She cringed at the cruel thought. It hadn't been like that; Megan had made a tough choice to protect her child, just like Ivy would for Joy.

So maybe she sounded more bitter than necessary when she said, "Why do you always rain on my parade, Mom?"

"It's not raining. It's just shining the light. Of truth." Then Mom softened. "You're going to get yourself hurt."

"I'm not expecting anything, therefore I can't be disappointed and I won't get hurt."

"Do you really believe that? If you're even thinking about going, then you've already set yourself up to get hurt."

Had she? "It's not like I'm falling in love with him. In fact, last week, he was just some guy who liked to show me pictures of his brand new granddaughter."

Mom close to shrieked. "Granddaughter? He's old enough to be your father?"

"He's fifty-two. And nowhere near old enough to be my father." Her father was in his seventies now.

Brett was... a silver fox. And Ivy liked it. A lot. Maybe too much.

"I've made up my mind, Mom. Joy and I are going. You should come with us."

"Tahoe?" Her voice rose with horror. "It's cold up there. I don't have the right outerwear."

That's just an excuse."

"What does an old lady like me want to go to Tahoe for?"

"You can play the penny slots."

"Do they even have penny slots anymore?"

"Of course they do." Ivy didn't have any idea.

"When does he want to go?"

"We'd leave on Wednesday, come back on Sunday." Not that it made a difference since her mother was retired.

But would anyone notice that she and Brett were both taking Wednesday off? Of course not. Lots of people would. Some even took the whole week off.

"I don't know."

"It's a free trip," Ivy cajoled.

"What about food?"

"All expenses paid." Brett had insisted on that, saying that the invitation was his and that he'd have had to pay for it if his daughter, her husband, and the in-laws had come. Ivy had stuffed down her guilt and agreed.

"There's no such thing as a free holiday," her mother said solemnly. Then she cackled. "But what the heck, let's take the man for all he's worth."

Ivy laughed. "You are so bad."

"I'm dying to see what he's like. And then I can make an informed judgment about whether he's trying to screw you over or not."

10

When the Wednesday before Thanksgiving arrived, Brett was at Ivy's door by nine in the morning to pick them up for the trip.

The previous Saturday, he'd taken her and Joy shopping. They needed hats, scarves, and mittens. Ivy had drawn the line at down jackets, which were far too much money. Instead she'd found cheap puff jackets that could be stuffed into small bags and would be more than adequate. She did let him buy plastic snow sleds for tobogganing, one for each of them. Except Ivy's Mom.

"This is getting out of hand," she'd whispered to him. "You're spending too much on us."

He'd yet again insisted that it was his invite and his responsibility. "I'm not letting you *layer*," he'd said with emphasis, because that's exactly what Ivy told him she was going to do.

He'd been a perfect gentleman the entire week since he'd made the invitation. No kisses. Barely even a touch. Sure she'd been insistent about not sleeping with him, but he could have at least kissed her.

Then again, it was a good thing he didn't. He was a huge complication she didn't need.

As if going away with him for a holiday trip wasn't.

She was so freaking mixed up. She hadn't called a lawyer. But she hadn't made a decision not to call one either. She hadn't made any decisions at all.

When she'd requested the day before Thanksgiving off, she'd felt an accompanying lurch of guilt. Like she was doing something wrong and illicit. As if she were lying to Jordana. The guilt heaped on when Jordana said Ivy deserved the time off because they'd all been working so hard to get ready for the darn audit. Jordana was spending the holiday with Grady and his family. Gloria was flying back to Connecticut to meet Parker's family. They *all* deserved a break before the onslaught.

But on Wednesday morning, Ivy put all those emotions behind her. She'd committed to making the trip, and she was damn well going to enjoy it. Especially with how ecstatic Joy was. Even her mother smiled politely when they picked her up. Archie was a perfect little angel sitting in her cat carrier between Mom and Joy in the backseat.

Ivy felt jittery and excited in the front next to Brett, his scent filling the car, surrounding her, heating her. With Joy chattering away, they didn't converse between themselves much, but it was lovely just looking at him as he drove, his big hands on the wheel, his smiles and laughter for Joy's enthusiasm, the brief shared glances when her daughter said something particularly amusing or silly.

Joy went into overdrive when they passed through Placerville and she got her first sight of snow, even if it was just a dusting on the ground at that level. "Look, Mommy, there's snow. *Snow.*" She bounced in her seat, hugging the stuffed sloth Brett had given her. She'd been using Rolf the sloth as a pillow on and off as she napped, but once they reached the mountains, she was wide-eyed with delight.

After the weekend storm, Tahoe reportedly had plenty of snow for Thanksgiving skiing.

"This is so cool," Joy said, sounding like a teenager. "Can I get out and touch it?"

"Let's wait till we get to Strawberry," Brett replied. "The snow should be deeper there."

"Do you want to play in the snow, Archie?" Joy leaned down to put her face close to the carrier.

Ivy leaned over the seat. "Archie will probably freak out."

Brett tapped the steering wheel. "Or she might escape and we'll never catch her."

"Okay." Joy agreed sweetly, then continued her travelogue of every exciting new sight they passed. As they rounded a big bend in the road, coming upon a waterfall flowing right out of the hillside, she squealed with glee. Archie meowed, either with excitement or terror. They passed through towns that were barely more than a restaurant or a store.

By the time they reached the town of Strawberry, the ground was covered by at least a foot of snow as far as the eye could see.

Brett pulled in behind several other cars parked next to a snow-covered field.

Joy was out of the car like a ball from a cannon. "Wait for us," Ivy called.

"I'll stay here and watch the cat," her mother said dryly.

"Don't you want to make a snow angel, Leonora?" Brett said with such a cheeky smile that Ivy swore there was an answering twitch on Mom's lips.

"Thank you, no," Mom replied with great dignity. "I'd never get back up without a crane. Now go on with you all before you lose Joy."

Joy was already packing a snowball, and it hit Brett square in the chest.

"You're in for it now," he called, grabbing up a handful of snow. And missed. On purpose, Ivy was sure, as Joy bounded away with exuberance.

The sun was bright across the snowy field dotted with revelers making snowmen, having snowball fights, and pulling little kids on sleds. The nippy air was alive with voices and laughter and shouts of pleasure. It didn't feel cold, not with the gloves Brett had bought her.

Then a snowball hit her square on the shoulder. "Why you dirty rotten." She pelted Brett with a great scoop of snow she didn't even bother to turn into a snowball.

He lunged at her, grabbing her around the waist and pulling her down, his big hard body half on top of her. She lost her breath, wanting to clutch him close. Wanting to raise her head off the pillow of snow until her lips touched his.

Their breaths mingled, frosting in the air. His eyes darkened, and she thought for a moment—oh God, yes, please—that he might kiss her right here on the sunlit snowscape.

She'd never wanted anything more in her life.

"Time for a snow angel," he whispered and rolled to his back beside her. "Come on, Joy," he called, his voice with a hint of huskiness. "Snow angels."

"How do I make a snow angel?" Joy stood over them.

"Like this." He waved his arms and legs back and forth. "Watch your mom, too."

Ivy dragged her limbs through the snow. Then Joy threw herself down beside her, arms and legs flying. It was wonderful, glorious fun. They were laughing and crying.

Brett pulled them both to their feet, dusting all the snow off them before it melted and made their jeans wet. Then they stood back to survey their artistry. He didn't let go of their hands, and somehow that was the most beautiful feeling of all. As if they were together, like a family.

Her heart felt close to breaking with wonder and joy.

"See, just like an angel. Snowman next." He was off, showing Joy how to roll the snow along the ground into big balls they could stack on top of one another.

"So you let him give Joy a cat." Her mother stood at her shoulder. Ivy hadn't heard her get out of the car.

"I didn't *let* him." She kept the bite out of her voice, though she badly wanted to snap. "His daughter had to give the cat away after her baby came. And he didn't want to send it to the pound."

"Right. And he couldn't take it. How much of a fight did you put up?"

"Mom." Of course, that wouldn't make her mother shut up.

And it didn't. "Do you think he really likes Joy or he's just trying to impress you?"

Brett was so good with Joy. Ivy's chest felt tight just watching them. For so many reasons. Because Joy never had a father. Because Brett made them all laugh so easily. Because Ivy was terrified her daughter would get too attached. And Brett would leave them devastated when he was gone.

"Or maybe he's just a pedophile."

"Mother," she hissed. "That isn't funny."

Her mother quirked a brow. "I thought it was. I mean, every TV show where you see a man with a kid he's not the father of, the guy turns out to be a pedophile. It's enough to make you start believing every unattached male is a secret pedophile."

Sometimes her mother was like a little kid—or a senile old lady—saying whatever popped into her head. "Would you stop saying that word. And especially don't say it in front of Brett. You need to behave yourself."

Mom snorted. "I'm not the one who was rolling around on the ground with a man on top of me right in front of my daughter."

"We weren't rolling."

"*Hmmph.*"

But it had felt for a moment like they were the only two people in the world.

It had been magic.

THE SUITE WAS AMAZING. ARCHIMEDES THE CAT HAD sniffed every corner, then plopped herself down on Joy's pillow.

The resort perched on a hilltop. The rooms were sumptuous, with a blazing fireplace in the living room and a view of the snow-covered mountains. The dining table sat eight, and the kitchen boasted every convenience, even a griddle. The clubhouse offered a spa, workout room, indoor and outdoor pool, hot tub, and restaurant. The interior walkways of their building overlooked an outdoor Jacuzzi that wafted steam into the air. Brett had told them all to pack swimsuits, though she doubted her mother had followed along.

Ivy had never stayed at a place like this in her life.

Thick down comforters and fluffy feather pillows blanketed the beds, and each room had an attached bathroom. The tub in hers was deep and roomy enough to fit two. She had a vivid image of candles all around the wide rim, champagne flutes, chocolate, bubbles.

And Brett lounging in the water with her.

"Look at the size of the bed, Mommy."

Ivy really needed to stop the daydreaming. She was with her daughter, for goodness sake. And her mother.

Joy bounced on the bed, rocking the pillow the cat had

commandeered. Then Joy flopped down and began making snow angels without the snow, knocking Rolf the sloth to the floor. "This is so cool, Mommy."

It was. And they better enjoy it while they had it because they weren't getting anything like this ever again.

Brett's bedroom was on the far side of the suite, while her mother's room was next door, the living room separating them from him.

"This is fabulous," she told him after unpacking both hers and Joy's suitcases and returning to the living room. "I don't know how to thank you."

"Just keep on having as much fun as we did making snowmen and snow angels." His smile did crazy things to her insides. "I thought we'd drive down to the grocery store and stock up. How about spaghetti for dinner?"

"I love spaghetti," Joy said behind her.

"I make a mean marinara with clams."

"*Ewwe.*" Joy made a face. She was used to hamburger.

He waggled his eyebrows at her. "Don't give me *ewwe*. You're gonna be begging for more. Go get your grandmother."

When she was gone, Ivy said, "At least let me pay for half the food. This is just too much."

"We had this discussion. I'd be buying for six if my daughter and the in-laws were here. I'm getting off cheap."

"I just don't feel comfortable."

He moved in on her, not quite touching, but enough that she had to tip her head back to look at him. His heat arced across the vacant space between them.

"You're doing me the favor by sharing your Thanksgiving with me. Let me do this for you. It's just a trip to the grocery store. And honestly, if you were paying for half, I'd feel guilty buying the things I really want." He grinned down at her. "I have very expensive tastes." Then he kissed the tip of her nose.

It was so... ordinary. Like something couples did. A sweet little nothing.

And yet it rocked her world.

She felt deep in her bones what a dangerous game she was playing. It wasn't only Joy who would get hurt when he left.

THE SPAGHETTI WITH CLAM SAUCE WAS A HIT. EVEN JOY liked it after her first two tentative bites.

Leonora Elliot had grudgingly admitted it was tasty. She was a tough woman to crack. But Brett wouldn't give up.

She might have been pretty when she was younger, but the years had turned her features hard. On a thin face without enough flesh, the lines stood out starkly. Probably once dark like Ivy's, her wiry gray hair curled in tight, permed ringlets. But it was her eyes that were brittle as ice.

"I'm not one you can win over easily," she told him bluntly.

Ivy was putting Joy to bed. They'd played several rounds of cards, demolished two bowls of popcorn, and after the long drive and all the excitement, Joy had almost fallen asleep over the last game.

"I know you aren't a pushover, Leonora. So tell me more about yourself. That way I can figure out how to get under your skin."

The fire crackled in the hearth, and they were drinking an excellent bottle of pinot noir.

"There's nothing to tell. I've got Ivy. She's got Joy. We're a teeny-tiny family. Self-contained."

In other words, they didn't need him.

But he wanted to know how Ivy had become the beautiful woman she was. He knew she'd lost her father and her beloved dog at the same time. That she was a single mother. That she was self-contained, like Leonora said. He didn't want secrets she wasn't ready to share. He just wanted to know where she came from.

"Ivy tells me you're retired."

Leonora snorted. "Retired makes me sound like I was some big executive. Or a nurse. Or something fancy. But I cleaned for a living. You don't retire from that. You just stop being able to get down on your hands and knees and scrub floors anymore." She held up her cracked, weathered fingers. "Look at these hands. Too much time spent in soapy water. I never did like those rubber gloves."

He could imagine how difficult her life had been. "But didn't Ivy's father give you some kind of support?"

Shrugging, she said, "His lawyer was better than mine. That woman was an idiot. But at least I got the house, and he has to pay the mortgage and taxes and utilities. For *life*." She said the word with relish. "It's the only way I could manage now on social security alone."

"But I understood from Ivy that you had to move after the divorce."

She raised a speculative eyebrow, obviously a comment on how much Ivy had shared. Then she shrugged, her shoulders bony beneath her sweater. "Even he couldn't afford the house we were in while paying for his new setup with that little secretary as well. So we sold it and he bought us something cheaper. I didn't mind. We had to economize, but at least we had a roof over our heads that no one could ever take away."

But she hadn't brought the dog. Maybe the animal had been part of her economizing, without realizing how important the pet was to Ivy.

"And I've been a pretty good saver over the years. So I squeak by now."

Ivy had learned her thriftiness from her mom. She'd learned to cook at home instead of eating out.

"And Ivy helps me, too."

He should have known. That's the kind of woman Ivy was, there for her daughter and her mother.

"I told her she should sue you."

He chuckled at her bluntness. "Thank you for the warning."

"You can't treat people like that." She shook her head, letting her eyes roll up briefly. "You wouldn't believe some of the crap I've had to listen to over the years. It's just not right."

"I agree. No one should have to take that." He didn't say that he wasn't the one who'd tossed out all those crazy accusations. But the buck stopped with him. Ultimately he was responsible for what went on in his office.

Then the elderly woman waved a hand. "These are some nice digs. I appreciate the invite."

"You're welcome."

"She should still sue you. But maybe for a little bit less than I originally thought."

He laughed outright. "Leonora, you're a card. I can tally up the cost of the trip and you can deduct it out of the settlement."

Leonora didn't know it, but she was telling him a lot about Ivy. He was beginning to understand her fierce independence. She was strong, she was generous, she was protective. Her family was everything.

If he had learned that when he was younger, he might not have lost his wife and daughter. It had taken years for Megan to truly forgive him for the divorce and for the times he wasn't there when she'd needed him.

Ivy padded barefoot into the living room. "She's exhausted. And Archie's curled up right beside her and Rolf the sloth."

His pulse kick-started as he remembered the feel of her beneath him on the snow. He had scrounged for every bit of willpower not to kiss her. She'd been so soft, smelled so sweet, her cheeks pink with the cold air, her eyes sparkling.

And right now she was delicious in a tight sweater and skinny jeans, her dark hair gleaming in the firelight.

Leonora slugged back the rest of her wine as if it were out of a box, so fast she couldn't taste the finer flavors. "I'm tired." She stood, her knees creaking audibly. "And that king-size bed is calling my name." She looked at him. "What's for breakfast?"

"Mother," Ivy admonished.

He addressed Leonora. "What would you like?"

"The works. Fried eggs, fried bacon, fried potatoes, fried tomatoes. And fried bread."

He lifted one brow. "Fried bread?"

Leonora nodded. "To die for. Cook it in the bacon fat. Everything gets cooked in the bacon fat. I haven't had it like that since I was a kid and they—" She looked pointedly to the ceiling at the powers that be. "—decided all that fat was bad for us. Of course my grandfather ate a full-fat, fried breakfast every Sunday his entire life and he lived to be a hundred. So there." She blew a raspberry at him and turned on her heel.

Ivy stared after her in horror until the bedroom closed with a snick.

"Your mother's pretty damn funny." He patted the couch beside him.

Ivy didn't sit. "She says when you get to be old, you can say whatever you want. I should have warned you she was a bit outspoken. But honestly, we don't need that kind of breakfast."

"I bought eggs, bacon, tomatoes, and bread. But no potatoes." He leaned forward to refill her wineglass. "Come and sit. Don't tell me it's your bedtime, too."

He didn't want to let her go yet.

In fact, he wanted her to stay all night.

11

Ivy slid down on the sofa beside him. A safe distance away. She didn't trust how his seductive voice might affect her with a romantic fire blazing in a cozy condo while the snow drifted outside. Though she didn't need the inviting fire or the snow to fall under his spell. All it took was the memory of his kiss.

And her desire for another.

She accepted the wine, then curled her legs beneath her, turning sideways, her arm on the back of the sofa. "Thank you. It's delicious. And the spaghetti was out of this world."

He chuckled. "Go ahead. Please keep complimenting me. I enjoy it."

"As busy as you are, how did you ever learn to cook?"

"Divorce," he said mildly. "I was used to home-cooked meals and hated eating out in restaurants all the time. I get enough of that when I'm traveling."

"What other culinary delights are you capable of? Besides bacon and eggs," she teased.

"I make a mean roast beef. Cooked to perfection."

"Yum."

She loved his voice. Low and deep, it struck a chord inside her. Sitting here with him was pleasant—no, God, it was so much more than pleasant. Sexy and intimate and wonderful, it made her heart flutter.

"I'm also good with a stir fry." He'd be good with anything he tried.

"So you're going to cook for us while we're here?"

"The way to a woman's heart is through her stomach," he quipped.

"I thought the old saying was the way to a man's heart."

He winked. "Maybe. But it seems to be working with your mom. She actually smiled at me."

"I'm shocked." It was a joke. Then again, her mother didn't fall easily under any man's spell. She hadn't dated while Ivy was growing up, claiming she never wanted to look after a man again. Neither his heart nor his stomach.

"I'll even admit to pumping her for information about you." His mouth lifted in a cheeky half smile. "It seemed a better bet than trying to pump you."

She flushed at the implication. And Brett didn't take back the double entendre he'd made with a twinkle in his eye.

She tried to laugh it off despite the heat she felt building down low. "So what did she tell you?"

"Not enough." He leaned closer, lowering his voice. "I want more."

Her pulse beat faster at her throat. He was an expert at seduction. She forgot his ulterior motive and that the day in Rhonda's office stood between them. Right now, he was just a man who wanted to seduce her for nothing more than herself.

Still, she couldn't hand him all the advantage by coming across as too eager. "You make it sound like I'm some sort of mystery woman."

"You are."

"Right, and like I know so much about you."

"You do. I've been divorced for eighteen years because I'm a workaholic. I've got a twenty-eight year daughter and now an adorable granddaughter."

"So there's nothing else to your life than that," she scoffed. There were the women he'd been with in the last eighteen years. Had he fallen in love? Why hadn't he married again?

"All right fine." He quirked an eyebrow like Spock on *Star Trek*. "Let's play a game. I ask a question, then you ask a question."

"What if I don't want to answer?"

"Then you forfeit your next question, and I get to ask another one." He waited a beat, his gaze traveling over her face, lighting on her hair, her eyelashes, her cheek, her mouth. She felt his scrutiny like the stroke of his fingers. "Are you game?"

"Who gets to go first?"

"I'll let you ask the first question." Somehow he was closer now, like a statue that moved only when you weren't looking. All her safe distance had melted away.

But really, what did she have to lose? If she didn't want to answer, she didn't have to. Until he ran out of questions.

"All right. How did you meet your wife?" She wanted to know about was his love life now, but wasn't ready to ask.

"We were college sweethearts. Got married right after I graduated. Megan was born seven months later. She's actually why I became a workaholic, wanting to buy a house, then a bigger house in a better neighborhood, sending Megan to private school, and so on."

She could only imagine being right out of college with a family already on the way. All that pressure.

"My turn," he said softly.

Her stomach tightened, but she nodded.

"Does Joy ever see her father?"

The unexpected question stole her breath. She'd thought he'd want to know about men she'd dated in the recent past.

"No." She pressed her lips together. Technically, she'd answered and he'd have to wait for another question to learn additional details. But more slipped out despite her intentions. "We weren't married, just living together." The word *just* was so inaccurate. She'd had all her hopes and dreams wrapped up in Rupert. "But he didn't want to have anything to do with a child." She swallowed, and suddenly she was saying the rest. "He didn't believe Joy was his, but she was. I was only with him."

"Asshole," he whispered.

Her mother said the same thing, but always with a hint of reproach. As if Ivy had been responsible, that all the bad choices had been hers, not Rupert's. It felt as if Brett were the first person who'd stood up for her.

Brett's daughter had been born seven months later, so he and his wife had to get married. But he hadn't run out on his responsibilities. Rupert had simply denied his.

"You must have loved him very much." He paused only a second. "Until he turned out to be an asshole."

She closed her eyes and admitted everything, as if she had no pride. But Brett seemed to understand. "I did. He was my professor at university. And I dropped out of college to go abroad with him." She'd thrown away her small scholarship, thrown away all the money she'd worked so hard to earn for college. That's what had pissed her mom off the most, the sheer waste of everything she'd done to get into university, then failing to get the degree she'd wanted so badly. All for a man who didn't really want her. A man Ivy had been terrified of losing right from the beginning. She suddenly saw how tawdry it all sounded. "I'm glad he's out of the picture now," she said defiantly. "We're better off on our own." She wrested back her dignity. "My turn." She asked the question she'd wanted an answer to before she had a chance to talk herself out of it. "Are you dating anyone?"

"No."

"But you have in the past. I mean, you're a handsome man and lots of women find you attractive and—" She stopped, feeling like an idiot with all her desires written between the lines of her question.

He didn't tell her it wasn't her turn. That she'd asked and he'd answered with one word. "I've dated women. I suppose you'd call them affairs because they weren't serious relationships." He gave back a little bit of truth, to match her truth. "I've certainly never brought a woman to Tahoe." He held her gaze. "There's no one I've wanted to bring before."

Which meant that she was special.

Or a woman who might sue his company and make him lose everything.

She put her wine on the coffee table, feeling suddenly lightheaded and out of her depth. It wasn't the wine. It was all him.

"My turn," he said, so softly she felt the ache of what his next question might be. "What was your major in college? What did you want to do with your life before your asshole professor sidetracked you?"

A rush of relief swamped her at the almost impersonal nature of the question, followed quickly by a wave of embarrassment that she'd never finished. Her cheeks grew hot, but she'd agreed to play this game. "Child psychology."

"Interesting." He smiled as if he saw a completely new facet of her.

"I wanted to work with children."

"You love kids. I can see that every time you interact with Joy."

She adored children. Maybe that's why she always loved looking at his baby pictures. Besides just being near him.

"Yeah. I wanted a huge family," she said, wistfulness blossoming in her chest like a flower.

"You're not old. You can still have the big family."

She thought of the discussion she'd had with Gloria and Jordana the day before she'd confronted Rhonda, before her life suddenly changed. She wanted the family, but she didn't want the partner who could walk out at any moment and leave her high and dry. "I'd rather have some kind of job where I work with children." Something where she depended on herself.

"Like what?"

She shrugged, the same as she had during that lunch. "Maybe something specializing in homeschooling. Not the actual homeschool curriculum, but setting up group activities, special programs just for homeschoolers." She felt herself warming to the idea. She'd forgotten about that discussion, which seemed to have taken place in another life. "Activities like visiting zoos and museums, something that's educational but also social. As well as team-building exercises like sports or tournaments. Spelling bees. Or even immersing themselves in another language, where they all have to speak the new language they're learning."

"Sounds great. And you seem so enthusiastic about it."

For a moment she'd been flying high with dreams. But reality was something else entirely. She hadn't finished her education. She didn't have the expertise. She'd never even homeschooled Joy, and her knowledge had been gleaned from websites. She didn't have the time to gain the experience, not while working forty hours a week.

Unless she sued the company. Then suddenly she would have the money she needed to go back to school, to get a degree, to learn everything she needed. She could erase all her failures.

Hiding the traitorous thought, she switched everything

back to him. "That was way more than one question. My turn now." God, what could she ask? "Did you always want to be a CFO?" It sounded so inane.

"I wanted to be a trapeze artist when I was a kid. And as a teenager, I wanted to be a vet."

She laughed. "A trapeze artist. Guess your parents didn't want you to run away to the circus."

"I tried, but my mother caught me."

It was endearing, giving her a glimpse of him as a sweet boy. "But why didn't you become a vet?"

"In the end, I went for the money instead." He breathed deeply and added, "I also couldn't hack it when one of my pets died. I had rabbits, hamsters, dogs, cats, fish, birds, even a bat. I was always rescuing animals." He smiled fondly, even sadly. "But I was a basket case when I couldn't save them. I couldn't have done that day in and day out."

He was strong, commanding. Yet the loss of an animal brought him low. The tenderness of his heart touched her, though she'd seen the evidence in his devotion to his daughter, his adoration of his grandbaby, his need to find a home for Archie. And most especially in how sweet he was with Joy.

He dropped his voice. "My question now." His smile turned wicked. "Have you ever fallen in love again? Do you date? Is there anyone in your life right now?"

Of course, they were all the questions she hadn't wanted to answer. Or think about. The questions that made her heart race and her skin turn prickly. She shook her head. And hoped he'd move on.

He reached out slowly, sliding his fingertips across her cheek, then gathered her hair and tucked it behind her ear. "So there's no one who's going to mind if I lean in and do this?" He cupped her nape, drew her closer until his lips caressed the shell of her ear.

"No," she whispered. "I don't date. Because of Joy. I mean, I don't ever bring a man home. Sometimes I go out, but..." She trailed off, the implication clear. She screwed them, but she never brought them home. "I don't want Joy to get attached to someone who's not going to stick around."

He kissed her earlobe, bit her lightly, sending a jolt straight down to her center. She was suddenly breathless and hot and wet.

She wanted to climb right into him.

"It's your turn for a question." He pushed her hair aside to kiss her throat.

She couldn't think. All she wanted to do was fist her hands in his sweater and pull him so tight to her that she could feel the heat of his skin through her clothes.

But they were playing a game she didn't want to stop. "Have you ever dated a woman from work? Have you ever slept with someone on the job?"

He trailed sweet, hot kisses down the vee of her top, answering with his breath against her neck. "I've never mixed business with pleasure. Since I decided on taking the business route, all I've ever wanted to do was take my company, one I've grown with my own ingenuity, to the pinnacle, the Fortune 500. Ultimate success." He licked lightly along the sensitive skin just below her jaw. "But now, all I want is this." Cupping her face in his hands, he kissed her openmouthed, taking complete possession.

She moaned. Her fingers clutched his sweater. She wanted to fall back on the sofa and pull him on top of her.

"My question," he murmured, his lips against hers. "How do you want me to make you feel good?"

She wanted to lie. She wanted the strength to push him away. Instead, she gave him the absolute truth. "I want your hands on me. I want your mouth on me. I want you to make me scream with pleasure. Because it's been so long."

She thought he'd dive on her then, give her everything she desired.

"But," he said, giving her lips a soft, slow swipe of his tongue, "you're not ready, are you. Not really. Not so you won't regret it in the morning."

"No," she said with equal truth.

"Your turn." He was so close, so hot, so hard, yet his voice was warm and inviting.

She needed an answer to one question more than any other. "Are you seducing me just so I won't go to a lawyer?"

He shook his head, his skin brushing hers. "I don't want you to sue. But I won't sleep with you to make sure that doesn't happen. I'm going to sleep with you because you excite my blood, you make my heart race. And the sight of your bare toes makes me as hard as a steel rod."

She laughed. It burst out of her, his words releasing all her tension. "My toes?"

He backed off, and she realized he'd been touching her with nothing more than his lips and hands. The rest was all her need, her desire.

"Your toes. The day we walked out at the park. When you took off your shoes. Now I keep wanting your toes."

"What do you want to do with them?"

"Lick them, rub them, caress them."

"You're crazy."

Laughter glinted in his eyes. "Crazy for you." Then he just as quickly turned serious. "While we're here, I don't care about the company. I don't care about Rhonda. I don't care about business versus pleasure. All I want is to spend time with you. Learn about you." His voice dropped a note. "Learn how you like to be touched. And kissed. How you like to be made love to. That's what I want, Ivy. But I won't take any of that until you're ready."

She looked at him for such a long moment. “My turn,” she said on a breath. “What if I’m never ready?”

He trailed a finger along her jaw, tipping her chin up until their lips were only a breath apart. “I don’t give up so easily. I won’t give up until you’re so ready that the word *no* doesn’t exist in your vocabulary anymore.”

The thought was so heady, so hot. A threat and a promise. She was pretty sure she’d already forgotten the word *no*.

It was Thanksgiving Day and Brett treated them with a ride up the gondola to the top of the ski slopes. The weather was sharp, the sky clear, the views magnificent. Joy had done a three-sixty trying to see everything.

He’d lain awake until the small hours, his hands stacked behind his head, watching the shadows on the bedroom ceiling. And thinking of Ivy. Remembering the sweet taste of her lips, the soft texture of her skin, the mesmerizing moan humming in her throat.

I want your hands on me. I want your mouth on me. I want you to make me scream with pleasure.

He’d wanted his hands and mouth on her right then. Because she hadn’t been talking about kisses and a little petting. She’d wanted him right down at her core, making her come so hard she pulled his hair until his scalp screamed with sensation and his body ached for pleasure.

He wanted to give her the things she hadn’t had in so long. She’d dated men, and he was sure that included sex, but he was equally sure those interludes hadn’t involved emotions intense enough to make her forget everything but the moment, the bliss, the ecstasy.

That was what he wanted to give her.

She’d been in love with the asshole university professor,

but the guy had trashed her. He'd ruined her, stealing away all her trust in a moment of blind self-preservation.

At least he knew what he was up against. Ivy would never believe he wanted her for herself and not because of some damn lawsuit. She'd asked, he'd answered, but he knew she didn't believe.

For him, the two were totally separate things.

Except he wasn't offering love. He wasn't offering forever.

For Joy, Ivy needed someone who thought in terms of forever. Someone Joy could get attached to without Ivy worrying about the future.

Somewhere in the middle of the night, he realized that before forever came, there had to be this, his desire for her, his need, his concern.

There had to be today, this trip, the delight he felt in being with her, and with Joy.

For breakfast he'd fried them all the deliciously greasy foods Leonora had requested. He'd die of a coronary if he ate like that every day, but damn if the fried bread wasn't freaking delicious.

He'd wanted it to be a perfect day, and so far, so good.

At the top, as well as the ski lifts and lodge, there was also an ice skating rink.

Racing out across the snow, Joy hung over the wire slung up as a railing around the makeshift rink, watching the skaters, her eyes wide and excited.

The rink was nowhere close to full, with perhaps ten skaters. Most people were here to ski.

"You wanna try?" he asked, squatting in front of Joy.

"Can I? Is it hard?"

He looked up at Ivy, saying, "You might be a bit wobbly at first, but you can hold my hand. I won't let you get hurt."

He wouldn't hurt Ivy either. No matter what happened, he wouldn't hurt either of them.

"Yay. Let's do it." Joy punched the air like she sixteen instead of six. "Mommy, you can hold Brett's other hand."

"Thank you. I appreciate you sharing him, sweetie," she said, her gaze on her daughter, her smile tongue-in-cheek, their exchange so touching, Brett's eyes teared up.

He told himself it was only the wind. "I'll get the skates. What are your sizes?"

Back in the lodge, Leonora sat at a table by the window, all their stuff piled around her.

"You up for some ice skating, Leonora?"

"Do I look like I'm an idiot who wants to break her brittle bones just to prove she's still as young as you whipper-snappers?"

"You most certainly don't look like an idiot."

"Besides, someone's got to watch all this crap." She waved a hand. "Plus it's colder than a witch's you know what out there."

He laughed. The lady was one plain speaker, that was for sure. "We'll be back. There's hot chocolate in that thermos if you want some while you're waiting."

Five minutes later, he was back with the skates. Ivy laced up her daughter, then herself, and they ventured onto the ice.

Joy promptly fell down, pulling Ivy with her, sending them both into fits of giggles.

His emotions welled up and his heart turned over again. They were delightful, they were perfect.

"Oops," he said, extending a hand to both of them. "I didn't do my job. I let you fall." He steadied them. "You can't walk. You have to slide." He demonstrated while they both stood stock still, their feet planted apart for balance.

"Give me your hands." He held his out to Joy, and she placed her palms trustingly in his. Gliding backwards, he pulled her slowly along, guiding her into the slide. When he finally let her go, she wobbled, steadied herself, glided for several seconds then wobbled and went down again, laughing.

He scooped her up, and they tried again. "You're doing great, sweetheart." They worked at it until finally she skated on her own. She forgot the rhythm for a moment, started to walk, realized her mistake, and settled into a slide once more, all without falling this time.

Ivy had been stumbling along the side, using the wire railing for balance, keeping her feet, but a grimace creased her lips.

"Your turn," he said, mimicking their Q&A last night. "Give me your hands."

She put hers in his as trustingly as Joy had. He wished she could trust him with everything else.

"You're so good with her." Her smile was a balm to his soul.

"Kids are naturals. And they don't care how many times they fall in the process of learning."

Joy was working her way round the edge of the rink, slowly, but without falling.

"Glide with me," he urged Ivy, slowly sliding backwards, pulling her. "Glide on one foot then shift to the other. Your foot goes out behind you and glides off the ice, then comes back around and takes over."

He guided her through it.

"Look at me, Mommy!" Joy called out, squealing with delight as she made a wide turn on the ice, heading back to them. She didn't wobble as much or pinwheel her arms as she had in the beginning.

"You're doing great," Ivy called back.

And lost her concentration, tipping sideways, and suddenly they were falling, sprawling across the ice. Joy burst into hysterical giggles as she approached them. Then Ivy did. He joined them.

This was what he'd missed all those years ago when he'd worked so hard for the bigger house and the better neighborhood and the private school. He'd missed all these special moments, watching his daughter grow up, teaching her how to navigate life, whether it was ice skating or dating boys.

Up here on top of the mountain, there was no lawsuit, no work, no conflict.

There was simply a second chance.

12

Ivy couldn't remember the last time she'd laughed so hard. "We won't be Olympic skaters any time soon."

"You're both absolutely gorgeous." Brett hugged Joy to him until she squealed with delight and adoration.

It was so... it was so... Oh God, Ivy was afraid she might cry. Rupert hadn't wanted this amazing creature they'd created together. He'd denied her. And yet this big, beautiful man held Joy like she was his own daughter.

Or his granddaughter.

That brought her up sharply.

Maybe he was reliving something he'd missed when he was fresh out of college and too busy taking care of his responsibilities to be with his family. Maybe she and Joy were substitutes.

Whatever. It didn't matter. Not right now. In this moment, Joy was the epitome of happiness.

"Come on, kids, we've got treats your grandmother is guarding back at the lodge." Outside the rink, Brett helped Joy off with her skates like a doting father. She ran ahead, giggling and laughing, watching the skiers lining up for the lifts, rushing back to two of them, chattering, laughing.

"Thank you," Ivy whispered, grateful for the happiness Brett had given her daughter. He was marvelous with her. Yes, maybe that's what he really wanted, to relive being a father, to offer Joy the attention he'd been too busy to give his daughter. Whatever the reason, Ivy rejoiced that Joy was having the time of her life, something Ivy could never have given her.

"It's my pleasure. You're all doing me the favor by being here this weekend. I'd rather be ice skating with you than spending the holiday at home by myself." He raised Ivy's hand to his lips, kissed her knuckles. "It means more than you can know."

Her heart was beating out a rapid melody by the time they joined her mother in the lodge. Where Mom seemed to make special note of Ivy's flushed cheeks, her shining eyes, and the smile she couldn't wipe off her face.

With a flourish, Brett pulled two thermoses from the backpack he'd carried up in the gondola. "We've got soup and hot chocolate." He leaned close to Joy and said with a huge smile, "There's even marshmallows in the hot chocolate."

"They've melted by now," Ivy's mother said drily.

But Joy was squirming excitedly on the chair.

"You know we could have just bought something in the cafeteria," Mom pointed out.

Brett didn't bat an eye at her negativism. "Some things are better when we make them ourselves. Especially when no one else has them."

So there, Ivy thought. She loved his attitude. It made the things he did for them so much more meaningful.

"I'm dying for the soup," she said, giving him the widest smile. Not that he needed her enthusiasm. Brett didn't seem the least bit bothered by anything her mother said.

He leaned close, ruffling her hair with his breath. "It's just ramen with extra spices." His backpack revealed four stacked bowls, cups, and spoons.

The ramen was peppery and spicy and delicious. Joy made a face at first bite, then took another. Then finally she giggled at him. "I like it. Lots better than that stuff over there." She pointed to another table with plates of hamburgers and French fries.

"I thought you'd like it."

Mom made a face, but she ate the whole bowl.

For dessert there was hot chocolate and Ghirardelli dark squares.

He was perfect. Kept them all laughing. And he was fantastic with Joy, talking on her level but not down to her. He asked questions about school and what she was learning and what she wanted to be when she grew up—a doctor, which somehow morphed into a zookeeper within the same conversation.

Was this what he wanted from them, to be a father again? It was strange and beautiful to watch.

Ivy watched her mother noticing, too.

When Joy blurted out, "Mommy, I have to go to the bathroom," the ladies in the group all trooped to the restrooms while Brett cleared up their leftovers.

On the way back, Joy hurtled ahead of them. She had only one speed, fast forward.

Her mother grabbed Ivy's arm, holding her back. "If you're not going to sue the man—" She shot a dark glance at Brett across the expanse of tables. "—then you better screw him."

"Mother!"

But Mom didn't stop. "And get yourself pregnant." She jutted her chin. "You're good at that."

Ivy stopped right there, as if all her muscles had ceased to work. She could only stare after her mother. Gaping.

Then, just as quickly as she'd been immobilized, she ran after her mother. "That is so unfair."

Mom simply shrugged. "I'm not slamming you. I'm just calling 'em like I see 'em."

"Mom." She spread her hands in exasperation. "I made one mistake."

Her mother imitated her splayed hands. "So make another one. He's obviously got money and a good job. He likes kids. He's good for Joy. What's the problem?"

She was acutely aware of Brett on the other side of dining room, his attention divided between Joy and the two of them. "I didn't get pregnant to force Rupert into marrying me."

"Well, you should have. He was just using you as his cleaning woman."

Ivy couldn't deny it. "Fine, you're right. I'm never making that mistake again."

"And that's why you're going to get this one to marry you."

"I don't want to get married."

"You need someone to support you."

She kept her voice low as people flowed around them to the restrooms. "No, I don't. Joy and I are perfectly fine just the way we are."

"Scrimping for every penny. That's no way to live. I did it with you, and I don't want it for Joy. It's no way to raise a child." She poked Ivy's shoulder. "You need to make the right choice this time. And he—" She stabbed her finger quite obviously in Brett's direction. "—is it."

Then her mother left Ivy standing alone, returning to her granddaughter.

And the man who was *it*.

IVY WAS UNCHARACTERISTICALLY QUIET AFTER RETURNING

from the ladies' room. With all the finger-pointing going on, he would have to be blind not to notice the exchange between Ivy and her mother.

The tension was unreadable. It wasn't anger. Ivy has simply fallen into extreme thoughtfulness. She didn't even react to Joy's enthusiasm about the trip back down in the gondola. Or his suggestion that they have Thanksgiving dinner out. Obviously, he couldn't roast a turkey and make all the trimmings in the two hours before dinnertime.

Ivy had merely said, "Sounds good."

She didn't even argue that once again it would be his treat.

What the hell had her mother said to her?

They'd all dressed for dinner. Ivy had packed a burgundy velvet skirt and a crisp white blouse for Joy.

But Ivy made his mouth water. She always dressed nicely at work, even sexy, but tonight, she blew all his male circuits. Her black evening dress ended halfway down her thighs, leaving an excess of toned leg covered in black stockings dipping down into mile-high black suede heels. Threads in her dress glittered with silver sparkles, and the bodice clung to her breasts, the neckline revealing a creamy swell of breast he wanted to lick like vanilla ice cream.

"You're going to freeze," Leonora declared.

Ivy returned to her room for a black velvet wrap.

"You're gorgeous." *And perfect. And sexy. And you make my head spin.*

"Thank you," she said softly.

Then he bent down to kiss the tip of Joy's nose. "You're the prettiest little girl I know."

"Prettier than your daughter?" she asked eagerly.

"Of course." It wasn't a lie. Megan wasn't a little girl anymore.

"And you, Leonora." He took both her hands in his. "You're a picture."

She laughed, almost a cackle. "You can't flatter me. I'm too old for that."

"It's not flattery if it's the truth."

Leonora was truly a picture. She reminded him of someone's maiden aunt who hadn't purchased a new dress in more than twenty years. And was extremely proud of the fact.

"You look quite dapper yourself."

"Thank you, Leonora." He wore suit and tie, aware it wouldn't impress Ivy since she saw him in the same attire every day.

But they all looked good together.

Like a family. Multigenerational.

As long as no one mistook him for Ivy's father.

"Shall we go, ladies?" He offered his arm to Leonora. It was the polite thing to do.

More than anything, he wanted to wrap Ivy close.

"Can I sit in the front seat?" Joy gazed up at him with sweetness and delight.

"What does your mom think?" he deferred to Ivy.

"Please, Mommy. I want to be a big girl just for tonight."

She smiled, and it struck him how much he'd missed her smiles since they'd left the lodge. "All right, sweetie."

He'd chosen the five-star restaurant in the MontBleu Casino, a short drive down the hill from their resort.

In the backseat, Leonora said, with no regard to who was listening, "Where did you get that dress and wrap? It must have cost a fortune."

"I bought it consignment years ago, before..." Ivy paused, glancing at Brett in the rearview mirror, then added, "Before Ivy."

Before she had to watch every dollar she spent. When she was with the asshole.

He could gladly grind the guy into pulp for what he'd done to her.

Though Joy was adorable, he wished for Ivy in the front seat so he could touch her, offer her the smallest amount of comfort.

The best he could do was laugh and say, “Girls, no fighting in the backseat.” He adjusted the mirror to see Leonora better.

“Who, me?” Leonora jabbed at her bony chest. “I would never do that.” She pointed at Ivy. “It’s all her. She’s always picking on me. In fact, I think I’m going to cry.”

Finally—thank God—Ivy laughed. “Sorry, Pops.” She used the name he insisted his granddaughter would learn to call him. “We’ll behave. Just don’t send us to our rooms.”

Meanwhile, Joy was staring bug-eyed over the fact that he’d scolded her mother and grandmother.

They had a private booth at the restaurant, with a red velvet curtain their waiter pulled across to give them extra privacy.

Ivy leaned close to Joy. “It matches your dress.”

Brett had helped his ladies into the booth, making sure he was last in and seated next to Ivy. So he could take her hand in his under the tablecloth.

For Thanksgiving, they had a special three-course meal. When Ivy was about to balk at the price, he squeezed her fingers. “It’s pretty damn reasonable.” Bending to her ear, he whispered, “So don’t get your panties bunched,” and let his breath tease her hair.

She shivered against him with a longing that matched his own.

“All right,” she said. “But no alcohol. It’ll double the price of the meal.”

He could compromise that much. It gave him reason to ply her with champagne when they returned to the resort.

Last night, he would gladly have made love to her on the couch. Or carried her into his room and shut out the world for a few hours. But he needed her to make the choice.

What was growing between them no longer had anything to do with the company.

When the waiter left them after taking their order—the Thanksgiving special all around—Joy asked, "What's lobster bi—"

"Bisque," Ivy said for her. "It's a deliciously creamy soup that's made with lobster broth."

"Am I going to like it?"

"We'll have to see, won't we."

Brett laced his fingers through Ivy's, well aware that Leonora's eagle eye detected something going on beneath the table. He didn't give a damn, especially when Ivy didn't pull away. When her thumb caressed the back of his hand.

It was the simple touches that got him going. Slipping her hair behind her ear. Trailing a finger along her jaw. Feeling her back beneath his hand as he guided her into the car or onto an elevator or up the stairs. The places he could touch her in front of her daughter and still stake a claim. Even if Ivy didn't know it.

Joy was delighted when the waiter arrived with their soup and asked, "Would the little Madame like ground pepper to season her bisque?"

She chattered about the exotic flavor and how amazing it was to have a curtain, like they were in their very own private restaurant where the waiters all wore ruffled tuxedo shirts.

"They look prissy," Leonora said.

Leonora often felt the need to point out the negative in anything positive.

How had Ivy, growing up in an atmosphere like that, still managed to maintain her sense of optimism?

When her meal arrived, Leonora's comment was, "At least the turkey isn't dry."

"I'm shocked you approve," Brett couldn't resist saying. With a smile, of course.

"I complimented your fried bread this morning," she added wryly.

"That you did, my dear."

"The bacon was perfect, exactly the way I like it," Ivy put in her two cents. "And your spaghetti was wonderful, too."

"It's a joy to cook for people who appreciate food."

"That's my name," Joy piped up. When her dessert arrived after the meal, she squealed with delight. The top of the lava cake burned with a flame the waiter let Joy blow out. It dripped with chocolate and ice cream.

Even Leonora said, though with a monotone, "It's to die for."

Ivy held tight to his hand as she spooned hers.

Something inside him blossomed. His heart filled up. He understood the true extent of what he'd lost when he was young, when work came before everything else. He'd lost this, family, belonging.

But surrounded by Ivy, her mother, her daughter, he'd found that missing *something*.

And he wasn't letting it go again.

13

The day had been perfect. They'd had so much fun. And the dinner was marvelous. Joy had never seen such a fancy restaurant or tasted food so different and delicious. She talked a mile a minute as Ivy helped her get ready for bed.

Her mother's comments didn't even bother her anymore.

Only Brett's touch was important, her hand in his, her thigh pressed to him.

"I want Brett to tuck me in," Joy said, Rolf clutched in her arms, Archie already curled up to the warm little-girl body and purring.

Hearing Joy's small voice, Brett suddenly appeared in the doorway. "Of course I'll tuck you in."

Ivy was utterly aware of him, his scent, musky and male, his big body, his warm skin. Her own skin thrummed in response.

She watched from the doorway as Brett sat beside Joy on the bed, pulling the covers to her chin. He leaned down to kiss the tip of her nose. "Did you have fun ice skating today?"

"It was so cool. Maybe I should become an ice skater. I

could skate in *Beauty and the Beast*. Mommy took me to see it once."

"That sounds great."

Ivy listened to the soft discussion, her heart melting and gooey in her chest. She still wore the black dress, stockings, and high heels because she loved the way Brett looked at her, his gaze traveling over every inch as if he imagined tasting her. The way he'd promised he wanted to.

"Okay, you gotta go to sleep now, sweetheart. You need to rest up for all the fun things I've got planned for tomorrow." He kissed Joy again and rose, waggling his fingers at her as he backed away. "Sleep tight."

When he turned, his smile was a tender caress, like the kiss on her daughter's forehead, light and sweet. Reaching Ivy's side, he took her hand in his, flipped off the light, and led her out.

With the door closed behind them, his touch suddenly turned hot.

Brett had poured champagne for them both and left the glasses on the coffee table. He was scrumptious in his suit and tie. She saw him dressed like this five days a week. But now he'd kissed her, hot, sexy, divine kisses that melted her right down to the core. Everything was so very different from what it had been two weeks ago.

Her mother's door was shut.

The hint wasn't even subtle.

If you're not going to sue the man, then you better screw him.

Ivy couldn't say when the change in her had happened. When she'd decided that resisting was impossible. Had it started when she was dressing for dinner with Brett in mind? When he twined his fingers with hers at the dinner table? When he made light of her mother's say-it-like-it-is attitude? When he'd scolded them for arguing in the backseat?

Or when he'd leaned close to whisper in her ear, *Don't get your panties in a bunch.*

He could make her feel totally sexual even with her family around her. She'd wanted to curl into him, nibble her way along his jaw, until she tasted his lips.

What made it even sexier was that she couldn't in front of her daughter. Or her mother.

There was something liberating and seductive about having *thoughts*, naughty, sexual thoughts in the privacy of her mind.

For so long, she'd been a mother, a daughter, an admin, a worker.

Brett made her feel like a lover.

She didn't want to think about Rhonda. Or work. Or her mother's unflattering comments. Or a potential lawsuit.

She wanted to know what it felt like to be his lover. Even if it was just for these few days, she needed to experience it all. She needed to store up memories for long, lonely nights.

Swooping a champagne glass from the table, she held it up.

"Thank you for a wonderful day and a perfect dinner." She clinked her flute with his and took a long drink. Her eyes on him.

"You're welcome."

She stepped closer, their bodies almost flush. "Do you remember what you said to me that night after the zoo?"

He didn't pretend not to understand. "I said I want to taste every inch of you."

"That," she said softly. "Yes, that was exactly what you said." She met his hot gaze, letting her eyes say everything.

"And last night you told me exactly where you want me to taste you." He slipped his fingers beneath her hair, the heat of his hand skating all the way down to her toes. And everywhere in between.

"I want that," she whispered. "I can't remember ever wanting anything so much."

"I thought you'd never ask." Then he tipped her head back for a mind-altering kiss.

Ivy tucked her champagne close to her body and leaned into his kiss, opening for him. The taste of male laced with champagne bubbles sizzled in her mouth.

"Don't make me scream," she whispered against his lips.

"How about a little moaning and groaning?"

She laughed, burying her face against his shoulder. "I can moan and groan for you."

"Good. I want to hear your sweet little noises telling me how good you feel."

She'd denied herself for so long, all the things that made her feel good. Hot sex, luxurious food, expensive clothes.

She'd denied Joy's happiness, too, always watching every penny, always saying no.

She needed to give her daughter more. Treats every once in a while.

She needed to treat herself with this big, gorgeous man. Just for the duration of the trip, she promised. Just late at night after her mother and daughter had gone to bed.

"You're thinking." Brett raised her hand and curled his fingers around hers. "You don't need to justify or rationalize."

"I wasn't—"

He stopped her with the sweetest touch of his lips. "You were. But this is just for us, just for now. No expectations, no demands. Okay?"

"No expectations," she agreed.

"Except pleasure," he added. "I do expect you to feel lots of pleasure. It's my mission. To make you feel so good you want to cry."

"God." She laughed. "Don't say things like that. You make me all shivery inside."

"That's the way I want you to be." He stepped back, holding her hand, leading her across the living room, past the dining table.

To the door of his room.

It was all too amazing. He was the CEO, for God's sake. She was just a secretary—despite her recent promotion.

He was so magnificent. Thick silver hair, penetrating eyes, a toned body that made her breath tight in her chest.

It was like a fairy tale. Like that movie *Pretty Woman*. Or *Sabrina*.

"I want to seduce you." His deep, low voice vibrated inside her. "Slowly, lingering over every moment."

After Rupert, she'd gotten used to slam-bam men, which had their own appeal. Get it done, move on. Short commercial breaks until she got back to her regularly programmed life.

Brett made it a full-length feature.

The door closed behind them. The bed seemed huge, the comforter thick, inviting, the pillows begging her to lay her head on them while he...

Clinking his glass to hers once more, he sipped the champagne, then set both flutes on the bedside table. Cupping her face in his hands, he put his mouth to hers, kissing her long and sweet, as if he were sipping the champagne right from her lips. Her legs felt weak, her heart raced, and she held onto his arms to keep herself steady as he shifted her foundation and tipped her world sideways.

His taste was like nothing she'd ever experienced, a heady mix of sweet champagne, chocolate lava cake, and sexy, hot male. She let him devour her and steal the very last breath from her body.

Until finally he set her back on her feet. She hadn't even realized she'd been floating.

"I want to undress you slowly, so I can enjoy every bit of flesh revealed."

Her body tingled, but suddenly her nerves got to her as well. "Then do I rip off your clothes all at once?" She tried to joke, to ease the tension welling up inside her.

"How about I remove one piece of your clothing, then you remove one of mine."

Just like the questions last night. A slow, languorous seduction. She would be pleading for him to touch her by the time they were both naked.

"You first." He laid her hand on his shoulder.

He'd already taken off his jacket, so she went for his tie. "You have an unfair advantage. You've got more clothes than me."

"Then we'll do two of mine for every one of yours." His eyes seemed lit with flame, burning right through to her center.

That was another thing about the men she'd been with since Rupert. Everything was so quick, she didn't have to think. She didn't have to consider the consequences. They were in and out of her life so fast, they were barely a blip on the monitor.

Brett made her think. And want. And decide.

"Tie first." She pulled until it loosened and fell free. His heart beat beneath the palm she rested on his chest, a fast, hard rhythm that said he was just as affected as she was.

"The buttons on your shirt," she said like she was reciting instructions. "I can't believe I'm doing this," her soft words whispered against his throat because she couldn't seem to look up.

"Why?"

"Because of who you are." Her fingers traveled down the row of buttons until his white T-shirt was revealed, dusky nipples visible beneath the material.

"Because I'm your boss?"

"Because you're the CEO." She pulled his shirt from the waistband of his dress slacks.

He put his thumb beneath her chin and tipped her head up until their eyes locked. "I'm just a man. If I wasn't, I couldn't want you so badly. And I do, Ivy. I want you under me. I want inside you. I want to taste you." He kissed her lips lightly. "And I want you to taste me. All of me. I want everything."

His voice mesmerized her. His gaze captured her. His lips owned her.

She undid his cuffs, and he tossed the shirt aside. "My turn." Like the game they'd played last night, his words heated her.

Sliding his hands down her arms to her hips, he dropped to one knee before her, his head tipped back to watch her. "Shoes. Watching you walk in them made me ache to have you."

He removed both, tossed them aside, then glided back up, fingers trailing over the skirt of her dress, raising it slightly and revealing a glimpse of thigh until he let the fabric slide back in place.

"Your turn. What do you want next, Ivy?"

If she wasn't nervous, if he wasn't Mr. Brett Baker, CEO, she'd drag every stitch off him all at once, go down on her knees, and taste him the way he wanted.

But her pulse was hammering with nerves, and when she knelt, all she did was remove his shoes and socks. As he helped her up, she asked, "Does that count as two items?"

"I'll let you have another."

She kept her eyes on his as she pulled his T-shirt from his pants. Sliding her fingers beneath the white cotton to his bare skin, she saw his eyes widen, only slightly, but enough to give her a delicious thrill. She was having her effect on him. His skin was hotter now. And he was harder.

She climbed her fingers up his abdomen, pulling the shirt slowly up, up, up.

"Tease," he whispered.

She grazed her thumbs over his nipples, feeling them go taut as hard pebbles. "Raise your arms," she told him. He followed her orders, and she skimmed the shirt up and over.

"Oh my God." The words were a gasp. "You're beautiful." His chest was furred with soft salt-and-pepper hair. She ran her fingers through the luxurious whorls, cupping his nipples.

"You're going to my head." A hand on her butt, he pulled her against him, letting her feel exactly which head he was talking about.

"You're a naughty man." Her tension was easing, flowing out of her, as heat flowed in.

"Are you a naughty woman?"

"How naughty?" She'd begun to enjoy the tease.

"Will you leave the lights on so you can see everything I do to you?"

She rubbed against him. "Yes, I'm naughty enough to leave the lights on so *you* can see what *I'm* doing to *you*."

"Perfect." He held her tight one more second. "My turn again." His arms slid around her back to the zipper of her dress.

She wasn't wearing much underneath it.

The zip glided down ever so slowly, her body leaning against his, his eyes darkening with the sound until finally he reached the bottom.

"Step out of it for me." He set her back a pace.

Ivy shimmied, slipping the dress off her shoulders, then letting it drop to the carpet.

"Jesus." His eyes were a liquid touch, tracing all her curves. "You're gorgeous enough to worship."

She was woman enough to love his words and his tone. She lifted a foot and kicked the dress aside to stand before him in a lacy, black push-up bra, tiny thong panties, and thigh-high stockings.

"God, I want to do you with those stockings on. They're so freaking sexy."

She viscerally felt how much her brief, clandestine affairs had been missing. The words, the looks, the sighs. The sense of his utter desire when he wasn't even touching her. It was pleasure all on its own. It made her wet for him.

"Take off your pants," she told him. "I want to watch." Making demands made her feel powerful and sexy.

He stripped out the belt, unzipped, then shucked his trousers. His thighs were big, muscled. His boxer briefs were tight, revealing everything yet somehow shrouding him in mystery, too.

"All of it," she ordered.

Then the boxers were gone, and there was just the magnificent, hard swell of him.

"You're more perfect than any man half your age."

"Perfect for you?"

She drew in a long, shaky breath. "I'm—" She had to take another breath to steady herself. "I'm so wet thinking of you inside me." She didn't want to be dirty or crude, but she needed to give him words that would make him as crazy as his did to her.

"I want inside you so badly I could throw you down and sink into you right this second." He was certainly hard enough. And so big. "But I've got so many things I need to do to you first."

She shivered imagining them all.

Then he moved, standing right there before her. Hooking his fingers in her thong, he dragged it over her hips, going slowly to his knees, sliding the delicate lace down her legs.

He tapped a foot for her to raise and whisked away the lingerie.

She might have been embarrassed. But the sound of awe rising from his throat turned her body to liquid.

He leaned in, his nose at the juncture of her thighs, and breathed deeply. "You smell so damn good. So hot and so wet. Spread your legs for me."

A quiver of desire raced through her, and she widened her stance.

"Look at you," he whispered. "So pretty and pink." His nose bumped her mound as he took another deep breath of her.

She had never known a man so sensual. He wanted to sink into her and yet he wanted to linger as well.

He clamped his big, warm hands on her butt, looked up at her, his eyes blazing. "I want to taste you just like this."

Then he put his mouth on her.

IVY MOANED, A LONG, DELICIOUS SOUND THAT WAS AS GOOD as her taste.

He buried his face against her, savoring her sweetness and the shudders coursing through her body. The sexy lace of her to-die-for stockings caressed his fingers and pushed him deeper into longing and need and desire. Into making her crazy.

Taking the hard bud of her sex between his lips, he drove her higher, only his hands on her beautiful sexy ass keeping her on her feet. She shoved her fingers through his hair, holding him tight to her center.

"Oh God, oh God, oh God." She panted, her head tipped back, pleasure rolling through her body.

He pulled away. She hadn't come yet. He wanted to tease

her to the edge, over and over, until finally she plunged headlong into ecstasy.

"Oh God," she murmured one last time, then looked down at him. "You make me crazy." Then she whispered, "I didn't scream, did I?"

He shook his head on a smile. "No." Then he climbed up her body to hold her flush against him, all that sweet, naked skin. "If you start to scream, do you want me to kiss you to shut you up?"

She cocked her hip and pressed her lips together. "I don't like any man shutting me up."

"Of course not. I'll let you go wild instead."

"But—" She held up a finger. "—in this instance, if I lose complete control and start to scream, please do shove your tongue down my throat to shut me up."

He laughed, hugging her tightly, savoring the sensual touch of her skin all along his. "I adore your sense of humor."

Sex was supposed to be fun, and despite the slight nervousness he'd sensed in her, he loved that she could still joke. When she started to feel instead of think, all those nerves would melt away.

She rubbed against him, and he did what came natural, what he was dying to do, kissing her long and deep with her taste on his tongue.

"Lie down on the bed," he whispered, throwing the covers aside. "I'm nowhere near done with you." Then, without even giving her the chance to move, he picked her up, dumping her on the mattress and following her down.

The lacy bra was a front clasp and he snapped it easily, then dragged the strap down her arm with his teeth.

Her laughter rippled against him, and he loved the sound of it, the feel of it.

Then all the laughter died as he plumped her breasts in his hand and took possession of her nipple. He tongued her to a hard peak, sucked her to a sweet sigh and a moan. He licked across the valley to give her other nipple the same treatment.

When she arched against him in pleasure, he slipped his hand between her legs and found her moist center again. Her body rocked with his rhythm, and she pushed her head back into the pillows. He played her until she quivered, sweet, soft gasps and moans falling from her lips. When he slipped a finger deep into her wetness, she tightened around him, thrusting up, her breast filling his mouth.

He pulled away, just as he had before, leaving her on the precipice.

"Oh my God, please. Brett." She gasped his name.

He loved the sound of that, too. She'd had yet to say his name when he had his hands on her this way. As if she were pretending he was someone else. Anyone but the CEO. But they'd passed another milestone.

"Not yet," he told her. "You're not quite ready."

"I am so ready." She squirmed on the bed, pushed his shoulders, ran her hands down his back.

"Not quite. I've got a lot more work to do."

She laughed at him. "It shouldn't be work."

"It's definitely a skill."

"Then get busy demonstrating how skilled you are." As quickly as she'd laughed, she sobered. "It's been such a long, long time. And now I think I'm going to die if I have to wait one more second."

He rose up, cupped her face, and kissed her with everything in him. "I feel like I've waited for you forever, Ivy. I didn't even know it, but now I'm crazy with it."

Crazy for the taste of her. Crazy for the sound of her pleasure. Crazy for the bliss he needed to give her.

Then he settled between her legs to give her everything.

14

Ivy fell into a wild, crazy zone of ultimate pleasure and need the moment his mouth covered her. His lips were magic, his tongue was pure heaven, and when he filled her with two fingers, she skyrocketed.

Pulling the pillow over her face, she drowned her cries as she rocked against him, her body undulating sinuously.

The peak she traveled was miles long, the ride lasting forever. Maybe because it had been so long. Maybe because he'd taken her *almost* there without letting her go off.

Or maybe it was just him.

Because no one, ever, absolutely-for-freaking *never* made her feel like this. Like she'd reached nirvana or heaven or any of those other places you went when the ecstasy was so good you didn't even remember your name.

But she remembered his name, and she cried it out over and over, burying the sound in the pillows.

She hadn't fully come down when he pulled the pillow off her face.

He nuzzled her cheeks, her hair, her ear, murmured sweet little nothings.

And she remembered what he'd said.

I've waited for you forever, Ivy.

"Our turn," he whispered. He reached beyond her, and she heard a crackle and rustle.

"Are you ready for me?" He donned a condom and held himself fisted in his hand. Big, thick, and beautiful. She wished she'd tasted him first, sipped from him.

Yet she wanted this, too, to feel him inside her, as deep as he could go.

"Now." She pushed his shoulders, directly him exactly where she wanted him.

God, the feel of him between her legs. The big, hard male weight of him. She'd longed for it, and yet she'd never suspected how miraculous it would feel.

Then he filled her, slowly, caressing all her secret, sensitive places inside.

"Oh God," she murmured. "You feel so right."

"Say my name."

"Brett. You fill me up." She drew her legs to his waist, dragging him deep, her body closing around him, tightening.

"Ivy," he said. She opened her eyes as he said, "You're the one filling me up in all the places I didn't know were empty."

He moved slowly, and her body spasmed around him. The slow, thick slide of him inside was overwhelming, and when he was buried deep, he stilled, simply flexing his muscles and driving her mad. Lowering his mouth to hers, he kissed her, slow and lingering.

"You're perfect." A slow, delicious slide out. "You feel so damn good." An amazing glide back in. He wasn't screwing her. He was stroking her with his body. "I can feel you around me, so tight, rippling all over me."

She shuddered, every muscle clamping down as a wave of pleasure rolled through her.

"Yeah. Jesus, baby. Just like that."

"Brett." It was all she could manage.

He took her lips again, sensing that's what she wanted, their mouths fused, their bodies one.

He rocked in, sending shockwaves to every inch of her. It was relentless pleasure, not quite an orgasm, not the hard twisting spasm, but a crazy kind of wild ecstasy that brought a cry to her voice when she said his name again.

He knew the moment she needed more, his body rocking faster, harder, their skin slick against each other.

She clasped her legs around his hips, her fingers digging into his butt. Until the moment it all burst inside her, shattering her, blinding her.

She reached ultimate pleasure as his mouth claimed hers.

Jesus.

His heart was still exploding and fireworks blasted off before his eyes.

He went there with Ivy, every step of the way. Drinking in her cries until finally they were gentle sobs of pure pleasure.

Their bodies began to settle, the aftershocks drifting away. He relished the feel of her in his arms, skin to skin, breath to breath, the silk of her stockings caressing his legs.

Then he pulled the covers over them.

"Perfect," he whispered against her hair. The word was inadequate. She was beyond perfection.

She snuggled deeper, and he never wanted to let her go. Returning home would change everything again, but he couldn't see himself letting her go, not even then. No matter what anyone said.

"You had condoms."

His heart clenched. She'd fallen off her high. She was analyzing, when he didn't want her to think at all.

"Did you plan all this?" she asked, her voice just a breath of sound in the room.

"I hoped. I certainly wanted to be prepared if it happened." He tipped her chin, and her eyes were a deep cocoa in the bedside lamplight. "I'm not going to lie and say I haven't dreamed about doing this since the moment I saw your bare toes out at the park."

Something brimmed in her gaze. He had no idea what until she said, "I've been dreaming about it since you showed me that first baby picture of your granddaughter. All of a sudden, you weren't just the CEO anymore. You were," she paused a long moment before adding, "so much more that I even admitted to myself."

She'd been so much more far longer than he'd ever admitted. Because he *had* stopped by her desk every day with a new picture, even the days he didn't absolutely need to walk across the landing to see Grady. And he hadn't wanted to leave.

He felt her swallow, her chin tipping slightly. "But this can be the only time."

His heart wailed in his chest. "It doesn't have to be."

She put her finger over his lips. "It does. Everything I told you about Joy hasn't changed. And my job hasn't changed."

Screw her job. He could take care of her and Joy.

Yet he knew without a doubt that very statement would have her jumping out of the bed.

Ivy Elliot didn't want any man taking care of her. She needed independence.

He damned the asshole who'd dumped her. He even damned her father, who'd started the whole problem by leaving his family high and dry.

"I better go." She was already pulling away, wrenching his insides.

He damn near had to grit his teeth and bunch his fists to

stop his muscles from working on their own, from grabbing, holding her to him.

"Thank you," she said.

He actually wanted to scream.

Her silky dark hair fell across her cheek. "I've never felt anything like that in my life." She leaned down, kissing him quickly, then backed off to retrieve her clothing, the sexy dress, the lacy bra, the mile-high heels.

God, the picture she made, all that beautiful, sleek skin, the mind-altering stockings.

Then it all disappeared beneath the dress. He could still remember, the feel of her, the taste, her scent, the tight muscles taking him to heaven.

He wanted to bound out of the bed. But all he did was say, "No one's ever done to me what you did. Made me lose my mind."

Made him lose his heart in less than two weeks.

His helpless, hopeless heart.

She picked up her shoes, carrying them. He might actually have died if she put them back on.

"Goodnight," she whispered.

When the door closed, he lay on the bed staring at the ceiling. It was a good night. The best damn night.

He swore it would not be the last night.

THEY HADN'T TURNED THE LIGHTS OUT IN THE LIVING room, and Ivy padded softly, switching everything off, until only the glow of the fire was left. She stood in the gentle radiance, feeling its warmth.

Then she slumped to her bottom, hugging her knees to her chest.

She couldn't go back to her room, to the bed she shared

with her daughter. Not after Brett. Not while her body still hummed with his touch.

She'd never done anything so hard as climbing out of his bed. All she'd wanted was to fall asleep in his arms, waking to do all those beautiful things again.

She hadn't had the chance to taste him.

And she wanted to ride him.

She wanted to see his face when he came.

But all of that would only drag her deeper. She would want more. Then more still.

Until her heart *needed* him.

She couldn't do that to Joy. She couldn't bring him so completely into their lives that it would devastate her daughter when he left again.

Joy was already attached. Ivy could only hope she wasn't *too* attached.

Maybe the trip had been a mistake. Yet she wouldn't steal her daughter's joy in her first snow, her first ice skating, her first ultra-fancy dinner. Or all the other firsts Brett had planned for her.

But it had to be over when their trip was over.

What had happened in his bedroom, every amazing moment of it, well, that was all over as of right now.

It *had* to be.

THE DAY FOLLOWING THAT GLORIOUS NIGHT, BRETT DIDN'T stop touching her. His arm around her shoulder one moment, the next guiding her into the car, then helping her out. His hand gliding across her back as he passed her on the way to the kitchen. A whisper of a kiss in her hair when Joy was racing ahead of them.

Every chance he got. Every excuse. Brett took it.

He was driving her completely crazy.

Ivy didn't know how she could resist. Because every time he touched her, even when he looked at her, she remembered last night. And she wanted to throw herself into his arms.

They took Joy to a snow park for sledding. Her mother stayed behind, saying someone had to look after Archie the cat so she didn't piddle in the corners.

The cat slept all day and didn't care one bit if no one was there, at least not until dinnertime. Or Joy returned.

Her mother's absence only encouraged Brett. They went down the hills separately, Joy screaming with delight. Then his sled broke and he insisted on sharing Ivy's.

How the hell did you break a plastic sled, even when you were as big as Brett?

Ivy was sure he'd sabotaged it just so he could con her into going with him.

She almost had an orgasm packed so tightly against him, wedged between his legs, feeling every hard and ready inch of him as they bounced and careened down the hill.

Her legs were weak and wobbly by the time the sun was starting to set.

And she was wild with need.

But Ivy maintained control. They were with her daughter after all, and she did not let one single iota of her chaotic emotions show. Not one.

"How about some hot tubbing?" Brett asked when they arrived back at the condo.

"It's snowing," Mom scoffed, throwing out an arm to indicate the flakes falling on the deck. "And I don't even own a swimsuit."

He wasn't daunted. "It's perfect. The tub is hot, and the snow falling all around you is magnificent." He bent down in front of Joy. "You can't come all the way to Tahoe and not do some hut tubbing in the snow."

Joy vibrated with anticipation. "Can we, Mommy, can we?"

Ivy wanted to shout, *Yes, yes, yes.* Despite how dangerous it was. Then she told herself her daughter would be chaperoning them. Except that Joy hadn't made any kind of chaperone at the snow park.

Brett had found a way to get his hands on Ivy anyway.

Joy put her palms together, pleading. "Mommy, please, please."

Really, how was she supposed to fight her daughter as well as herself?

So she caved. "All right."

Brett had the grace not to crow.

The hot tub was in the middle of the complex and open to the sky, with all the suites surrounding it and four floors above it so the tub was sheltered from wind.

They wore the thick terry robes provided by the resort until they stepped into the bubbling waters.

"Look, Mommy, it's snowing." Joy held out her hands to catch the flakes.

"It's snowing," she said to Brett, a catch of laughter in her voice. "This is crazy."

He did another of his sneaky maneuvers, tucking his fingers beneath her hair and pulling her against him briefly. "That's why it's so fun." Then he threw off his robe and plunged into the water. "Last one in's a rotten egg!"

His chest was gorgeous and naked, bringing back every tactile memory of last night.

Joy wasn't about to be a rotten egg, and she plunged after Brett.

Ivy was more sedate, slipping off her flip-flops, hanging her towel and robe on the hooks provided, hanging theirs, too.

She wore a one-piece bathing suit with the hips cut high, the back dipping low, and a deep vee into her cleavage.

"Doesn't your mother look beautiful?"

"Huh?" Joy gave him a puzzled gaze. "She looks like Mommy."

He laughed and swooped in to give Joy a big hug. "Yes, she does."

"Oh my God." Ivy moaned, closing her eyes, as she let the hot, bubbling water suck her down.

"Told you it was worth it." He waggled his brows.

"You are so right." She tossed a smile at him. "I don't know why I ever doubt you." With the cold air around them, the steam rising off the water, and the snow falling lightly, it was paradise. Especially after the cold blast of the wind all afternoon while they were sledding.

Joy stuck out her tongue, trying to catch the snowflakes. The stars miraculously peeked through the clouds, and the falling snow against the star-studded backdrop was amazing.

Brett's leg brushed hers under the water. His toes slid up her calf. She gave him a stern warning glare.

"Mommy, catch the snowflakes with me."

Ivy sank down into the middle of the tub beside her daughter and tilted her head, sticking her tongue out to taste the flakes.

Brett joined them and they all held hands, leaning back to see the sky and capture the snow.

It was beautiful and serene. It was terrifyingly perfect.

It was almost like they were a family.

THE MAN WAS TO DIE FOR. HONESTLY.

He was on his best behavior, too, if you didn't count trying to touch her at every opportunity. He'd managed a lot of contact in the hot tub, even with Joy there, a stroke down

Ivy's leg, a caress along the center of her back, a quick kiss on her shoulder.

For dinner, Brett treated them to homemade pizza, the cheese deliciously gooey, the toppings spicy and mouthwatering. Then he made popcorn and hot chocolate while they played cards.

Even Ivy's mother enjoyed herself.

The day had been long with lots of activity, and Joy tuckered out just after nine o'clock. They all decided to have an early night—at least Ivy made the decision for them—especially since tomorrow Brett planned a drive around the lake.

Of course, the early night was her way of avoiding Brett. Because if she left Joy alone in the bed and returned to the living room, she wouldn't be able to resist him.

Everything about the man was a treat.

Everything about the man was a seduction.

Joy insisted on having Brett tuck her in again. Ivy insisted on shutting the door behind him when he left, no matter how much it melted her heart to watch him with her daughter. Now she lay in bed beside her sleeping child, the purr of the cat like music that should have lulled her to sleep. Outside, the wind sang through the pines.

She should have been able to fall asleep. Yet she lay on her back staring at the ceiling and watching shadows flit across it as the trees outside swayed in the wind.

She should have known Brett was like a drug and one night would only make her crave another. And another.

It was a dilemma for single mothers everywhere. How much did you let a man in? How close did you let him get to your children before they became too attached to let him go? She'd solved that problem by never bringing a man home and keeping her affairs brief. She didn't indulge often, but every few months, she just needed *something*. She'd never wanted a single one of them to be anything more.

Until Brett. He was like a storm trooper barging his way in.

Especially after last night.

Because now she knew just how good he was. Where most realities didn't live up to the fantasy, Brett surpassed it.

She told herself one more time couldn't hurt. Tonight was no different than last night. And God how she wanted everything she hadn't gotten the chance to do. Touching him, tasting him. She wanted wild, she wanted crazy. She wanted to drive him over the edge.

She wanted to be the one who had to kiss him to shut him up.

Ivy quietly climbed out of the bed.

HIS DOOR WAS OPEN, THE LIGHTS STILL ON. HE LAY ON THE bed, hands stacked behind his head.

Brett didn't consider her a sure thing. The open door was simply hopeful.

Hope won out. She stood in the doorway, hands on both jambs, a granny nightgown covering her from neck to ankles.

It was the sexiest damn thing he'd ever seen.

Then she closed the door, her footsteps barely audible on the plush carpet.

Standing beside the bed, she said, "I forgot one thing last night." Her face was scrubbed clean, her skin glowing without makeup.

"What did you forget?" His heart did a fast thump in his chest.

"I need to taste you." Her skin flushed as she said it. "Just once." Her voice dipped low. "I have to know. So I can remember."

"You can have it as often as you like, Ivy. It doesn't have to be just a memory."

She shook her head, her hair flying across her cheek. "That can never work. But we're here. And this is like some special place—" A magical place, he thought. "—where anything is possible."

He wasn't going to fight that fight now. "Everything is possible." He lifted the covers, inviting her in. "Now come and taste me."

She crawled under the comforter with him, her body fragrant and warm. "My turn," she whispered, hiking her nightgown up so she could straddle him.

He fell deliciously into the juncture of thighs. Only his pajama bottoms separated them.

"First, I want to kiss you." She leaned over his chest, her breasts already peaked, and touched his cheeks with her fingers. Her kiss was utterly sweet, her mouth barely parted. Then she licked the seam of his lips, kissed him softly, opening fully. She tasted him, her tongue against his. Her thighs shifted, and she clasped him tighter between her legs, her hips moving with the rhythm of her mouth against his.

He was hard. He'd been hard since the moment he'd climbed into bed with the anticipation that she'd come to him. Putting his hands to her hips, he held her down, caressing her with his body, rocking them gently as she kissed him.

"Mmm," she murmured. "All minty toothpaste. I wonder what the rest of you tastes like."

He loved her this way, flirty and sexy, bold and take-charge. Last night, she'd been nervous, tentative. He'd made love to her rather than doing it together. But he loved it both ways.

She kissed along his jaw. "You shaved."

"I wanted to be ready if you decided to come."

"Oh, I've decided to come all right." Her laughter puffed against his skin. "But I'm going to have my wicked way with you first." She rubbed her breasts against him, then sat up. "We need total nakedness for this."

She'd left the lights on, and she was glorious on his lap as she pulled the nightgown up and over her head, tossing it aside. Her breasts bounced, and it was all he could do not to touch and taste and savor. But she wanted the control tonight.

Arms curled around her head, she moved on him, her hips undulating, his erection pulsing as she rode him.

Then she lifted her leg as if she were dismounting a horse, and pulled his pajamas off. They joined her nightgown on the floor.

Wrapping her hand around him, she stroked slowly, lightly. "Look at you," she crooned.

"Jesus," he whispered, the pleasure heightening as she squeezed. "You're perfect like this. Playing the dominant."

She batted her lashes at him. "I'm playing CEO." Then she climbed on again, clasping him between her thighs and driving him crazy with a skin-on-skin shimmy.

Draping herself over his chest, she licked his nipple, bit lightly, then harder.

An exquisite pleasure-pain shot down to his erection, and he arched involuntarily. "God, you make me freaking crazy."

She laughed. This was a side of her he hadn't seen, and he wanted more.

She gave it to him, crawling down his body, trailing kisses in her wake. Until she was *right* there, her breath making his skin jump. She licked him, one long swipe up his shaft. And looked up at him, her smile as wicked as Salome doing her dance.

"My turn," she said, blowing on him. Then her lips were

all over him. She took him deep, sucked hard on the way back up, working her lips over his tip.

His legs quaked with how good it was.

"Jesus, lady." The words seemed torn from his throat. He was up on the cliff ready to dive so fast that his mind whirled. "Don't make me come, Jesus, not yet. I need to be inside you."

She let him go long enough to tell him, "Hush." Looking at him, seconds ticked away as her eyes darkened seductively. "We have all night." She went at him again, her lips, her hand, her mouth, her tongue. She reached under him, squeezed gently, and another rush of pleasure washed through him. He gritted his teeth, fought off the climax. "Jesus, please."

But she was too much, hitting all his hot spots, driving him close to insanity, close to screaming. He fisted his hands in the sheets, bared his teeth. "God, nothing—" It was all he could manage, because *nothing* had ever felt like this. Nothing had ever felt as good as Ivy letting go of all her inhibitions and taking him. Driving him. Owning him.

When the explosion hit, he stuffed his face into the pillow as his body bucked beneath her. She didn't let go, working him, squeezing every last ounce of pleasure out of him. She took everything he had to give, every drop.

There was a space of time when he might have lost consciousness. He wasn't even aware of her climbing his body, resting against him, her face in the crook of his neck.

"Crazy good," he whispered.

She kissed his ear, his jaw, his cheek. Then she put her lips to his and whispered, "Kiss me now."

He'd kissed her last night with her taste still on his tongue. She wanted to share, too.

So he took, kissing her soft then hard, tasting his own saltiness, tasting her pleasure in what she'd done to him.

Together, they tasted like power.

15

"That was number one," she whispered against his mouth.

"What's next?"

"I want to ride you. On top."

He rolled her, spreading her with his knee between her legs.

She loved feeling him come for her, the way his body shook, the corded muscles of his neck, the arch of his body. He'd gone rigid, his breath a series of gasps. Though he'd tried to mask them beneath the pillow, she heard his hoarse cries.

His taste was luscious in her mouth, the feel of him magnificent. She'd felt alive, in control, powerful.

Sex had never been like that for her.

It was a new and wonderful experience he'd given her. Or that he'd allowed her to take.

No, she'd simply taken it. He was a man who didn't fear a woman taking anything from him.

He was a CEO. He was all about power. She couldn't have

imagined he would give her what she wanted. But he'd done it so willingly.

He bent to her lips and murmured, "My turn first. Before you get to ride." Then his fingers began a languorous stroll down her belly. "I want to watch you come. I want to hold you in my arms and watch every emotion play over your face." He bent to her lips for a quick kiss. "Which means I'm only going to use my fingers on you. Because I need you tucked close to me just like this." He held her beneath him, his arm wrapped around her.

Her skin jumped as he circled her nipple with his fingernail.

"I think I'm going to like it that way." She'd never been watched. It was like being on exhibition. The idea sent a sexy thrill through her. "Yes, watch me come. Please."

"Your skin is so damn soft and smooth." He drew slow, gentle circles down her torso to her belly, then beyond. He dipped inside. "God, you're wet. And I didn't even touch you."

"I rubbed myself all over you." His skin against her, his erection, his kiss, his taste, all was an aphrodisiac.

He slipped between her folds, finding the sensitive button that made her body jump. She gave a moue of pleasure.

"You were marking me."

She laughed, then her breath hitched as he circled and pressed. "You're a marked man, now."

"Hell, yes, I am."

God, it was good. Amazing. His voice, his touch, his eyes on her, his fingers all over her, inside her.

Everything turned liquid and hot. She grabbed his arm, sank her nails into him. Bit her lip as the pleasure mounted.

"Let me hear you, all those delicious little noises," he whispered against her ear, then pulled back to look at her once more, his fingers ceaseless, the intensity building.

"Brett." She gasped, moaned deep in her throat, and gave him all the sounds of pleasure he wanted. "Oh, oh, God."

Her body started to move on its own, rolling with the swish of his fingers, her hips rising, her butt tensing.

"Look at me." His voice seemed far off.

"Oh, God, I can't. I—" She clung to him, her hand on his shoulder. She wanted to bury her face against him, but he wanted to watch. Oh, God, sweet Jesus, having him watch her was as intense as his touch.

"Let it go, baby."

She opened her mouth, gasped air. Then the wave crashed, dragging her down, splintering her. She writhed in his arms, riding the peak. Until finally she started to laugh. Softly. Because it was crazy. So good. So perfect. So insane.

She opened her eyes. His arms still held her, his hand caressing her hip.

"That was the most beautiful thing I've ever seen."

She caught her breath. "You did that to me."

"Yeah. Pretty damn hot. And you did it to me, too. With your mouth."

"I like it. Coming for you. Making you come for me. If we come at the same time, we don't get to experience what the other is feeling."

He stroked the hair back from her face. "Simultaneous orgasm is pretty freaking hot, too. When you get so tight around me, your body squeezing me, it damn near makes my head explode."

She trailed her finger down his nose. "We can do that, too."

"We have all night." He paused. "Until you go back to your bed."

She couldn't be sure whether he was saying he understood that she had to leave. Or if he was telling her she had to go.

For the first time since she'd closed the door, her belly

clenched. She remembered time limits. She remembered that they'd be going home on Sunday. Only two days left.

Only two nights.

There was no longer a doubt that she would be crawling back into his bed tomorrow night. She'd been lying to herself thinking it could only be one more time.

She would take as much as she could get.

She would do all the things she'd dreamed of.

"I want to be on top." She couldn't say why it was so important, but she needed it. Then she whispered, maybe meaning it only for herself, "What else do I want?"

He adjusted her in his arms till they lay on the bed facing each other. "What are your fantasies?"

She bit her lip, smiling at him. "Nothing kinky."

"Kinky is good, but not absolutely necessary."

"Hmm." She closed her eyes, considering. "I'd like it back to front. On our knees." She leaned close to whisper, "With your fingers on me."

"Or your fingers."

She gasped. "You're bad."

"But very fun."

Oh yes, he was so very fun. "Then there's the lotus position." She wasn't even sure if that's what it was called.

But he knew it. "With you in my lap and our legs around each other."

"And you have to lift me. Very slowly."

He chuckled. "I love the way you think."

"What's your fantasy?"

He stroked her hair, pushing it behind her ear. "My fantasy is playing out your fantasies."

She pulled him close, caressing him with her whole body. "My turn. Are you ready to let me ride?"

"I'm ready for anything you want." His kiss was hard and fast, but it seared her to her soul.

Did men really give a woman anything she wanted? Maybe. For tonight, tomorrow night. She was going to take it.

And face the consequences later.

SHE TURNED HIM ABSOLUTELY NUTS.

She'd rolled on the condom, making his skin buzz and jump with each leisurely, sexy move. Then she'd taken him inside, so damn slowly his hands had itched to grab her hips and slam into her.

Yet the pleasure was exquisite.

She'd smiled, moving on him like she was sitting in a western saddle.

Until, Jesus, she'd really gotten into it, her arms high, her hands in her hair, riding him straight up to heaven.

The orgasm had been simultaneous, cataclysmic, mind-blowing. And just when he would have shouted out his pleasure, she kissed him, swallowing both their cries.

They'd made love. To each other. With each other. It was beyond mere sex.

Then she'd fallen asleep in his arms.

Somehow, holding her as she slept was as momentous as making love. All her defenses were down, and she clasped him to her as if she'd never let go.

He didn't want to let her go. Not back to her bed. Not back to the life she'd had.

Yet he knew when she woke, that's exactly what she'd do, walk back to her own life. Her separate life.

If he told her he wanted more, she'd ask him for how long. She wouldn't believe him if he said forever.

Finally he slept, too.

In the morning, just as he'd thought—just as he'd feared—she was gone.

"SO," HER MOTHER SAID. "IS HE ANY GOOD?"

"Mother!"

This morning Brett had driven them around the lake, stopping at Emerald Bay, where he and Joy were sledding. The man never stopped being perfect.

Her mother never stopped pushing.

"Don't try to pretend you haven't been sneaking into his room. I'm no dummy."

"That's none of your business."

Her mother harrumphed. "I'm not condemning you. I say good for you."

Joy hooted as she hit the bottom of the hill first, before Brett, winning whatever race they'd been running. He'd probably let her win, but that didn't seem to matter to Joy.

"In fact, I say use the guy for all he's worth before he dumps you."

She could only stare at her mother.

She shrugged. "Well, he will. He divorced his wife eighteen years ago. He hasn't had a real girlfriend since—"

"How do you know that?"

Her mother made a face. "We talk. And what I'm saying is that he's not a relationship kind of man. He's a workaholic. So have your fun while you can. Make him give you some gifts, too. Jewelry would be good in case you need to pawn it later."

"I cannot believe some of the things that come out of your mouth." She could. Her mother had always been candid.

"Well, since you aren't going to sue him, you need to at least get yourself *something*. And I don't mean just hot sex."

Ivy blushed. She was never more glad to have her daughter on a hill where neither she nor Brett could overhear her mother.

"I haven't said I'm not going to sue him."

Mom snorted. "Right. Like you're actually going to call a lawyer. Sweetheart, you're in too deep to ever do that to Brett now."

Ivy could only stare at the snow-covered hill as Joy squealed with delight, and Brett acted like a bigger kid than she was.

Her mother was absolutely right. She couldn't sue Brett. She couldn't sue the company. She couldn't even sue Rhonda.

She simply wouldn't do that to him.

How long would he stick around once he figured that out?

IVY WASN'T GOING TO SUE. BUT SHE WASN'T GETTING IN any deeper, for Joy's sake and for her own as well. Once they were back home, everything had to be all business.

Which meant she had one more night.

She didn't even pretend this time. Before taking Joy off to bed, she asked Brett to pour her another glass of champagne. To her mother, she said, "Mom, didn't you want to use that big jet tub in your room one last time before we leave tomorrow."

Her mother gave her a snarky, knowing smile. "Yes, of course, dear. Since I'll never see another tub like that in my life." She actually swished her hips as she retired to her room.

Brett was giving Ivy the eye as if he suspected something was going on. He'd be an idiot if he didn't.

Following their usual ritual, Joy needed a goodnight hug and kiss from both Ivy and Brett. The champagne was waiting for them when they returned to the living room.

Sitting on the couch, Brett stretched out a hand to Ivy. "So what's going on between you and Leonora?"

She sat next to him, arm along the back of the couch, legs

tucked beneath her. Sipping her champagne, she played with the thick hair at Brett's collar. "She's giving me advice. But I haven't taken my mother's advice since I left home for college."

"Advice about what?"

"What do you think?"

He pointed to his chest, raising an eyebrow.

Ivy nodded.

"What did she advise you to do?"

She smiled, letting it grow slowly, hoping it was sexy and seductive. "She told me I should do everything I wanted."

He quirked one eyebrow. "You mean..."

"S-E-X," she spelled for him. Okay, it wasn't the whole truth. Her mother wanted her to ask for a lot more. But Ivy wanted only the sex part.

"I'd be happy to help you out."

He stroked his chin, freshly shaven after dinner. Like he expected her to come to his room. Or maybe he was just hopeful, the same as when he'd bought the condoms. What did she care anyway whether he expected, anticipated, or hoped? She *was* going to his room tonight, and she wasn't leaving until she'd done all those sexy positions they'd talked about last night.

She leaned in, licked his ear, and smiled when he shuddered. Then she told him the complete and utter truth. "I like the way you make me feel." She put her finger over his lips when he opened his mouth. "Not just S-E-X. But the way you let me take charge when I want to. The way you like the things I do to you. You make me feel it's all about me instead of about you."

He caught her hand, pressed his lips to her knuckles. "It *is* all about you. It should always be all about the woman. Lovemaking is so much better that way, so much hotter."

Lovemaking. She'd called it *S-E-X.*

A thrill shimmied through her at the words he used.

"That's why I want to know your fantasies. Because playing them out for you is the sexiest thing a man could ever do."

Had he done that with his other women? The ones he wasn't having a relationship with?

Or was she special?

Ivy couldn't ask. But God, how she wanted to.

He laced his fingers with hers, then curled her hand in and kissed the back. It was so romantic, so intimate.

"Let me show you tonight. How good it can be when all your fantasies are fulfilled."

She followed him to his room. She'd follow him anywhere. What woman wouldn't want every fantasy fulfilled.

Even if it was only for one night.

16

He didn't lose himself to the pleasure, not yet. He wanted first to give her the fantasies she'd asked for. On the big bed in his room, he pressed her spine to his chest, tipping her head back against his shoulder as he kissed the creamy skin of her neck.

"Do you want it like this?" he murmured in her ear.

She moaned. "God yes."

Sitting back on his haunches, he spread her legs over him, her knees fitted tight to his thighs. She'd already done the honors with the condom, nearly driving him to madness while she touched him. And now he slid inside her. Slowly.

Her eyelashes fluttered down, and a moan welled up from deep inside her. "Brett. Oh my God. That is so perfect."

She didn't know the half of it. Her eyes were closed. She couldn't see the picture they made in the long mirror opposite the bed. He hadn't planned to pose in front of it, yet he couldn't tear his eyes away from the pure carnality of their scene.

Hands on her hips, raising her, pulling her back again, he watched as he filled her. It was no porn movie. It was perfection, her skin flushed, her breasts high, nipples peaked, her lips slightly parted as she gasped and panted. His darker skin against her creamy tones. Her black hair tangled with his. The beauty of his erection sliding deep inside her, her pink flesh claiming him.

The man's hand in the mirror slid over the taut tummy, tunneling down, down, down to their joining, and the hot button nestled there. Her body gripped him tightly, and when he put his finger on her, slipping in all the moisture they'd created together, she contracted, like a fist stroking him.

"Jesus." He breathed. Maintained control. Barely.

Her body moved against him, rising, falling, their flesh slip-sliding as she gained momentum, her moans increasingly desperate.

"Touch yourself for me." But she was too far gone with the pleasure to hear him or understand.

He guided her hand down, holding her there with his own, their fingers playing her like a duet.

In the mirror, they were stunning. As if they were one, with one goal in mind, her pleasure. Her movements were completely abandoned, her eyes closed, her body nothing but sensation. He had never seen anything more exquisite in his life, and he held himself back simply to watch her, as her skin pinkened, her nipples turned to taut beads, and her moisture slipped onto their fingers. She writhed, her body arching, milking him inside her, tugging him toward that simultaneous orgasm.

But he needed this more, the sight of them in the mirror, almost one body, one mind, one heart, their only need being her satisfaction.

"Look at us," he whispered, yet the command in his voice forced her to open her eyes.

"Oh my God." She retreated an infinitesimal distance from him, seeing everything. The slightly new position intensified the pressure on her, inside her, hitting that special spot with precision.

Her body imploded around him, close to dragging him over the edge with her. He managed not to fall with his last measure of will. Her mouth fell open, a cry welling up. He slid his finger between her teeth, letting her bite down, the pain and the pleasure so intense they threatened his will. And yet he held.

He watched.

He fell into the mirror's perfection. Fell into her.

Fell completely for her.

THE SIGHT OF THEM IN THE MIRROR WAS EROTIC. Brilliant, sensual. And terrifying. She'd abandoned herself completely to him. The mirror showed it all, the flush of her skin, the wild, crazy need, with Brett right *there*, filling her, a physical part of her. She belonged to *him*. She had never, ever felt like this with anyone. She'd never given everything, lost total control. Lost *herself*.

Yet in the next moment, none of that mattered. There was just Brett filling her up and the crash of pleasure through her. Squeezing her eyes tight, she rode it, biting down on his finger to trap the screams in her throat, while every muscle inside her convulsed.

She must have lost all her senses to the pleasure, because she surfaced to find herself nestled in his lap, facing him, her legs wrapped around him just the way she'd described last night. He was still buried inside her, stealing the very air she needed to breathe.

"What are you doing to me?" she whispered.

"Giving you every fantasy you want."

Oh God. It was too much. Too good. She could want this

all the time. She could need it.

"Trust me," he murmured, putting his mouth on hers, whispering the trust into her, mesmerizing her with it.

She had no choice but to give everything to him. She was in too deep. She couldn't back out now. She could only wrap her arms around his neck and let him take her. His hands on her butt, he moved her in a slow, undulating rise and fall, his body caressing every nerve, inside and out. He stroked sensitive places she hadn't known existed.

"Brett," she breathed his name against his ear.

"Take me, baby. Like this. Jesus, just like this."

If he'd picked up the pace, she would have shattered, and it would be over. But his moves were slow, insanely perfect, and she was losing it all over again.

"Brett, Oh God." She panted his name, then, "please, please," begging for something she couldn't name. The pleasure was an endless crest, stretching out forever.

She opened her mouth, a low moan rising up her throat. He took it all, covering her lips with his, making love to her tongue, his moves inside her unstoppable.

"Come for me, baby," he whispered, then took her mouth again.

She had to obey, her body spasming around him. Tightened her legs, she squeezed him. His hands rocked her harder, faster, wilder. Until he went rigid, throbbing deep inside her, reaching up, up, to her chest, her heart.

She couldn't say how long she sat in his lap, his body filling her, his arms holding her. The feeling was as blissful as the orgasms he'd given her. Just to be held, his skin against hers, his scent all over her, his hair brushing her cheek.

Finally he rolled her, taking her down to lie flat on the bed beneath him. Stroking the hair from her face, he said, "I'll be right back."

As he pulled out and climbed from the bed, she heard his

words again. *Trust me.* Without him, the bed was colder, her body empty. His words sent a chill down her spine.

She couldn't remember what she was supposed to trust. She couldn't remember why he'd even said it. Trust him to give her pleasure? To make all her fantasies come true?

He couldn't know all her fantasies. They had nothing to do with sex.

She could hear him in the bathroom, the water running.

No man could make her dreams come true. She could depend only on herself. Joy could depend only on her.

She'd been good with that truth. She understood it. She did everything to live up to it.

But these last three nights with Brett made her want more. It made her want him to come back. The mirror had shown it all. She'd lost herself to him, let him become a part of her, two halves of the same whole.

The problem was that she and Joy were like Archie the cat. As soon as they did something to disappoint or they were no longer necessary, they'd be out. No one could blame Brett's daughter. Her priorities had changed.

No one would blame Brett for his priority. It had always been the company. Had always been making sure she didn't get in the way.

The water shut off. Ivy squeezed her eyes tight as if that could shut out the ache around her heart. The bathroom light went dark.

She moved before he came back into the room, crawling off the bed, searching for her nightgown.

"Hey, where you going?"

Brett's arms wrapped around her, hauling back against his warm, hard body.

She sank into him, relishing the security even as she knew it was so much better to pull away. "I don't want Joy to wake up without me."

"Lie with me for a while." His words against her ear were so sweet, so warm, so enticing. "Let's catch our breath. Together."

"But—" she started.

He pulled her down onto the bed. "I want to feel you against me."

She didn't have the strength to pull away. She wanted to feel him surrounding her. She wanted his skin against hers, his scent all over her.

They lay for a long, delicious moment she wanted to hang onto forever. But when she opened her eyes, she saw them in the mirror.

She saw a woman who wanted too much. She saw a man in the shadows behind her, his arm across her belly holding her to him.

A shadow that would be gone when the sun came up.

Then Brett shifted, rolling her beneath him, kissing her again.

She forgot the image in the mirror. Because Brett could make her forget anything.

At least for tonight.

SHE WAS WARM, SOFT, AND FRAGRANT IN HIS ARMS, HER breath soft in sleep. If he hadn't exhausted her with pleasure, she'd already be gone, back to her other life. Her other room on the opposite end of the condo, as if it were on the other side of the world.

Their loving was like nothing he'd ever known. Yet when it ended, she seemed to escape from him again.

Like a butterfly he couldn't hold onto.

He couldn't say exactly which thing he'd done had distanced her. For long, beautiful moments, they were close enough to be one being.

In the next, she was gone again.

You're pushing her too hard.

He'd barreled into her life, rushed her, bringing her here to Tahoe. He'd wanted the lovemaking to bring them closer, but he feared she was further away than ever.

If he wanted more with her, he was going to have to give her space.

You're crowding her.

He always listened to his inner voice.

Early on, he'd thought of her as a dazzling butterfly whose wings they were pulling off. But *he* was the one pulling off her wings, forcing her to accept the things he wanted to give her. Even when she wasn't ready.

She'd been abandoned twice, as a child, then again as an adult. She'd avoided men so her daughter wouldn't get attached to anyone who might potentially leave her. Ivy was courageously protective.

Right now, her body was warm and her skin silky smooth against him. He relished her sweet woman scent with every breath.

If he wasn't careful, he'd smother her. Then he'd lose her.

He couldn't accept that as a possibility.

So when she woke deep in the night and slipped from his bed, he let her go. It was the only way to make sure she came back again.

God how he wanted her back again. He wasn't ready to admit even to himself exactly what that meant. He would allow only the fact that letting her get away wasn't an option.

HER DAUGHTER WAS MADLY IN LOVE. SUNDAY WAS THEIR go-home day, and from the backseat, Joy hadn't stopped talking about every wonderful thing they'd done. She'd wanted to sit in the front seat with Brett, but he'd nixed it with, "Sorry, sweetheart, but that's your mom's spot."

After what they'd done last night, Ivy had expected Brett to hold her hand, stroke her knee, or find another excuse to touch her, but he hadn't. He'd simply answered any question Joy put to him from the backseat, his eyes flicking to the rearview mirror.

The questioning went on and on.

Joy: "Can you teach my mommy to make pancakes like yours?"

Brett: "I'm sure her pancakes are perfect," said with a wink in Ivy's direction.

Joy: "Are you going to come see Archie so she doesn't miss you?"

Brett: "Archie has fallen for you. She's not going to miss me," said with a half-smile, a shake of his head, and another glance at Ivy.

Ivy: "Honey, stop pestering Brett with questions."

Brett: "She's not pestering me."

Mom: "Ivy, the child is just excited about all the marvelous, wonderful, fabulous things Brett showed her this weekend. Let her enjoy," said with definite reminder of what she'd gone on about yesterday. *Get whatever you can before he dumps you.*

Ivy loved her daughter's exuberance, her interest in everything. Her zest for life. She never wanted to shut that down.

But Joy had gone gaga over Brett.

That was all Ivy's fault.

Ivy had wanted the holiday. Ivy had wanted those three sexy, seductive nights filled with orgasmic pleasure. She wanted to hang onto the memory of them forever.

God help her, she wanted more nights with him.

She just didn't want her life to change. She didn't want Joy to get involved and attached, then ultimately hurt. She didn't want to hear her mother harping on what she should do.

If only the sex between them hadn't been so amazing. If only she didn't crave more.

If only she hadn't seen in the mirror exactly what Brett could do to her. How he'd made her feel utterly connected to him.

Now she wasn't sure she could let him go even as much as she knew it was the right thing.

It used to be about Rhonda and the lawsuit and work.

But all that stopped being a consideration days ago. Now it was how badly her daughter could be hurt—how badly Ivy would be hurt—when her mother's predictions came true.

So what was she supposed to do if Brett wanted to come in tonight, into her apartment, into her bed, into her body?

Into her heart.

How was she supposed to tell him the longer this thing went on, the greater the potential for damage?

By the time they got home after dropping off her mother, Ivy's head ached with all the thoughts pounding through it.

The only thing she could be glad for was that Joy had fallen asleep.

"I'll carry her upstairs," Brett said, stooping through the car door to pick up Joy.

Ivy's heart twisted. He looked so wonderful, this big beautiful man cradling a small child so gently in his arms.

She had to turn away before she burst into tears. Ivy had never had a man Joy could love, a man to carry her, to tuck her in. A man to look up to.

She leaned into the car's backseat for the cat carrier.

Archie mewled, and Ivy held the cage high a moment, putting her face up to the cat's. "We're almost home, sweetie pie, and you can come out."

Archie started to purr as if she understood.

Reaching the top of the stairs, Ivy pulled out her keys and unlocked the door for Brett. Joy hadn't moved.

"Megan used to be like this," Brett said softly. "Sleeping through anything."

Ivy smiled despite her raging emotions. "Joy can do her share of getting cranky when she's overtired."

"They all can." He carried his precious bundle down the short hall. Ivy stood in the doorway as he laid Joy on the bed and pulled off her shoes. With her feet clad only in socks, Joy pulled her legs up and curled into a ball.

The sight was so endearing.

How could her daughter *not* fall head over heels for this man? It was impossible. He was so good, his shoulders big and wide to offer comfort to any little girl who needed a cry. He was interested in everything, asking all the right questions, exclaiming at just the right moment. He also knew to say *no* when *no* needed to be said.

He was perfect for Joy.

He was so utterly perfect for Ivy.

Except that he was temporary.

She pulled away from the doorjamb, from the sight of him. From the ache around her heart. "I'll get her ready for bed later."

"I'll just cover her up." Brett settled a blanket over Joy with such tenderness.

She wondered again if her daughter was part of what he wanted. To be the good guy providing all the fun things to do.

He should have learned the first time around that fun things were great. Until you walked out the door again.

She turned. "I'll get our stuff out of the car."

"Coming with you."

He followed her out, and together they carried all the paraphernalia up the stairs and dumped it on the living room carpet so she could sort it out later.

From his carrier, Archie gave a sharp mewl.

"Oh sweetie pie, I'm so sorry. I forgot all about you." She looked at Brett, knocking her temple with her knuckles.

Free, Archie immediately ran to Brett and stretched high up his legs until he picked her up.

"She wants to come home with you again."

Scratching the cat under the chin, he shook his head. "She's switched allegiance to Joy now."

As if she understood the name, the cat squirmed out of his arms and raced down the hall, disappearing into Joy's room.

Alone with him, Ivy was suddenly tongue-tied. What now? Would he ask to stay the night? Maybe he'd just want a quick tumble in her bed.

She'd had sex with the man three nights in a row. That was a first since Joy had been born. She saw a man for a few nights or weeks, then he was gone. There were no trips, no sleepovers, no man to carry Joy upstairs and tuck her into bed.

"Well," she said, her hands clasped together, until she realized it could be mistaken for hand-wringing. "Thanks for such a wonderful trip. We'll never forget it. Joy probably won't stop talking about it for a month." She sounded overly bright. Bordering on maniacal.

Brett suddenly moved in on her. She went up against the hallway wall, ready for his touch, his lips on hers. But he just cupped her face in his hand. "That was the best Thanksgiving in a long, long time. And those were the three best nights of my life."

"Except for the night Valerie was born," she added for him, her breathing fast, her heart racing. She just had to make a joke or cry.

He laughed softly, his breath warm and enticing across her cheek. "Totally different kind of best." He tipped her chin up with his thumb. "You are the sexiest, hottest woman I know. And I love your fantasies." He kissed her quickly, long enough to set her on fire, too short to satisfy. "You need to think up a few more."

Then he stepped back. "You'll want to put stuff away, get settled before work tomorrow. And it was totally my pleasure having you."

She hadn't found her voice by the time the door was closing behind him.

She couldn't believe he'd walked out. She'd been thinking all day what she'd do if he wanted to stay the night.

And he'd left. Just like that. Without even an honest-to-goodness, bone-melting kiss.

Suddenly it was worse not having to deal with him at all.

What did he mean? She was the hottest, sexiest woman. He loved her fantasies. He wanted her to think up a few more. What the hell did he *mean*?

Right now, she had only one fantasy.

"I just want more," she whispered to the quiet apartment. More of his kisses, his touch, his body, his voice, his scent. More of *him*.

That was when she knew she'd truly lost her mind.

17

Monday was even worse. Mitch Redmond of The Des Moines Group and his troupe of auditors arrived. Everyone was on high alert. They were given the main conference room the executives used, so Ivy saw them every time she passed by to get to Jordana's office, even when she had to use the lady's room, which was right outside the main door.

It meant she had to see Brett, too. His office was on the second floor, but in the opposite quadrant. There were two card-keyed doors and the big landing between them. She didn't run into him much unless he was coming to see Grady.

But now he was a constant specter. She didn't have a clue how to act around him.

She almost bumped into him coming out of the conference room, a coffee pot in his hand. "The damn water line's stopped working in there."

The words could have been angry, especially with *damn* in there. But his eyes on her said something else. So did the slight smile curving his lips when he saw her.

Or maybe that was her imagination.

"I'll make coffee in the breakroom," she said, trying to take the carafe out of his hand. He held it away so she had to shift close enough to smell his spicy male scent.

It almost sent her into a hypnotic trance, unable to move, just stand there feeling the heat of his body tempting her to do something crazy.

"You don't have to do that. But I'd appreciate it if you'd call my secretary and have her send Maintenance in."

"Sure. But I can also make a pot and bring it in so you have something right now." She wanted to step back. She *should* step back. But she'd had dreams about him last night. Wild, crazy, sexual dreams.

"You're a supervisor, Ivy." He was so tall, so gorgeous, looking down at her with eyes that melted her insides. Especially with a smile that seemed to say something entirely different. "You don't need to do that kind of stuff anymore."

"You're carrying the coffee pot. Weren't you going to do it yourself? And you're the CEO." The big bad CEO who did naughty, sexy, kinky things to her. She reached again. They were so close. Too close. If anyone walked out that door. If anyone pushed aside the closed blinds in the conference room. If anyone turned the corner or entered from the landing.

All she could think of were his parting words last night. *It was totally my pleasure having you.* He'd had her in every way, man on top, woman riding man, front to back, lotus position, in front of a mirror.

And he wanted more of her fantasies.

"Give it to me," she said softly.

She meant it exactly the way it sounded. She wanted *it*. She was crazy but she didn't care. She wanted him bad.

If he'd dropped the pot and hauled her up against the wall, she'd have been powerless to stop him. They'd have gone up in flames together.

"Of course, Ivy." His voice was low, deep, harsher than normal. She'd heard that voice in his bedroom. "You can have it." He gave her the coffee pot. "Thanks for taking care of my needs."

The conference door opened then. Ivy almost shrieked and jumped back. Almost. Before she got hold of herself. Instead, Brett turned, the distance between them widening without being noticeable.

The man who walked out was big and tall, far more muscle than fat, and a handsome, ruddy complexion that said he spent lots of time outdoors.

"Not to worry, Mitch," Brett said. "We've got the coffee on the way before the troops melt down."

The man's laugh boomed in the hallway outside the conference room. "Not to worry. I'm just making a pit stop."

Brett pointed to the door leading out to the landing. "That way. Make sure you keep your card key with you. You'll need it to get back in."

Mitch—Ivy knew it was Mitch Redmond—patted his pocket. "Got it." But he didn't leave, and his gaze flashed between Brett and her.

Brett made the introduction. "This is our HR Supervisor, Ivy Elliot."

"Sooo nice to meet you." He strung out the first word. His grip as he shook her hand was relaxed, yet he held on a fraction too long.

Or maybe it felt that way when she saw Brett looking at their clasped hands.

"Nice to meet you, too." She gestured with the pot. "Coffee. It'll be ready soon."

Mitch smiled as big as he was tall. "Thank you, ma'am."

Brett added, "Thank you, Ivy."

She turned sharply and marched into the breakroom for the fresh pot. As it filled, she sagged back against the counter, catching her breath. The rich aroma of coffee surrounded her, making her mouth water.

Or maybe that was Brett.

They hadn't said a single personal word, yet her knees were weak and her heart was racing at the speed of light.

Had she read something into his words he hadn't put there? Or was he talking in sexy riddles no one else but her would understand?

Then there was Mitch Redmond. She wasn't sure if there'd been anything in that look he'd shot from Brett to her. Maybe it was just a pointed reminder for a polite introduction.

Or he'd smelled something in the air between them. Like a hound dog picking up the scent of a female in heat.

Her legs still hadn't regained total control when Gloria sashayed into the breakroom. Gloria was everything Ivy could want to be, elegant, intelligent, confident. With Parker Hunt in her life, she'd also become sexy in a very classy way. It seemed unconscious, just a look she wore, as if she knew she was desired by the man she loved.

Sometimes it was almost too intimate to watch, as if Ivy could see right into her life.

"Hey, thanks for getting the coffee. Brett asked me to bring it in."

"He asked you? You're the CFO."

"I know," Gloria said, sidestepping Ivy to get to the coffee machine. "And I can tie my own shoes, too."

"I didn't mean—"

Gloria nudged her. "I'm giving you a bad time." Then she turned, eying Ivy, her hand on the pot's handle. "Are you okay? You look a little out of sorts."

"I'm fine," Ivy said quickly. "Just peachy."

"Thanksgiving good?"

She felt a damning blush creep into her cheeks. "It was

great. My Mom, Joy, you know." She shrugged, then quickly turned it back on Gloria. "How was Connecticut?"

Gloria shivered. "Cold. But Parker's family was great." Then she sighed dreamily. "We had to stay in an adorable bed-and-breakfast because his mom's house couldn't handle the whole crowd."

That was the reason for Gloria's sashay, a romantic holiday in a snowbound B&B.

"I was a little nervous meeting his family," she confided. "Especially since I'm a little older than him and his mom certainly isn't getting any grandchildren out of me." She rolled her eyes. "But they were all super."

Ivy had never thought of it before, but what would Brett's family think of her? Not that it mattered. She and Brett were nothing like Gloria and Parker. They were in love. Her relationship with Brett... Well, they were two people who'd had sex over the course of three nights.

Ivy stifled the thought. "That's wonderful, Gloria." She wouldn't be surprised if there was a wedding soon. Heck, she wouldn't be surprised if there were two weddings, Jordana and Grady as well.

Gloria touched her arm. "But are you sure everything's okay? You look a little flushed. You're not coming down with anything? Holidays can do that to you, all the rushing around. And afterwards we just crash."

Did she look that bad? Or worse, did she look that good, her skin pink with reaction to her close encounter with Brett.

"Honest, I'm fine." She waved a hand. "Just getting into the swing with a new job."

That was enough to distract Gloria, thank God. "How's the temp?"

"Good. A quick learner."

"I'm so glad everything is working out. I better get this

coffee in there before the hoard goes crazy." Gloria grabbed up the pot and pivoted.

"Good luck. Oh and tell Brett I'll have his secretary call about the water line for the machine in there."

Gloria gave her a thumbs up. "Thanks. You're the best."

Actually, Brett was the best. He could get her going without saying a single salacious word. Just breathing him in was enough.

That ability made him the worst thing for her, too. Mitch Redmond had sensed a vibe. Gloria had noticed a flush. If anyone saw Ivy mooning over Brett, there'd be a price to pay.

And she'd be the one who paid it, not him. After all, he was the CEO. She was just a secretary. Whether or not she'd gotten a promotion.

BRETT HAD SETTLED THE AUDITORS IN THE CONFERENCE room, which was a good central location. Of course, they'd be spending most of their time with the various VPs and employees.

The room was a low murmur of conversation before the meeting began. His VPs were in attendance, including Jordana filling in for Rhonda.

Like a polite host, he poured himself the last cup of coffee left in the pot, making sure everyone else had theirs first.

"Your girl Ivy makes a good cup." Mitch poured cream into his mug.

"She's not my secretary. She's a supervisor in HR." He was a bit pissed *his* secretary hadn't taken care of the coffee before the meeting started. She would have known the machine wasn't working and Maintenance could already have been up here.

"I meant the universal *your*, as in your company rather than mine."

He wondered if Redmond was fishing, but the guy seemed pleasant enough. Brett had liked him on his last trip out here. His voice was overloud, but he was a big guy with a big chest and big lungs.

Redmond turned, leaning back against the counter as Brett doctored up his coffee. Everything was informal right now, some chitchat, how was the flight, et cetera.

"Gloria and Hunt look made for each other, don't they."

It was the last thing Brett expected out of the man's mouth.

Gloria and Parker were in deep conversation with the audit manager. There wasn't a thing that spoke of the relationship between them. Parker didn't stand too close, didn't look too long.

Brett had been standing closer to Ivy out in the hall.

Yeah, he'd been standing a lot closer. Too close. For a moment, all he could remember was how she tasted. He'd been in danger of losing his focus.

But hell if he didn't like it. A man liked a woman to tilt his world off kilter every once in a while. Ivy was damn good at throwing him into a spin.

Best not to starting spinning at work, though, especially with the auditors here.

"I guess the best man won," Redmond mused.

"Do not tell me you were hitting on my VP the last time you were here."

The man grinned big once again. "Hitting on her isn't the right terminology. I simply asked her to dinner. And she said no."

"Mixing business and pleasure is never a good idea." Brett told himself he wasn't mixing. He and Ivy were strictly after office hours. Just like he'd ordained with Parker and Gloria as well as Grady and Jordana. *Do not bring your personal life into the office.*

Yet he thought of the things he'd said to Ivy out there in the hall. Hidden messages. Double entendres. He'd been mixing way too much.

Then Mitch Redmond had walked in on exchange.

"I wouldn't call it mixing. I hadn't decided to give you money at that point," Mitch confessed.

Brett shot him a look. "Are you saying—"

"Hell, no," Redmond countered. "I wasn't using Gloria as a bargaining chip." He leaned in, lowered his voice. "Since I lost, if she was any kind of payoff, you never would have gotten the money. But I don't work like that."

"Good to know. Just don't make a habit of hitting on my employees."

Redmond held up his hand in a who-me gesture.

Yeah, you. "I saw you eyeing Miss Elliot." The moment the words were out, he wondered whether he would have said something if any other woman was involved.

Because he knew damn well he was hypersensitive about Ivy. He'd wanted to growl when Redmond shook her hand.

"Eyeing her is different than simply introducing myself to a beautiful woman." Redmond shrugged. "After all, we'll be business partners, if everything goes well."

He'd have to watch the guy.

Mitch Redmond noticed too much. If he was noticing Ivy, he might also see that Brett couldn't stop looking at her either.

Better yet, Brett needed to watch himself at work. No more hallway tête-à-têtes steeped in double entendres.

He'd have to save all that for the night.

Brett had ignored her the rest of the day. After their brief encounter outside the conference that morning, he seemed to go out of his way to avoid her.

It was a subtle change, something no one else would notice. If he saw her in the hall, he turned the other way. If he had to pass by her, he barely smiled, hardly looked. He hadn't even shown her a baby picture. Nor had he called her since she'd arrived home from work that evening.

He'd acknowledged her far more before they'd had sex.

Ivy shouldn't make comparisons, but the whole thing reminded her of Rupert. Everything with Rupert had been done in secret, because she was his student. Even after they'd returned from their long trip abroad, when she'd moved in with him, she was still never invited to faculty functions, never met his university colleagues. Like she was his dirty little secret.

Until finally he'd found another dirty little secret and dumped Ivy.

She hadn't been able to hide her agitation when she'd been speed-walking with Hannah Fall at lunch. Even Joy was picking up on it now.

"Isn't Brett coming for dinner?" Joy asked.

Ivy sat at the kitchen table chewing on a hangnail. She'd been lost in thought. "No, honey, he's not. He's a really busy man." But she'd waited to start cooking, hoping she'd hear from him, until Joy's stomach growled loud enough to be heard.

He hadn't said he'd come by. He hadn't actually said he'd ever see her again. Except for that part about wanting to know more of her fantasies.

It was totally contrary to be hurt that he hadn't called or texted. She wasn't supposed to be any expectations. It was so much better if she forgot all about him.

But she wouldn't.

She would keep wanting things that were bad for her, just the way she'd kept on wanting Rupert.

"But he has to eat," Joy said, with the hint of a whine.

"He's going out to dinner with the auditors we've got visiting this week."

"I guess he won't be here to tuck Archie into bed then." Joy's face caved, her lower lip jutting in a pout.

"You can tuck Archie into bed instead." But what Joy really wanted was for Brett to tuck her in the way he had in Tahoe. "Archie can be your best pal now."

Ivy's heart sank even deeper. Joy was completely attached. Just as she was attached to Archimedes, the poor little psycho cat who was no longer wanted when the new baby came home.

"Dinner will be ready in just a couple of minutes. Tater puffs, you love those."

Her child brightened. "And chicken tenders?"

Ivy nodded, forcing herself to smile. She'd made the tenders out of real chicken strips and shredded real potatoes for homemade tots because she had no idea what was really in the frozen ones.

With the mention of chicken tenders and tater puffs, Joy's blues were dashed away.

If only Ivy's worries were so easily forgotten.

18

Brett texted Ivy just before nine o'clock that evening. The meetings had gone long past six, and the dinner conversation had droned on and on.

He was tired. His body ached from too much sitting and too much food. He hadn't planned to bother her tonight. But the moment he climbed in his car, he was on the phone, texting to ask if he could come over.

He should have texted earlier. That had always been one of his wife's complaints, busy with work, he often forgot to call to say where he was or when he was coming home.

But he didn't want Ivy to think he expected to come over.

Her answer was quick. *Joy's already in bed.*

I can kiss her goodnight without waking her. He needed to see Ivy, if only to gather her in his arms and feel her warmth for a few minutes.

He wasn't pushing or rushing. It was just contact. *I want to kiss you goodnight, too.*

Her answer took forever to come. He'd already put his phone down and started the engine when his cell beeped.

All right. For a little while.

The day's tension drained out of him. As if she were a muscle relaxant. A pillow to lay his head on. A glass of wine to soothe him.

Being with her had become so much more than making love.

Ivy opened the door, a finger to her lips as she said softly, "Don't go in to see Joy. I don't want you to wake her."

He was about to tell her that he'd be as quiet as a mouse. But of course, Archie would be with Joy. And if he was the mouse, the cat would chase.

Ivy led him into the kitchen. "Long day?"

Her bare feet were his potential undoing, but he maintained a light tone. "Yeah. Not bad, just long."

"A glass of wine?" she asked.

"I had some with dinner. Best not to have any more." All he really wanted to drink was her. "But thanks."

They stood still, the kitchen clock ticking on the wall above the door. Until he needed to touch her so badly he couldn't stop himself. "Come here."

Hand at her nape, he reeled her in. At first, all he did was hold her. Finally her arms slid around him.

"You're so warm and soft," he whispered.

He tipped her chin up with his thumb and sipped on her lips, tasting gently, licking until she opened. The kiss was long and languorous, a gentle glide of tongue against tongue, soft breaths, audible sighs.

He might have kept himself sane if he hadn't let his hands wander. Down her back, to her tight buns in the leggings. He squeezed, pulled her closer. Until there was no doubt about the hardness between them.

Even then, he would have stopped. But he sensed the change in her, skin heating, nipples peaking, the sweet aroma of arousal. Both hers and his.

Without taking his mouth off hers, he hauled her up,

setting her on the counter, and stepped between her legs. Her breath hitched, and she locked her ankles at his back, his erection riding her center.

They were out of control in seconds, like a fire in backdraft.

There was no taste better than hers, no skin smoother, nobody hotter.

He drew back to breathe, to beg. "I want you. Jesus, I need you."

"The bedroom," she whispered.

He didn't wait for another word, grabbing her up, carrying her with her legs still circling his waist. Her room was the first door on the right. She closed it with a soft click of the lock.

He got impressions of pastel colors, a thick comforter, pillows, and clothing thrown on a chair by the bureau.

"I need to taste you." Holding her tight to him, he kissed her long and deep. But that wasn't the only taste he needed.

Skipping the slow strip tease, they were already tearing at each other's clothes by the time he let her down onto the bed. When her panties were hanging on the lampshade and they were finally skin to skin, he slid down her body to the crown jewel between her legs.

"Do you have any idea how many times today I dreamed of doing this?"

"Stop dreaming," she said, her voice husky as she raised her hips, a temptation he couldn't resist.

She was sweet ambrosia. Her breaths coming faster, she writhed beneath him on the bed, and the button between her legs was hard and tight. Inside she was wet and so freaking ready for him. She soaked his fingers, and he savored each delicious drop. His tongue buried against her, he watched as the flush spread up her body. She grabbed the brass rails at the head of her bed, her hips rocking with him. Sounds worked their way up her throat, a hum, a mewl, a moan, soft as if she were trying to force them back down.

She didn't cry out when she came, but her taste flooded him and she bucked beneath him, riding wave after wave.

He climbed her body before she came all the way down. The only coherent thing he'd done before throwing his suit across the room was to lay a condom on the side table. Now he rolled it on and plunged deep into her.

He'd wanted to fulfill every one of her fantasies. But maybe this was all they needed, a cataclysmic coming together. The moment their flesh merged, she rolled into another orgasm. She was so damn tight around him that it was only seconds before he fell after her, his body becoming part of hers.

Their hearts beating like one.

IVY LAY CUDDLED IN HIS ARMS, HER BODY SATED, HER muscles barely able to move. With her head on his chest, his heart pumped against her ear, a steady, comforting thud. Plastered to his side, she was warm. She could stay this way all night, lusciously relaxed after two orgasms.

"Jesus," he whispered, his breath fluttering through her hair. "I needed that." His fingers moved in rhythmic circles on her arm, and she snuggled deeper into him. She'd needed it, too.

It was frightening to think how badly she'd needed it.

His voice was low, gentle, lulling. "You're the only thing that kept me sane today. The thought of coming home to you, making love to you."

Coming home. Making love.

She wanted to deny it. To say that wasn't what they'd done.

And yet, with him deep inside her, even with his mouth on her, that's what it was. *Making love.*

She couldn't call it anything else. The feelings were too potent for denial.

She was far too attached. She wanted more nights like this. God help her, she didn't want him to leave now. The thought of waking up next to him in the morning was so delicious, it was terrifying.

"You make me crazy with how good it feels," she told him, needing to offer something besides the ball of fear germinating in her stomach.

His fingers trailed her arm, up, down, soothing and exciting all at once. "I didn't mean to jump on you the moment I walked in the door."

"I liked it." She loved knowing that he desired her. It made her forget that he'd ignored her most of the day.

It was like a game. Pretend nothing had happened all day long. Then jump each other the moment they were alone.

It would be utterly perfect if Joy wasn't starting to count on him being there. It would be totally amazing, if only Ivy wasn't starting to need him. If she didn't feel the crushing weight of fear that he'd leave when the whole business with the auditors was over. And when a lawsuit was no longer a threat.

She could have asked him what he really wanted, but she was afraid of the truth. Nor could she bear the lies.

Things were so much easier when she had discreet, short-lived affairs. When Joy wasn't involved. When Ivy didn't worry about her own heart. She wanted that with Brett. Hot, carefree sex. Wild, crazy, going at each other.

Then home to their separate lives.

That's what she needed. Something controlled. She hadn't like the way she'd felt this evening, waiting for him to show up for dinner, angry that he hadn't texted, that he'd ignored her at work this afternoon. She hadn't liked that needy woman at all.

Yet without the emotion, would she have the ecstasy?

"You're quiet," he said.

"Just enjoying the feel of you against me."

"I love the sound of that."

God, how she enjoyed it. But could she have it? Could she enjoy the times they had together without freaking out that he would leave?

If she didn't have Joy's feelings to worry about, was it possible?

Maybe all she really needed to do was manage the time she spent with him. Keep him in his proper corner of her life. No trips to Tahoe or excursions to the zoo. No dinners with Joy. Just hot sex in the middle of the night. God, how divine that would be. Maybe she could even manage a night away from home, at his place, where she could let out all the cries she had to stifle.

Her mother had told her to get everything she could before he dumped her. Mom might even be willing to babysit a couple of times.

Yes, it could work. Keep the man in his place and she wouldn't feel so attached.

She shifted, glancing at the clock. "It's late," she whispered. "I better check on Joy. I hope we didn't wake her."

"We were very quiet. The bed didn't even creak."

But she had so wanted to shout out her pleasure. To scream his name. "I can only hope," she said, shifting, slipping out of his arms.

"Don't go yet." He tried to hold on.

He couldn't know how hard it was to leave him. But it had to be done. She needed to put him into a separate corner of her life, starting right now. Before she was in so deep she couldn't live without him.

"We can't stay here all night." It was exactly where she wanted to be. She kissed him quickly, her eyes closed because looking at him would make her lose all her resolve.

She grabbed her clothes, sliding into them, gave him a wind-up motion with her hand. Finally he got dressed, too.

Joy was sleeping. When Brett bent to kiss her forehead, neither she nor Archie stirred.

"Sleeping like a baby," he said outside the door, his voice low. "Let's go back to bed."

She laughed softly, feeling anything but funny. She was needy enough to haul him against her and beg. But she didn't. "Don't be silly. You've got another long day tomorrow." She pushed him to the front door before she could drag him back into the bedroom. "After good sex, you should sleep like a baby, too."

"Ivy."

She opened the door and kissed him quickly. "See you tomorrow."

Like it was no big deal. Like none of this really mattered.

Then she somehow managed to push him out.

She could do this. She could protect Joy from disappointment. She could keep herself from getting too involved or too dependent. And she could still have the divinely hot sex on the side. Like she'd always done since Joy was born.

Except that not one single man she'd been with had shown her the ecstasy that Brett did.

SHE COULDN'T GET HIM OUT OF THERE FAST ENOUGH.

After good sex, he'd sleep like a baby?

What the hell was up?

She'd acted like none of it meant anything. But there was so much more in her kiss, so much more in the ways she touched him, her fingertips on his skin, her sighs against his ear.

He'd known she'd never let him spend the night. Ivy didn't want Joy finding him in her mother's bed in the morning. He understood that.

But he'd wanted a longer, sweeter, slower lovemaking. He'd wanted a few more hours of her in his arms.

Maybe he'd screwed up by texting her after his dinner, showing up on her doorstep, and jumping her immediately, tearing her clothes off. Afterward, she'd gotten distant, saying the right words, words she thought he wanted to hear, but without the feeling. As if she'd totally disconnected from him.

He'd rushed her. And she was taking a big emotional step back.

But he wasn't giving up. No way.

Tomorrow night, he'd get it right. Or as many nights as it took.

"GOOD MORNING, IVY."

Ivy almost shrieked. Which was stupid because she'd been waiting all morning for one sight of Brett. One breathtaking glimpse. Then bam, he was right in front of her as she returned from the restroom. The conference door was open, voices filtering out. It was ridiculously embarrassing, but her face flamed anyway, as if everyone inside could guess what they'd done last night.

"Oh, yes, good morning." She almost stuttered on the words.

Why, why, why? Last night she was so confident in her resolve. She had a plan. Then the moment she saw him, she got all weak-kneed again.

Control yourself, Ivy.

"I'm looking for Jordana," Brett said. "The auditors want to review the headcount estimates for next year."

Of course, *he* wasn't thinking about last night. He knew how to separate the night from the day.

"She's just—"

The outer door opened behind them, and Brett said, "There you are." Ivy turned to find Jordana, her lipstick freshened. "I was just asking Ivy if she'd seen you. The auditors want the headcount data. Can you be ready for them in half an hour?"

"Sure." Jordana smiled with assurance. "Anytime. I'm totally ready."

Jordana had been studying the numbers all morning, making sure she understood Rhonda's budgeting. She'd had Ivy run down a couple of things, too. But she came across as if she knew it all right off the top of her head.

Ivy wished she could exude the same confidence.

"Great. Thanks. I'll let them know." Brett gave her a gorgeous smile. Okay, it wasn't any different than the thousand smiles she'd seen since she'd started working at the company. But now she was stunned by how utterly magnificent he was.

"Ivy." He nodded, melting her down to the bones with another of those smiles, then closed himself off in the conference room again.

She was completely tongue-tied, mesmerized. She'd wanted to kiss him. Today wasn't any different than yesterday, when she'd wanted to drag him off to some secret lair and have her wicked way with him.

Maybe it would have been better if he'd ignored her the way he had yesterday afternoon. Instead of making her crazy.

Tonight. She'd do all the dirty, kinky things flashing

through her mind. She'd kiss him till he went cross-eyed. She'd go down on her knees and—

"Earth to Ivy."

"Sorry. Just deep in thought." Deep in sexual fantasies. "You need some more help with the headcount?"

Jordana grabbed her arm, pulled her around the corner—away from the conference room door—and down the short aisle to her office, where Jordana promptly closed the door. "Are you okay?"

"Yeah, I'm fine." She had the immediate afterthought, *Sure, I'm fine, except that I keep reliving Brett's mouth on me, making me come until I almost screamed out loud.*

"Gloria said you seemed out of sorts yesterday." Jordana pushed a thick lock of brunette hair behind her ear as if that might somehow allow her to see Ivy better. "You look a bit dazed. Was Brett giving you a hard time about Rhonda?"

"Of course not. We were right outside the conference room. With the door open. He's not going to talk about it there."

"Yeah. Right. I know that." Then her gaze went soft, the same way it did when she was talking with an unhappy employee. "But you seem a little off. He hasn't been pressuring you, has he? I mean, he might be the CEO, but I'm acting HR guru, and I don't care who he is, he can't pressure you into not suing if that's what you want to do."

It was the last thing she wanted. She hadn't seriously considered it since Brett had started coming to her house for dinner. She'd certainly made up her mind after Tahoe that she wasn't going to sue. But the damn issue was still hanging over her head.

"He's never even mentioned it." He was too busy pleasuring her.

"That's good."

Oh yes, he was very, very good.

"But if he does—if *anyone* does, tell me, and I'll take care of it."

"Jordana, you work for the company. You're supposed to be on their side."

"I'm on the employee's side first, the company comes second. And *you* are my friend. So you're before employees *and* company."

"That's so nice of you. I really appreciate it." But she wasn't sure how Jordana would feel if she knew Brett Baker was leaving work and crawling into Ivy's bed. Maybe there were boundaries in friendship.

"If you need to talk, come to me, okay? Or Gloria. We'll both do anything we can."

Before Ivy could blink them away, tears pricked her eyes. She had friends. She felt like she'd been alone so long. "Thank you. Have I ever told you that I don't have a lot of friends?" She didn't wait for Jordana. "Okay, try none. Until you and Gloria. I just can't believe how nice you are to me. How supportive."

"Right." Jordana gave an eye-roll. "We're so supportive that we goaded you into taking Rhonda head on. And look at that disaster."

It was the day Brett had changed her life.

She couldn't go back three weeks and undo it all. She didn't even want to.

"You're wrong. It wasn't a disaster. I have a new job thanks to all of you." And she had a smokin' hot CEO dying to be in her bed. "Really, things are looking up." Or they would be if she could wrap her mind around Brett and her as friends with benefits. All she had to do was manage it properly. "You know, I feel a lot better." Of course, that was an admission to Jordana that she'd been feeling bad. "Thank you."

"Look, when the auditors are outta here, you, me, and Gloria need a lunch. Okay?"

"Deal." She tipped her head. "What do you think about inviting Hannah from Customer Service?" That way they wouldn't concentrate on Ivy. "We've been walking out in the park at lunch. And I like her."

Warmth curled in her chest. She had friends. She wasn't alone. She might not be able to talk about Brett with them, but she wasn't completely alone anymore.

In an uncertain world, friends felt wonderful.

19

Tonight was going to be a repeat of last night, so Brett texted Ivy right after her workday ended.

Can't make dinner tonight. With the auditors. But I can drop by to tuck in Joy.

He sat at the end of the conference table, the auditors going back and forth with Mitch or Knox or Finn. Lucy Perez had been in for a while, but she'd taken one of the team over to her office to demonstrate the standard cost roll-up.

With a moment free from questions, Brett's mind immediately flew to Ivy. He'd seen her in passing, and every time, the need to touch her had been next to overwhelming. Just a touch, a proprietary hand on her back, fingers cupping her elbow, the kind of touches he'd given her when they were in Tahoe. A tactile connection.

Of course he could never so much as lay a finger on her. Her reputation was paramount. More important than any investment they'd receive from The Nelson Group.

The thought was a shock. Because nothing had been more important. He wanted the company public; he wanted it to soar up the stock exchange. He wanted the Fortune

500. And he needed this investment to put them on that road.

But suddenly he needed Ivy even more.

The good thing was that he could have both. They weren't mutually exclusive, one or the other.

She finally texted him back. *Don't come until later. Joy has homework. I'll get her to bed first.*

All right, new rule. She didn't want to disrupt Joy's homework time and regular schedule. But it also felt like Ivy was cutting him out of a huge piece of her life.

For sure he'd rushed her. Now she was backing up a mile a second. But she wasn't shutting him down completely. There was hope. He could work his way back in with patience.

Tonight, he wouldn't drag her to the bedroom right away. They'd talk first, maybe have a glass of wine. He had a bottle of something sweet in his car that he thought she might like.

But Ivy shocked the shoes right off his feet when she dragged him to the bedroom the moment she'd closed the front door behind him.

Not that he wasn't willing. "I brought you wine."

"You're so sweet. Thank you." She set it on the bureau. "Later."

Later was just fine with him.

She fisted her fingers in the lapels of his suit jacket. "Last night," she said softly, "you did some very naughty things to me with your mouth." She went up on her toes to kiss him. "Now it's my turn."

His breath had already ratchetted up at the first touch. She wore a tight sweater that showed off all her curves, and with her body pressed so close, he was already hard and aching. "I'm not sure I can wait long enough to let you have your turn. I want inside you right now."

She pushed the jacket off his shoulders. "This will be just as divine."

His tie flew across the room, and she plucked the shirt buttons out of their holes, stripping him down while she was still dressed.

Standing naked before her was one of the most erotic experiences he'd ever had.

When she sank to her knees in front of him, he was close to losing it.

"Look at you," she crooned to his erection. "You're already hard for me."

"Aching," he whispered.

She wrapped her fist around him. Then looked up, her eyes deep as the earth. "You can't come until I say so."

"I won't." It was a promise. A prayer. He adored how she took charge. Taking what she wanted.

"I want you to come in my mouth when I finally allow you."

"I want to come inside you."

She smiled up at him coquettishly. "You can do that later. You're good for more than twice."

He might be over fifty, but she made him feel like a young man who could keep it up forever.

"In your mouth," he whispered.

"All right. Good. Go sit in the chair." She pointed to the corner chair, which was now empty of clothing. Ivy had been planning what she wanted, and his pulse rate shot higher.

He sat naked in her chair, his erection beckoning her.

Ivy stalked him, crawling across the carpet like a predator hunting her prey. Her eyes gleamed in the dim lamplight of the bedside table.

When she reached him, she spread his legs, crawling between them. Then finally she cupped his sac in her warm hand and squeezed. Before she'd even touched his erection, he was full and heavy, so ready for her.

"Here's what I want," she whispered, her lips puckered enticingly. "Hold yourself up. Like you're offering it to me."

"Jesus." The sound fell from his lips, more a gasp than anything else.

He'd told her he wanted her fantasies. And this was what she came up with. She craved power. She needed him complicit in his own undoing. God help him, he wanted to give it to her.

His erection in his hand, he stroked, base to tip, back down again. "I'm all yours."

She took the tip in her mouth. He thought he'd explode. She circled and swirled her tongue all over him, around the swollen head, the sensitive ridge, then dipping down to meet his fingers. There was something about the kiss of her lips on his hand that made his body rage, rising up to meet her, his grip falling away so that she took him deep down her throat.

"Nothing. God. Never like that." His head fell back, his eyes closed, and he was just a machine pumping into her mouth. She took him all, her throat relaxing. He wanted to know who had taught her that, then just as quickly never wanted to know. Better to imagine she'd learned it for him alone.

She drove him mad then, with her hand, her tongue, her mouth. When his legs started to shake and his body bucked, she backed off long enough to order, "Not yet."

The immense will it took to keep himself in check made the scene all the hotter. Her head bobbed in his lap, and it was the sexiest damn thing he'd ever seen, her hair cascading over her face, the short locks bouncing, the wet sound of her lips on him.

"God. Ivy. I can't stop it." He gripped the arms of the chairs, nails digging in, his body rising and falling with her rhythm as if he were making love to her, not just her mouth. The intensity built inside him, the pleasure relentless, overwhelming, and he was sure no amount of willpower could stop him.

Then she lifted for one microsecond. "Now." Giving him permission.

He exploded in her mouth, his teeth gritted to keep from shouting out her name. The pleasure was grinding, overpowering, as if he were losing everything he was to her.

Ivy took it, swallowing, drinking it all, stroking him with her hands and her lips until he was completely drained. If he hadn't been sitting already, he would have fallen.

He was barely aware of her climbing onto his lap, but he felt her lips over his, tasted her triumph, tasted his undoing. Snaking his arms around her, he hugged her tight to his body. He was still half hard between her legs, and he rocked her.

"You're crazy," he whispered into her hair.

"But did I make *you* crazy?" Her words fluttered across his mind.

"God, yes."

"That was my fantasy. To make you crazy."

He laughed softly. "Then I totally delivered on it."

"Oh you did. I'm not done though. I have more fantasies."

"I want to fulfill them all." He kept his eyes closed, all the better to relish the feel of her. "What's next?"

She licked his ear, sending a shiver through him. "I would like three hours for one night where you make me come so hard I scream."

"Oh, I can do that." He could do it all night long. "But what about Joy?"

"I'll ask my mother to babysit. And you can take me to your house."

He'd never wanted anything more than to have her in his bed. Except to make love to her for a full night and wake up with her in his arms. Straight from his gut, he wanted to beg for those extra hours. Three would never be enough. But he'd promised himself he wouldn't push. Instead he'd wait for the day she asked for more. For now, it was enough that she wanted three hours alone in his bed. Enough that she was escalating their relationship.

"You've got it. My house. Three hours. All the screaming you can take." He stroked her hair back and tipped her chin up to see her face. Her lips were plump, swollen from all the attention she'd given him, her skin flushed a gorgeous pink. "But what else do you want tonight?"

"I can't decide," she said, the corners of her mouth rising in a smile. "Maybe you should tell me your fantasy."

A lifetime of her in his bed. The thought rushed in so quickly it shocked him. But he felt the rightness of it. A lifetime of exploring Ivy. Making love to her. Waking up beside her. Taking care of her. Taking care of her daughter. Yeah. That was his fantasy.

If that was love, then he'd fallen.

But Ivy had asked for his sexual fantasy. And he gave her the one that had tortured him. "I want to watch you in the mirror again, stand behind you, make you come with my fingers in you. I want to see every expression on your face."

She pulled back, the movement slight, but he felt it just the same. Then she swallowed hard, as if something were stuck in her throat. "I thought you wanted to be inside me."

"I want to watch your eyes glaze over." With the passion only he could give her. "I want to see your brow furrow with concentration as you strive for the peak." The one to which only he could take her. "I want to feel your body's tremors as you fall into sheer bliss." The bliss only he brought her to.

She flapped a hand negligently at the long mirror on the back of her door. "I'd rather feel you inside me." She wriggled on his lap to entice him.

He got it then. She was afraid to see herself in the mirror. Afraid she'd see that he truly was the only one who could give her all those things. She'd been afraid that last night in Tahoe when he'd made love to her in front of the mirror.

To push. Or not to push.

Maybe tonight wasn't the night. The right time might very well be during the three hours she spent at his house. The night he would convince her to stay forever.

"All right, then let me come inside you. Now." He held her down to show her he was ready again. He would always be ready for her.

He stripped her out of the few clothes she was wearing and carried her to the bed. There he made love to her, filled her up, filled them both. Until he smothered both their cries with his mouth.

And dreamed of the night when she let go with everything she felt.

HE WAS DIVINE.

"No, don't move," Ivy told him. "I like your weight on me." The solid weight of a man. Of Brett. Still inside her. She could stay this way all night.

Of course, she wouldn't.

But the sex had been *sooooo* good. She'd relished her power over him when he was deep in her mouth. She adored the sweet, simple missionary position just as much. Explosive.

"I'm too heavy."

She wrapped her arms tighter, keeping him in place. "You're just right. Please don't move." His body felt so, so good.

Everything was going exactly according to plan. Except for that fantasy of his about watching her in the mirror. She couldn't take that. Even if she closed her eyes, she was sure he'd see something she didn't want to reveal. Some mutant need to have him all night. To have... more.

But three hours screaming in his bed. Oh yeah. She could take that. It was a brilliant idea. If her mom wouldn't babysit, she'd find a regular sitter for Joy.

She drifted down into the aftermath of pleasure, reliving the sensations, talking almost without thinking. "I love having you in my mouth. I love your taste. I love the way you feel inside me." He flexed and she felt him all over again. Then she flexed for him, too, dragging a groan out of him. "I love how hard you come for me." She was using the word *love* a bit too much. But she loved the way he made her feel. And she had to say it again. "I love how hard you make me come."

"I could do it again." There was a hint of laughter in his voice.

"Again? So soon?" Then she dropped to a whispered laugh. "I thought men needed to recharge."

"With you, I can keep going all night." He licked her neck, sending a shiver through her. "Let me prove it to you."

His words suddenly made her realize she wasn't pushing him off. She'd been begging him to stay. *Please don't move.* Almost like saying, *Please don't go.*

But he had to go. The only way she could maintain control was by making him go.

She sighed—it felt like regret—then said, "You're right, you're getting too heavy now." She pushed his shoulders.

He didn't move for the longest time, and she thought he might keep her trapped beneath him all night.

Then he slid to the side.

She did feel regret. But she couldn't pull him back.

"Just a little while longer," he said.

"That's not a good idea. You could fall asleep. We both could fall asleep."

"But we slept together in Tahoe," he said in the most rational tone.

"Right. But I could always sneak back to my room before Joy woke up." The word bothered her. *Sneak*. Like they were doing something illicit. Somehow she felt the need to explain. "I don't want Joy finding you here and getting all dependent on you."

Ivy didn't want to get dependent.

She slid away from him, to the edge of the bed, though that was the last place she wanted to go. She'd rather stay in his arms, under him, feeling his delicious weight on her again.

There would be another night. She could have more. But she had to stick to the plan.

She kept her back to him because she didn't want to see his face.

"I like feeling that Joy needs me." His words made her squirm. "I like tucking her into bed. I could even read her a story. I don't mind, Ivy. I'd love that."

"It's not a good idea," she said, shaking her head.

She stood, searching for her clothes.

"Why not?"

She couldn't answer. She couldn't tell him about her utter terror. She didn't want Joy to care too much about him. She didn't want Joy to know how badly it hurt when someone you cared about walked away.

The only way to ensure that was to keep their sex in the proper place, in the bedroom, after office hours, long after Joy was in bed.

And to send Brett home before she begged him to stay.

20

"I'm tired." Ivy found her panties and leggings, stepping into them. "It's time for me to get to bed."

Brett hadn't wanted the confrontation now. He didn't want a confrontation at all. His plan was simple: get her used to having him around, to spending the night with him, a gradual transition. Until she admitted how good they were together, and she'd never leave him.

But she was taking things away rather than giving them. Now she didn't even want him around her daughter.

"I don't mind if Joy starts to care about me. I care about her. It's not dependency."

She was getting dressed. He had to do the same, gathering his clothes from around the room where he'd thrown them before she'd so exquisitely turned him inside out.

"All right, it's not dependency." She shrugged braless into her sweater. "But she's still going to get hurt."

He stopped in the midst of buttoning his shirt. "How is she going to get hurt?"

"When you're not interested in her anymore," she said

with a huff, as if he should have it all figured out. As if she had *him* figured out.

"I care about her. I'm not going to walk out without a word."

She huffed again. He found his tie.

"Look, we're having hot sex. My daughter really doesn't need to be a part of the relationship."

He didn't know whether to be pissed at her lackadaisical terminology and or grab onto the fact that she'd used the word *relationship*.

But the way she meant it was the same as calling him her fuck buddy. And he wasn't about to be put in the same category as one of her nameless guys who satisfied an itch and moved on.

"That's *all* you think we're doing? Having hot sex?"

For the first time, she hesitated, as if she recognized the harsh warning in his voice. "Isn't it?"

He wanted to grab her up, shake her, make her see. He'd wanted to give her time. But time would only push her further away. Having hot sex instead of making love would only let her shore up her walls.

Until one day he wouldn't be able to tear them down.

"That's not what *I'm* doing." Emotion rasped in his throat. "I'm making love. With you."

She turned away from him then, straightening the sheets they had mussed, as if she needed to hide that the emotions were just as true for her. "You haven't even known me that long. It's been three weeks."

"I've known you a lot longer. I know how competent you are, how loyal, how kind. Kind enough to smile at a grandfather's devotion."

She balled the edge of a sheet in her hand. "I don't think of you as a grandfather."

He stepped closer, dropped his voice. "Do you think of me as a lover?"

"Yes," she whispered, still holding the sheet but doing nothing with it. Her short hair had fallen forward, shielding her face from him.

"Then we're making love." He touched her arm. "Not just having sex."

"It's terminology," she said, then drew in a deep, shaky breath.

"It's not just terminology. It's a feeling. I am making love to you, Ivy." Then he said it all. "I don't want to crawl into your bed after Joy goes to sleep. I don't want to have sex with you for an hour, then sneak off again. I don't even want three hours at my house where you can let loose all the sounds I'm dying to hear. And then go home again."

The silence pounded between them. The longer he kept his mouth shut, the harder it was for her not to ask the question he was begging for.

And finally she did. "Then what do you want?"

"I want you." He chanced sliding his hand up her arm, dipping beneath the silky fall of hair at her nape. "I want Joy." That had huge meaning, too. "I want to take care of you both. I want to be a part of your life. I don't want to hide in a tidy little corner. I want to come home to you, make love to you, sleep with you, wake up with you." He traced her ear with his thumb. "I want to fall in love with you if you'll give me half a chance."

Deep, deep breath, her chest expanding. Then she shot it out. "So you're not in love with me now."

"I care deeply. I can't think about anything except you."

"But you don't know if you love me yet."

He was old enough to know that the intense emotion you felt for someone in the first blush of a relationship wasn't always love. She was right, too, that he'd only felt this intensity for her over the past three weeks. Was that love?

"I want the chance to find out. I want to be with you, look after you, look after Joy. I want to give you everything I can."

She was breathing quickly now, as if some pent-up emotion threatened to break free. "But you can't guarantee you'll still want to do that three months from now. Or six. Or a year."

"Ivy."

"Because your track record so far isn't particularly good. Even you admitted you didn't give your family what they needed. That work came first."

"I've learned a helluva lot since then."

"Really." She turned on him then, looked him full in the face. "I can take care of Joy. I can take care of myself. And I'm wondering if the best way to do that is get a lawyer and see whether I actually have a case after what Rhonda did."

There wasn't much more that could have shut him up. She was threatening to sue.

She took a step toward him. "Your work has always been the most important thing in your life. The Fortune 500 means more than anything else. How do I know you're not telling me you'll take care of me just so I won't sue you and ruin all your plans?"

He actually took a step back. As if she'd stabbed him in the heart. "Because you know *me.* Because you know I wouldn't hold that over your head. That choice has always been yours."

Ivy was relentless. "For you, the company is the most important thing. For me, it's my daughter. She comes first. So what if I told you I was putting her first and the best thing I can do for her is hire a lawyer?"

Ivy's blood roared in her ears. She'd never meant to start this. God, she'd just wanted to keep Brett in her bedroom, separate from everything. Why couldn't he just do that instead of asking for more?

But now she'd gone too far and there was no going back.

She asked the question that had been burning a hole through her heart since the day he'd taken them to the zoo. "Do you still want me if I'm suing you?"

"You don't need to sue me, Ivy. I won't bring Rhonda back if you don't want me to. I realized our mistake and I'm correcting your salary, your job title."

"Plus you've slept with me. And offered to take care of me and my daughter. I should be satisfied with that. I should let it all rest. I should stop thinking about being a failure. As an employee. As a single mother. I should just forget everything Rhonda said because you've made it all better."

She took another step at him, forcing him back. All her fears rolled over her like a tsunami. "What happens after you pass this audit with flying colors and The Nelson Group gives you everything you want? Where will you be then?"

"I'll be right here. It's not about the money."

"But I don't know that," she snapped. "I have no idea what it's about. Other than hot sex. So you can have the hot sex, because that's really good. But you can't have the rest of my life until—" She stopped right there. Because somehow the rest was unthinkable.

Brett heard it anyway. "Until I prove myself to you."

She didn't deny it. Yet she knew how godawful much she was asking for. If any man had ever tested her like this, she'd have walked out. Rupert had never asked her. She'd simply given it all anyway.

"I can't prove it, Ivy. You have to trust me."

She couldn't. She'd trusted Rupert, and he'd thrown her away. Men had always thrown her away. When Joy came, she'd had to put aside her own desires and needs. She'd put Joy first.

"I'm not the one that has to trust you. Joy does. Because she's the one who'll be hurt when you walk away from me. I would take the risk if it were just me. But I can't with Joy."

He stared at her for so long that her chest was about to explode with her inability to breathe.

Then he smiled. It was just a rise of one corner of his mouth, but so much emotion filled it. "You wouldn't take the risk, with or without Ivy. You want a sure thing. I'm old enough to admit I can't promise that. But sometimes you just have to take a chance. Because three months from now, six months, even a year—" He threw her words back at her. "—you'll regret never finding out what could have been."

He sliced her up with that terrible image, her, Joy. And nothing else but regret.

"I don't want a corner of your life and your bed. I want more." He shrugged. "I'm not willing to settle. You have to decide how much you're willing to settle for." Then he added the zinger. "And how much you're willing to let Joy settle for."

She thought he'd walk out then, but he reached for her, took her chin in his hand, holding her gently. And kissed her. So soft. So sweet. So beautiful she wanted to cry.

"Goodnight, Ivy."

When she heard the front door close, she wanted to run after him.

God, did she really just get rid of him? For good?

Joy stood in the hallway, rubbing her eyes. "Mommy. I heard you talking."

She chose her daughter, grabbing Joy up in her arms. "I'm sorry I woke you up, baby. Let's get you back to bed."

She tucked Joy in, kissed her forehead, then scratched Archie under the chin.

She wasn't making Joy settle. She was keeping her from getting hurt.

As badly as she might want to take the risk for herself, Ivy couldn't risk her daughter. No matter what Brett said.

She returned to her bedroom, and the light sparkled through the bottle of wine he'd brought her. A man bearing gifts. Brett had always given, not taken.

How long would that last?

She had to do the right thing.

But the right thing didn't mean she wouldn't cry herself to sleep, hugging the pillow as if it were Brett.

THE ACHE WAS SO BAD HE THOUGHT HE WAS HAVING A heart attack.

Lying in his cold, empty bed, Brett thought of the three hours she'd wanted. He should have shut his mouth and given them to her.

If he had, he would never have to face the fact that she didn't trust him. That she'd probably never trust him.

For God's sake, she still thought he cared about a lawsuit. He didn't give a damn. The Nelson Group would give them the money or they wouldn't. And if they didn't, he'd find the money elsewhere.

He could have his dream.

But he wanted Ivy, too.

The dream would be worth nothing if she wasn't there.

He should have said he loved her. It wouldn't have been a lie. His heart was bursting with emotion for her.

But was it truly love? He'd loved his wife. He never would have left her if she hadn't gotten tired of his workaholic ways.

Yet once he was gone, he'd missed Megan so much more than he'd ever missed his wife. What he'd learned was that love came and love went. There were no guarantees. Especially not after three weeks.

He'd never lost his drive to reach his goals. When his wife was gone, he'd filled himself up with his work.

But Jesus, without Ivy, his soul felt torn in half.

Walking out that door was the hardest thing he'd ever done, but he was old enough to know *she* had to make the choice. He was willing to risk everything. He was willing to be there every day, for her, for Joy. And every night just for Ivy.

But she had to trust him enough to believe it.

21

It actually hurt to see Brett, a physical clenching of her stomach and a fist squeezing her heart. Ivy couldn't breathe when she encountered him in the hall. Her legs turned rubbery when passed by her to get to Grady's office without stopping to show her a photo of Valerie.

It was Wednesday, the third day of the audit. Gloria said it was going well. Jordana thought it was cool to be on the team presenting to them.

Brett hadn't ignored Ivy. He hadn't looked right through her as if she didn't exist. He'd been polite and solicitous. Like he'd been before he'd ever touched her. As if she were just another employee. He hadn't asked her to rethink what she'd said last night. He hadn't texted her.

When she left at the end of the day to pick up Joy, there was still no text, and for a moment, sitting there in her car with the engine running, tears burned her eyes.

He meant what he said. She had to make the first move. She wanted to be angry, as if he'd turned it into a game. But this was no game. He was a strong man. He'd said what he wanted. She had to decide if she could give it to him.

And she was the one left with the aching heart.

"What do you say we go to Grandma's house for dinner tonight?" She tried to sound cheery and normal after Joy was buckled in.

Ivy needed to talk. While her know-it-all, I-told-you-so mother was probably one of the worst choices, she didn't have another. She couldn't explain the whole issue to Gloria or Jordana. But her mother knew it intimately.

"Yay," Joy crowed. "Can we have hot dogs and baked beans?"

Her mother fed Joy things Ivy would never think of. Hot dogs weren't even real meat and the baked beans her mother preferred were loaded with sugar and sodium. But once in a while, a kid needed to be a kid.

Just as a woman had to talk to her mother because sometimes she needed to listen to things she didn't want to hear.

Grandma had the beans baking and the hot dogs boiling by the time they arrived.

Joy ran to her, throwing her arms around her grandmother's aproned hips. Mom bent to kiss her head. "To what do I owe this pleasure?"

"Mom had a fight with Brett last night."

"Joy!" Ivy burst out. They hadn't been talking loud enough for it to be called a fight. Nor had Joy said a thing about hearing Brett's voice. "We were not fighting."

Her mother raised a brow. "Maybe you were doing something else that little ears shouldn't hear."

"We were not."

Mom merely shrugged, made a face, and rescued the hot dogs from the boiling water.

Dinner was set on the table, hot dogs, beans, and French fries. Not a vegetable in sight, but Ivy didn't say a thing. When you invited yourself over, you got what you got.

"So how was school, honey?" Ivy's mother salted her beans.

"Mom, you don't need extra salt."

She pursed her lips, then said, "I want it."

Ivy took the salt away when Joy started to do the same.

"School was okay," Joy said into the middle of the tussle. "But I liked it when Brett helped me with my homework. When's he coming back, Mommy?"

"He didn't help you with your homework, sweetheart."

"He asked me questions," she said stubbornly.

To her mother's credit, she didn't ask what the so-called fight with Brett had been about. At least not yet. Instead she said, "We've got ice cream for dessert."

"What kind?" Joy asked, her eyes wide.

"Your favorite."

Joy punched her fork in the air. "Chocolate chip cookie dough!"

Ivy was grateful to her mother. After that, Joy seemed to forget how wonderful Brett was and began describing in detail every single minute of her day.

When dinner was done, Ivy helped her mother do the dishes while Joy took her homework into the living room and worked on the coffee table.

"All right. Spit it out. What did you do wrong?"

Ivy clucked her tongue. "I didn't do anything wrong."

"Then why did he dump you? I told you to hang on and get everything you could *before* he dumped you."

Ivy stacked the rinsed dishes in the dishwasher. "He started making demands I couldn't meet."

"Oh my God. Don't tell me he asked to have sex in public. Or wanted to take you to a BDSM club."

Ivy rolled her eyes and sighed. "You really watch too much TV."

"I get that from erotic romance novels, my dear."

The thought of her mother reading anything vaguely erotic... she couldn't think about it. "He wanted to spend more time with me. And with Joy. He didn't like it when I said he could only come over after Joy went to bed. He said he wants to take care of us, whatever that means."

Her mom washed the pans, and Ivy dried. "So you told him he could only come over for sex. And he *didn't* like that? What's wrong with him? Most men would kill for that." She shrugged. "But he is kind of old. Maybe it was too much pressure."

"Mo-om." Her mother never failed to shock her. And sometimes even to make her laugh. Still, Ivy was sure she didn't mean a thing she said. "He just wanted a bigger piece of our lives than I'm willing to give."

With the pans put away, her mother leaned on the counter and looked at Ivy. "Why?"

"Why what?"

"Why couldn't you give a little more? He was great with Joy, and she adored him. And he was a sweetheart to you. So why not give him a little more?"

"You know why. I don't want Joy getting hurt." She folded the dish towel and hung it over the oven rail. "You were the one who said he'd dump us. I'm just protecting Ivy against that."

"You're protecting yourself."

"If I was protecting myself, why would I let him come around at all?"

"Because that's how you like your men, in bitesize pieces. A night here, a night there, maybe over a couple of weeks, then it's sayonara, baby."

Her skin prickled. "What are you talking about?"

"I'm not an idiot, Ivy. I know what you're doing when you ask me to babysit. It's a pattern. First it's a Friday or Saturday night. Then maybe two, three, and a couple of times, even four weekends in a row. You look real sexy when you drop Joy off. And messy sexy when you pick her up. Then bam, it's months before you need me to babysit again."

She could only stare at her mother. She had no clue she'd been that transparent. Then she had to justify herself. Because between mothers and daughters, you always had to justify. "It was better that way for Ivy. She didn't get attached to some guy who wasn't going to stick around."

"You didn't know they weren't going to stick around."

"Oh, I knew, believe me."

"Then it was because you didn't choose the type that would stick around. You didn't want a man who would stay."

She felt a bit militant now, and put her hands on her hips, facing her mom down. "Since when did you start believing there was *any* type of man that would actually stick around?"

"We're not talking about me. We're talking about you. Brett wasn't so bad. If he wanted to take care of you, what's the big deal?"

"Because it wouldn't last."

"So what? Nothing lasts. You take what you can get."

"I don't want to just take what I can get." The words snapped out despite her best intentions.

"Well, you sure act like you do. You never ask for more. And you don't give anyone more."

"Right. Look what happened the last time I gave someone more. He dumped me and wouldn't even admit Joy was his child."

"Rupert was an ass. He preyed on his female students."

The bluntness hurt, to actually know that her mother viewed her as prey. But she'd come to her mother for just this bluntness. "So you don't think Brett is preying on his female employees?"

"I don't think he's taking any of his other female

employees to Tahoe and wining and dining their mothers and daughters."

"But what about the lawsuit? You're the one who said he just wants to keep me happy so I won't sue."

"Are you trying to get me to reassure you?"

Yes. Hell, yes. "I'm just asking what you think. Because your views seem completely different than before."

"All right. You want to know what I think? Even if you don't like it?"

"Yes." Maybe not.

"You're not going to blame me later?"

"I won't blame you." That didn't mean she wouldn't be hurt.

"All right. You got messed over by one asshole, now they're all assholes."

Wow. Mom could say that to herself, too.

"Most of them *are* assholes," her mother affirmed. "But this guy is offering to take care of you. And you need taking care of, Ivy."

"I've done a damn good job of taking care of myself so far."

"Right. That's why you're constantly moaning that you have to live month to month. That you can never save. That you have to scrimp on everything. That you can't afford to send Joy to a private school. That you never got to finish college. That you couldn't sue the bastard who got you pregnant because he might decide later that he wanted to take the child away. You're a victim, Ivy."

She opened her mouth to defend herself. She'd asked for it, but she couldn't believe her mother would actually say it. Not like that.

Mom didn't give her time to put up a defense. "You're a victim of yourself, Ivy. You're so afraid you're going to get hurt that you don't do anything at all. Well, make a stand.

Make a choice. If you don't want this guy to take care of you, then sue his ass. You always say you want to be strong and take care of your kid. Well, be strong and defend yourself in court if you're not going to take what this man is offering you."

She didn't even know what Brett was offering.

"And don't use me as an excuse either, just because I got dumped and had to look after you all by myself. You're not me. My choices aren't your choices. Maybe I never wanted another man in my life. Maybe I didn't even want the one I had."

"What?" Her mother had *always* blamed her father.

"I was getting older, and I wanted a baby. And in the olden days, you needed a husband."

"It was the eighties, Mom, not the *olden* days."

"I didn't make enough to raise a kid on my own. That didn't mean I didn't make him a good wife. But he was never my first priority." Her mother's voice dropped, softened. "You were." After a deep breath, she added, "And I hated the way you let that Rupert man treat you. I wanted better for you." She touched Ivy's arm gently. "Maybe this one could be the better kind you've always deserved."

It was the kindest thing she could ever remember her mother saying to her. On top of the shocker that her mom had never loved her father. Now she had to wrap her mind around a huge change to the way she'd thought her childhood played out. Maybe her father had left because he was looking for the love his wife couldn't give him.

But that didn't excuse that he'd left his daughter behind. And it had nothing to do with the way had Rupert treated her.

"But I don't want a man to take care of me, Mom. Not even Brett."

"Maybe you need to change your definition of being taken

care of. It's not just money. It's emotional support. A man who believes in you."

"Brett doesn't know me well enough to believe in me."

"That's crap. I saw him look at you. He's got *belief* written all over him."

Ivy spread out the dish towel on the oven rail, making sure it didn't have a single wrinkle, thinking so hard her head hurt.

"The only person who doesn't believe in you is you."

She looked at her mother's worn face and the lines that were so much more than age. But she didn't ask, because implicit in her mother's words were that *she* believed in Ivy, despite everything she'd ever said over the years. "Am I really a victim?"

"Anyone who's afraid is a victim."

Her mother had always been snarky. She'd never been afraid to say what she thought. She'd never been hesitant to show her disapproval. But Ivy saw something she hadn't appreciated before. "Mom, sometimes you're amazingly profound."

Her mother made a face. "I'm just brutally honest. Most people don't care for it."

You might not want to hear it, but sometimes you needed it. Ivy *was* a victim, not of the men in her life, but of her own fears. She was so afraid of how things could go wrong that she couldn't even allow a good man into her life. She could only give him pieces of herself.

Because she didn't trust anyone not to screw her over.

Last night she'd even threatened to sue Brett. Just to see what he'd do. Like a test. *Can I trust you to stay even if I do something you don't like? Even if I screw over all your life goals?*

It was an unconscionable thing to do to him.

The seeds of last night had started growing the day she let Brett solve her problem with Rhonda. *She* needed to confront

Rhonda about everything she'd said that day. It wasn't about a lawsuit. It was standing up to the person who'd wronged her. It was acting instead of being acted upon. Ivy hadn't been able face her fears the day it happened because she'd actually believed Rhonda was right. She believed she was a failure. Then she'd let Brett try to fix it for her. The task had been impossible, but he'd given it his all.

And she'd thrown everything back in his face.

She finally did something she rarely gave her mother, putting an arm around her shoulder. "I'm not going to be a victim anymore. I'm not going to sue either. I'm going to the horse's mouth and say what I should have said then, instead of running away."

"You're going to give that bitch a piece of your mind?"

"I'm not giving her anything else of mine. I'm just going to point out the errors in her impression of me."

Her mother knuckled her in the ribs. "Oh," she cooed, "You sound so diplomatic. Go for it, honey."

"Then I'm going to tell Brett the truth."

Her mother reached up, the skin of her hand papery with age and the years of soapy water. "Good for you. I love you."

"Mom, I love you, too." She realized how rarely they said that to each other. "Thank you for your wisdom."

She wouldn't waste that wisdom.

And she couldn't waste the rest of her life by being afraid.

22

The next morning, Ivy didn't consider the ethical ramifications of looking up Rhonda's address in the employee database. Or rather, she considered it and decided the circumstances outweighed the ethics.

She found Rhonda in Palo Alto, her street only ten minutes from the office. Ivy cancelled her walk with Hannah and headed out just before lunch.

She hadn't seen Brett except through the window of the conference room. That was a good thing. She needed to take care of Rhonda before she could talk to him.

Rhonda's home was an Eichler style with a pitched roof and an interior atrium, sage green siding and a turquoise front door, which somehow all fit together seamlessly. Ivy hoped Rhonda was home. She'd decided not to call ahead and give her any warning. Of course that meant she ran the risk of pressing the doorbell on an empty house.

She'd almost given up after the second ring and was turning away when the turquoise door opened.

Rhonda's sweats looked baggy, as if she'd lost weight. She'd scraped her hair back into a very short ponytail. The atrium behind her, which probably bloomed with brilliant flowers in the spring, looked barren now. The hydrangeas in pots had been cut back to stumps.

"Ivy." That was all Rhonda said, her name, with no inflection.

"Hi, Rhonda. Can we talk inside?" Ivy didn't want to recite her spiel out on the front walk.

Rhonda opened the door wider. Ivy could then see the camellia bushes were still lush and green, ready for buds in just a few weeks. Azaleas waited for the sun, too. Not everything was winter dead. In the summer, it would be lovely to sit at the small café table.

Sadly, there was only one chair.

On the atrium's opposite side was another turquoise door beneath an overhang, this one flanked by floor to ceiling windows.

The entry was an aggregate stone that matched the stone walks in the atrium, and led straight down two steps into a sunken living room backed by a wall of windows.

It was beautiful, filled with light falling through all the glass.

"This must be like coming home to a garden," she told Rhonda. A sanctuary. Except that in front of the TV, there was only a loveseat with one side table, a small coffee table, and a single footstool. And no other furniture in the room.

"I've got coffee," Rhonda offered.

Ivy hadn't intended to ask for anything. She'd wanted only to say her piece and go. But there was something about Rhonda, the single chair at the café table, the house that was both gorgeous yet strangely empty. So she said, "That would be great. Thank you."

"You like sugar and cream, right?" Rhonda's face, usually blotchy red, was now merely pale.

"Yes."

Rhonda disappeared into the kitchen off to the left, returned with two cups, and stepped down into the living room. Ivy realized she would have to sit on the small loveseat with Rhonda, which was slightly unnerving, as if she'd be invading Rhonda's personal space. And vice versa.

Rhonda settled, holding the mug between her hands as if she needed warmth. "Is Brett going to fire me?"

"I have no idea."

"I know he promoted you and gave you a raise." Rhonda's spies had been talking. She still didn't drink.

Ivy's mug was hot, and she didn't know how Rhonda could hold hers so tightly without burning herself. "Yes. I got a promotion. But that wasn't what I came to ask you for that day. I only wanted compensation for the extra work."

"That's what you told me."

There was no reason not to say exactly what she'd come here for. "What you accused me of was wrong. I'm not money-grubbing. I'm not a blackmailer. I'm a single mother and proud of it, but I'm not asking for handouts. I worked hard for you. All I expected was recognition of the extra effort. I would have been satisfied if you'd told me I would be reimbursed for my extra day care expenses and paid for my overtime at home. All I wanted was to be treated fairly."

She didn't add that she wasn't a loser or a failure or that she wasn't replaceable. Those were emotional judgments and she didn't want to deal with emotion right now, only with what was right and wrong. "You didn't provide any solution to the problem. As my boss, that was your job."

Rhonda swallowed without even tasting her coffee.

Ivy had coached herself not to expect Rhonda to say all her complaints were justified. People like Rhonda never admitted they were wrong.

It was enough that Ivy had called her on it.

Because she wasn't expecting vindication, she almost

dropped her coffee mug when Rhonda said, "You were a convenient target. And I blamed all my problems on you just because you were there. I'm sorry."

Ivy couldn't believe her. "I'm not going to sue you or the company, so you don't have to mouth platitudes."

"I deserve that. You have every reason to doubt my sincerity." Color started to blotch Rhonda's cheeks. That usually meant agitation. "I said a lot of terrible things to you. I called you a failure, but the truth is I admire your selfless dedication to your daughter. In fact I'm jealous of that. The only thing I've ever been dedicated to was my job."

Ivy had expected another fight. She had no intention of winning, because you couldn't win against a crazy person who wouldn't listen.

But Rhonda didn't seem so crazy now. She wasn't the fire-breathing dragon lady she'd been that day in her office.

"Because I treated you abominably, you deserve to know the truth." Rhonda tapped the side of her mug, still without drinking. "I like to win. I like to be in control. Sometimes that means I don't always play fair or nice. I make enemies. I have a lot of enemies at the company. Mostly that's my fault. I could have had Jordana on my side, but instead I decided to make war on her." She glanced at Ivy. "I'd appreciate it if you wouldn't repeat any of this to anyone. It would be embarrassing. But sitting here alone all day with nothing but soap operas, game shows, Dr. Phil, and Judge Judy, I've had to think hard about what I'm going to say to Brett when he finally comes back to talk to me after The Nelson Group auditors leave."

Ivy could have said something, asked a question, made Rhonda's confession easier on her. But she kept her mouth shut.

"Brett wanted to give me time to think about what I'd done." Rhonda laughed softly, her voice a little rough, probably because she never laughed. At least not that Ivy had seen. "Sort of like a kid in time out," she added.

"There's a resemblance," Ivy agreed, banking the sudden urge to smile.

"I've done a lot of thinking. I'm tired of fighting with everyone. It's exhausting."

Maybe Rhonda was more like Ivy than either of them thought. They were both afraid. Rhonda's fear came out in constant bickering and struggling to stay on top. Ivy's came out in keeping away anyone who might betray her. She didn't say it, of course, not wanting to sound like she was psychoanalyzing Rhonda. She had enough trouble analyzing herself.

"How about this, Rhonda? Let's make a pact that we're not going to fight anymore. I can't say what Brett will decide after the auditors leave, but if he wants you to come back, then I'll agree to work with you."

"And what about your promotion if I come back?" Rhonda's face remained blank.

Ivy couldn't decide if the woman felt fear or anger. Or simply resignation. "I'll do a good job for you as supervisor. And I believe you'll need the help." Brett had said the same thing the night she'd questioned him, but for the first time, Ivy saw herself as an asset to HR. To Rhonda. She'd deserved that promotion. "But this will be a two-way street. I'll need you to agree to listen. If I come to you with a problem, I'm not there because I'm stupid or because I can't handle it myself or because I just need to whine. I'm there because I want your opinion. But you have to be willing to listen to mine, too."

"I used to be good at listening," Rhonda mused, staring out the floor-to-ceiling windows at a backyard resplendent with trees. "I don't know when I lost that capacity. Maybe it happened when I became VP, and I decided everyone would try to take it away from me."

"You have to stop being so paranoid."

Rhonda put her hand over her mouth and stifled another laugh. Two in one day was amazing. "I deserve that. You know, watching daytime TV is eye-opening. Dr. Phil is all touchy-feely, getting people to talk things out. While Judge Judy just says it like it is, and she doesn't take any nonsense. I need to learn to be somewhere in the middle. To be what *that* person—" She pointed emphatically. "—needs me to be in *that* moment. Instead of trying to figure out what kind of angle they have or how they're out to get me." She laughed again. "I do sound paranoid, don't I."

"Yeah. Totally."

They laughed together. Just like Ivy had needed to hug her mom last night and tell her she loved her, she needed to laugh with Rhonda right now.

"Here's what I'm going to do." Ivy set her mug, still mostly full, on the coffee table. "I'll tell Brett I can work with you again. The decision to bring you back is up to him, but I'll let him know we've come to an accord." She held up a finger. "But I'm trusting you to keep up your end, too."

"Why don't we just say we'll trust each other?"

Trust. She hadn't been able to give it to Brett the other night. But here she was dishing it out to Rhonda.

"Deal." Ivy stuck out her hand.

They shook.

When she left Rhonda, she had a plan. She owed Brett the truth. She'd been afraid to trust him, but she didn't want to end up like Rhonda, living in a house with one café chair, one footstool, and a loveseat that wasn't really meant for two.

Three months from now, or six, or even a year, she absolutely did not want to regret that she'd never discovered how good she and Brett could be together.

She didn't want to be a woman who was too afraid to trust.

She wanted to leap.

And she wanted to trust that Brett would catch her.

THE AUDITORS WERE IN AND OUT OF THE CONFERENCE room. So were his VPs. Mitch Redmond liked to sit and contemplate the future. So Brett made himself available, often joining them in the conference room. Like now. Through the open window blinds facing the interior hall, he observed his employees passing to and fro. He saw Ivy leave for lunch. He noted her return. He was aware that his gaze followed her. That with everyone who passed the windows, he was waiting for a glimpse of her.

He hadn't talked to her about the scene between them two nights ago, even as badly as he'd wanted to. Just a couple of words. Just to see the dark chocolate of her eyes. Just to take a breath of her.

But he couldn't push her. He'd already done that and walked away in disaster. So he'd left everything up to her.

If she didn't want to regret.

If she decided to take the risk.

If she could live without a guarantee.

He'd backed them both into a corner. Ultimatums were never a good idea. They meant one person had to back down. One person had to give in. It turned the whole thing into a battle only one of them could win.

All he really wanted to win was Ivy.

In any way he could.

Because *he* didn't want any regrets.

He couldn't give her a guarantee. He'd thought his marriage was a guarantee, but he'd learned that nothing in life ever was. People, places, jobs, lives, everything changed. Ivy couldn't guarantee her feelings either.

But he could do something to show her he had the best intentions. He could prove to her that she and Joy were more important than a job or goal. He could make a first move.

There was only one thing he could do that would mean anything to her.

So he left the auditors, left his VPs, left Mitch, left the conference room to make a phone call. Then another. Followed by another. Until he had everything he needed.

Now he had to hand it all over to Ivy. And abide by what she decided.

23

Ivy sent him a text in the middle of the afternoon. Brett had planned on stopping by her apartment after he finished with the auditors for the day. But she'd already decided she wanted to see him.

Can we get together? I can come by your place after work.

His heart beat hard enough to feel its pumping against his chest. He wanted to write back *Hell, yes.* He was willing to take anything she offered. Meeting at his place said so much. She wanted her three hours. She wanted to scream out her passion with him. But it also shouted status quo, that she wanted to go back to the way things were, as if their argument had never happened.

He couldn't go back. He'd come far enough to know that he wanted her in his life, and not in half measures.

We can talk at my place. I'll be done here by 6:30. He added in his address.

Great. Mom says she'll take Joy.

He had his three hours. All he had to do was convince her they should last a lifetime.

She was a shadow in her car parked on the street when he

pulled into his garage. He lived in a quiet, tree-lined neighborhood in the Belmont Hills where people were wary of strangers sitting in cars. After parking, he crossed the street to fetch her.

She was already climbing out.

Everything inside him stilled, all his focus coming down to her. Her skirt was short, her legs endless in sexy high heels. She was the Ivy she'd been before all the crap with Rhonda, before she'd even started working for the evil queen of HR. She'd dressed just this side of sexy, her skirts a little short, her necklines a little lower. And always perfection.

An overwhelming urge beat inside him to grab her up and carry her off like a caveman. Into his house. His bed. His life.

All he said was, "Hey."

"Hey." Then she smiled and his heart lit up.

Jesus, he had it bad. But he didn't touch her. If he allowed himself even one kiss, he'd never get to all the things he needed to tell her.

"Fancy digs," she said, indicating his house. It was a split level with large front windows, two large patches of green grass on either side of the walkway, and lots of flowering bushes that were now dormant in winter.

"It works for someone who needs a home office." But it wasn't a home. It was a place he stayed. He realized he hadn't had a home since he'd divorced. *Home* was a state of mind, the people you returned to, the ones who mattered. "The deck in back is better, with a view across the hills."

He was anxious to show her, dreamed of sitting out there with her in the summertime, watching Joy play in the yard.

He took her through the open garage and into the kitchen.

"Wow, now I see how you got to be such a fabulous cook with all this at your disposal."

She gazed around the sparkling granite, the gadgets on the

counter, the center island with copper pots hanging within easy reach.

"I like to cook. It relaxes me."

He still hadn't kissed her, but his pulse was pounding with desire while his head pounded with the need to tell her everything. "I want to give you this." He reached inside his suit jacket for the list he'd stored there. A short list, the best of the best.

He laid the envelope on the counter beside her.

"What's this?" She didn't touch it, her gaze suddenly growing wary.

"A list of lawyers."

Her face lost its color. "What for?"

He moved in on her, close enough to touch, but he didn't. Not yet. "You believe I'm only hanging around you because I'm afraid you'll sue the company. That once the auditors are gone and we get the money, I'll be done with you." He picked up the envelope, took her hand in his, and placed it in her palm. "So sue me. All these lawyers are good. I made some calls and got the best names. Do whatever you need to do." He dropped his voice. "But that won't change how much I want to be with you. I'm not going away. No matter what you do."

She stared at the white envelope. Then she looked at him, her eyes dark, her lips lush. "But it could ruin everything for you."

"I don't give a damn." He cupped her cheek, smoothed his thumb along her lips. "I can't imagine being without you. My heart hurts if I even think about it. If that's not the definition of love, then I don't know what the hell is. I love you, no qualifications."

She didn't say a word, and everything inside him was about to burst wide open.

"Give us a chance, Ivy. I'll be there for you. For Joy."

"But you'd hate me," she whispered, "if I ruined everything. You want to go all the way. The Fortune 500."

He touched his lips to hers, barely there, just to feel the connection if only for a moment. "I'm no longer that thirty-year-old workaholic who has something to prove. I have goals, but they aren't going to mean a damn thing if you and Joy aren't there with me."

She closed her eyes and leaned into his cupped hand.

"Trust me," he murmured. "Trust yourself."

Ivy leaned into his touch. The gentleness in his big hand was the sweetest thing she'd ever felt in her life.

I love you.

She'd heard those words before, and they hadn't meant much or lasted for long.

But this was Brett. And he was giving her the whole world in a list of lawyers.

Ivy didn't have to think a second longer. She'd only taken so long because she couldn't believe anyone would ever offer what he had. Not just love, but letting her hold his future in her hand. Giving her the power.

Ivy tore the envelope in half without opening it, then again, into fours, and threw it on the counter. "I went to see Rhonda this afternoon." Everything she had to say to him started there. "I thought I'd have to point out to her how everything she said about me was wrong."

"You shouldn't have to confront her on your own." He stood so close she could breathe him in as if he were part of her.

"I had to look her in the eye and make myself believe that the things she said weren't true."

"Jesus, Ivy, they were never true."

He was so good, so beautiful. And he believed in her. "Going there helped me figure that out. Even before she answered the door. The funny thing was that she actually apologized before I said everything I'd intended to."

"She damn well better. She was wrong."

She loved that he stood up for her. But just because he supported her didn't mean she couldn't do it all for herself. His caring didn't diminish her.

"I finally see that. She *was* wrong. I've been so afraid of trusting someone because they might let me down. But I understand that the real thing I've always feared is failure. Rhonda hit all my sore spots that day." She pressed close, tipping her head back to meet his gaze. "I was afraid that if I let you take care of things, it meant I was incapable. That if I let you too close to Joy, I might lose her. That if I let you too close to me, you'd see I couldn't handle things on my own."

"I never thought that."

"I know you didn't. I trust you, Brett." She smoothed her palms over the lapels of his suit jacket. "I trust that you'll stay. I trust that you'll be good for Joy." Going up on her tiptoes, she put her lips on his and whispered, "I trust that you'll be good for me."

Slipping his hand beneath her hair, he slanted his mouth over hers, parting her lips with a deep kiss. He tasted like the heaven she'd always been searching for.

When he let her breathe on her own again, she clung to him. "I won't let myself be afraid. I love you, and I never want to have any regrets. Not in three months, or six, or a year. Not in this lifetime." Looping her arms around his neck," she whispered against his ear, "We need you. Joy and I need you in our lives so badly."

HE THOUGHT HE'D HAVE TO KEEP FIGHTING HER FEARS. BUT she'd given him everything. More than he'd ever hoped for.

Holding her as close as two bodies could get without actually merging into one, he murmured against her hair, "How long do we have before you have to pick Joy up?"

"We have all night."

If hearts could burst from sheer joy, his was about to. He laughed softly. "Thank God it's more than three hours."

She held his face in her hands. "All my hours. All my nights. Every single one. I'm not afraid anymore. I love you."

He would never tire of hearing her say those words. He knew how much they cost Ivy. He knew they were almost like giving up her freedom.

Relishing the feel of her skin against his fingers, he whispered, "I'm going to make love to you so good that you can't help screaming."

Her eyes glittered. "I'll make you come so hard that you shout my name."

"Always. Only your name, ever."

"Then take me to your bed."

"Your wish is my command." He gathered her up in his arms, carrying her like a bride. He didn't show her the house. There would be time for that later. Now all he wanted was her. To seal the promises they'd made to each other. With touch. With love.

In the bedroom, he set her on her feet at the end of his bed. Straight across from the mirrored doors of his closet.

She stared at their images, then fisted her hand in his shirt. "Do you remember the fantasy you told me you wanted?" In the mirror, she met his gaze.

"I remember." He wanted to stand her in front of the mirror and make her come with his fingers. So he could watch every emotion play across her face.

He'd known, too, that it frightened her.

"Do it now." Her voice was soft, low, seductive. "Touch me and make me come. Watch me in the mirror. Take off all my clothes and leave all yours on."

This was the moment she truly gave him her trust. Before, it had been the mirror of her fears. Now it was the mirror of their love, their desire, their trust.

He removed every stitch of her clothing, the deliciously short skirt, the top that hinted at all the creamy skin beneath. The lacy bra, the naughty thong.

"I'm leaving the shoes. I want them." Then he removed nothing else but his suit jacket. "Jesus, you're beautiful," he whispered with all the awe filling him.

He stood behind her, almost a head taller, her glossy black hair reaching only to his chin. Her skin was pale against his dark suit, her breasts high and firm, her body slender and perfect.

"Spread your legs," he whispered in her ear.

She stood proud and seductive in the mirror. She wasn't the woman in Tahoe. She wasn't the woman of two nights ago. She was new. She was confident.

And she was his.

He cupped her breasts in his hands, pulling her against him. "Feel what you do to me." He was hard against the small of her back.

"Touch me," she whispered. "Everywhere."

The man in the mirror bent to kiss the delicate flesh between her neck and shoulder. She tipped her head to the side, giving him greater access. He kissed his way up to her ear. With his breath on her, he pinched her nipples.

She moaned, the sound welling up, full-throated with all her pleasure. "More," she begged.

He skimmed his hands down her belly. "Watch us."

She didn't close her eyes, her gaze tracking the movement of his fingers. Until he slipped into her folds. She sucked in a breath, said his name. Everything between them had been whispers and sighs, gasps and bitten lips, everything kept inside, never letting it out.

His name on her lips was soft. But it held the promise of so much more to come.

So many more hours.

So many more nights.

A lifetime of nights just like this.

It hadn't been merely the need to be quiet so her daughter didn't wake. It had been the need to keep everything secret, hidden from the world.

She was wet, her body already trembling. He swirled his fingers over the pearl buried between her legs. "Tell me how it feels."

"Oh God, Brett." She leaned her head back on his shoulder, curling her arm around his neck, anchoring her body to his. "It's so good. So hot. It burns and it makes me shake inside." She gasped, moaned. Then she cried out. "God. Yes. Please. Don't stop. Please don't ever stop."

She undulated against him like waves against a shore. In the mirror, her lips were parted, her chest a rising and falling swell of desire as her breath puffed harder.

His hand was dark against her, and nothing had ever been so erotic as the sight of his fingers buried in her. Making her feel so much pleasure. She was slick against his touch, her skin warm and flushed with arousal.

She made him feel young again, totally alive, in his prime and primal.

"Do you want to come?" he asked softly, blowing warm air against her ear, making her squirm.

"Yes, please. I need to come."

"I don't think you're ready yet. You're not making enough noise."

"I'm ready. I'm so ready." She rocked against him, increasing the friction. "Please."

"Look at us. Look how beautiful you are."

He held her up with one hand banded beneath her breasts. She watched his fingers on her, the endless circle of his touch, round and round, down, sliding inside and back up.

"Yes, yes, yes," she chanted, her voice growing louder.

"Watch us. Don't stop."

He wanted her to see everything. The way he saw it. The taut lines of her face, the need etched around her mouth. He would know when she was ready. It would be written on her face. The moment she was so lost that she couldn't keep her eyes open, the moment she became nothing more than sensation.

She was like fireworks going off in his hand. Her body began to shake, bowing against him. With his fingers inside her, he felt her contractions.

Then she cried his name, her voice throaty, filling the room, filling him. He held her tight as she bucked, a rush of moist pleasure on his fingers, her moans and cries ringing.

Then she collapsed, dragging him down to the carpet with her. He held her, his back against the foot of the bed, his breathing hard, hers even harder, his body aching for her.

"God, yes, God, yes." Her voice was low and hungry. She crawled into his lap, pulled at his slacks, her eyes glazed, crazy with desire. "I need you in me. Right now. Brett. Please. Where's the condom?" She was patting his pants, searching his pockets.

She stopped. As if a switch had flipped. "Do you trust me?" she whispered, her eyes hot.

"I trust you."

"Then come inside me. Just like this. Skin to skin. I'm on the pill."

He held her tight, his heart so big it felt like it couldn't fit in his chest anymore. "I don't care if you're not. I want you this way."

She slid him out of his pants and into her heat. His tie was still around his neck, his shirt buttoned, his shoes on his feet.

But she eclipsed everything with the feel of her body surrounding him completely. Fully. Wholly.

"This is making love," she said, her breath fluttering against his lips. She moved on him, a subtle rhythm that was enough to drive him crazy.

"Making love," he murmured.

"I will always make love to you. It will never be anything else." She kissed him, short, sweet, and deep. "Even if it's kinky and dirty."

"It will always be making love."

The words were a vow between them.

Then she made him lose his mind.

WHEN SHE CAME, SHE SCREAMED, ALL HER PLEASURE RACING through it, all her emotions letting go completely for him.

"Always," she cried out, her body spasming around him.

Then he shouted his release, coming with her. God, she loved the smooth, hard feel of him inside her.

She loved him.

Collapsing on his chest, she breathed hard and heavy, his breaths matching hers until finally, ages later, they calmed.

"Jesus. You're fantastic."

She laughed against him. "I love that you still have all your clothes on. It's kinky and naughty."

He stroked her hair. "I couldn't wait to have you. It will always be like this. The need to get my hands on you, to get inside you."

In all her nameless nights over the last six years, she'd never had this crazy, wild need. She'd never had anyone want her this way.

And she'd never wanted anyone so badly.

"Always," she whispered against his neck. "I will always trust you to be there for us."

He slid his hands into her hair, pulling her up to look at him. "I will always put you first."

She laid a finger on his lips. "Within reason. I do know you're going to have late nights. And times when you have to cancel plans." She kissed him quickly. "Because you're my big, adorable CEO, a very important man. But I have one big complaint." She stroked his nipple through his shirt.

He shivered and said, "What?"

"You said you had a toe fetish. That you wanted to lick mine, kiss them, caress them." She wrinkled her nose. "You haven't done that yet. And I'm very curious how it feels."

He laughed. "I am so remiss. Before the night is out, I'm going to lick your toes until you come."

"You're very kinky." She loved him that way. She loved the way he laughed, the way he made her laugh.

"Just don't tell my daughter." He nuzzled her hair, his voice softening. "I want you to meet Megan. And Valerie."

She'd forgotten about his daughter. "What will Megan think... about... well, you know."

"She'll love you. She'll love Joy. Joy will be like Valerie's big sister." His gaze turned serious and sweet. "It's what I've always wanted. A family. Megan wants it for me, too." He chuckled. "At least she's wanted it since she grew up and stopped hating me for the divorce."

"Do you know what I love about you?" Her voice felt soft and dreamy in the dark bedroom.

"What?"

"That you want Joy to be a part of your life, too." She'd once feared that he'd wanted her *only* so he could have a family. As if Joy could help him erase the sins of his past fatherhood. But she knew so much more now. "You want us both. A package deal."

"I already love her, too."

"I know. That's what makes you so special." She'd known these things about him all along, deep in her heart. But her fears had gotten in the way, giving her false readings. "I don't need to be afraid anymore."

"Not of me." He trailed his fingers along her chin, to her mouth, tracing her lips.

"No. Not of you." And not of a lot of other things. Facing Rhonda today had taught her something about herself. She could stand on her own, stand up for herself. She *was* strong, even if she'd doubted herself many times along the way. "I've got a proposition for you."

"That sounds interesting." He held her hips down, flexing inside her, letting her feel just how interested he was. Again. "I love being propositioned, if it's from you."

"I want you to bring Rhonda back."

His face went blank, all expression gone, his body still as stone. "Why?"

"Because everyone deserves a second chance. I truly believe she sees how many mistakes she's made. She was afraid." Ivy understood fear. "She didn't want to lose her position. She felt like people were always fighting her. All those woman-in a-man's-world issues."

"Gloria doesn't have those problems. She's reasonable, rational."

"Rhonda can be, too. She's seen the error of her ways."

"You can really say that after what she did to you?"

"Yes, I can."

His gaze tracked his face, roaming from her eyes to her

mouth. "You're an amazing woman to be able to forgive so easily."

"It wasn't easy. But I realized that if I was ever going to change—" If she was ever going to allow herself to believe in Brett. "—I had to confront Rhonda. I can work with her. I want to try, at least. My gut says she wants to work well with everyone this time. If you give her a chance."

"But what about you, your promotion? Don't you think she'll try to take that away from you?"

He didn't say that he'd stop Rhonda if she tried, and she loved him for his belief in her. "I already told her I'm not giving the promotion back."

Brett pulled her in for a long kiss. "You go, girl."

She laughed at his valley-girl imitation. "So will you do it?"

"I'll do anything for you."

"But will you blame me if I'm wrong and she screws up again?" Her heart started a staccato beat in her chest.

"I trust your judgment. If it's the wrong decision, then we're both wrong. And we'll move on."

She should have known that's what he'd say. Trust worked both ways.

Then she laughed, suddenly seeing the kinkiness in the situation.

"What?"

"Here we are talking about work and Rhonda and meeting your daughter." She leaned in, kissing him hard. "While you're still inside me," she added with a husky whisper.

"That's real life. We talk about work while we're making love. We make hot, dirty love while your daughter is sleeping in the next room. We just have to be quiet." He kissed her, plunging deep into her mouth, rocking her body exquisitely. "Then there will be the nights where we take Joy to your mother or hire a sitter so we can get a hotel room where I make you scream all night long." He groaned

Ivy gave him a matching moan as sensation built deep inside her.

"That's life," he said, a slight crack in his voice. "And I want it all with you."

She wanted it, too.

"So when are you going to marry me and make us a real family?"

It might have been the most unromantic proposal. Except that he was inside her. Her body was on fire for him. And nothing could have been more romantic.

"As soon as you want." She felt him slide deep, the pleasure close to unbearable. "Yes. Now. We can do it right this minute."

Then she screamed his name. Because screaming for him felt so absolutely perfect.

And marriage with him would be heaven.

24

"I can't believe Brett's actually bringing Rhonda back." Jordana stabbed a slice of mandarin hiding in the lettuce of her Chinese chicken salad. She was following in Gloria's footsteps with her lunch choice.

The auditors had left last Friday, along with everyone from The Nelson Group. The audit had taken a full two weeks. Now it was time for a girl lunch to celebrate. They would have done it yesterday, but there was the regular executive staff meeting on Mondays.

"I have to say I never had a hard time with her." Hannah Fall had joined them at Ivy's invitation, with Jordana's and Gloria's wholehearted agreement.

Jordana laughed. "That's because you always came to me for everything."

Hannah pursed her lips to hide her smile, but it broke free. "I try to make the smart move as often as possible."

Gloria set her water glass down after taking a sip. "I have a premonition Rhonda is going to be completely different this time around. She actually apologized to everyone in the staff meeting. Even Knox Turner."

They all knew how Rhonda felt about Knox. Her first day back yesterday had forced her to dive right into the Monday staff meeting. Talk about a trial by fire.

"At least she didn't try to demote you, Ivy." Jordana stabbed her fork in the air. "I would never have let her get away with it, I promise."

"Thank you. I know you wouldn't." But Ivy had already fought that battle herself. The new dynamic was working out. She was learning so much. Jordana was a great teacher. Given time, she hoped Rhonda would be, too.

"I have an announcement." Ivy held up her water glass. The other ladies raised theirs. "I'm going back to college."

Gloria gasped. "That's fabulous."

"Are you going to study Human Relations?" Hannah asked. It was a logical choice.

"I'll be majoring in child development. I've been thinking a lot about what I want to do." She and Brett had discussed her future. *Their* future. She'd mentioned it once, when they were in Tahoe, but he'd remembered. "I've always wanted to stay home with Joy. Homeschooling."

"You talked about that." Jordana sounded disappointed. As if she'd enjoyed mentoring Ivy.

"Right. And you both gave me the brilliant idea. When I'm done with school, I'd like to start a homeschool program. Something where I get all the homeschooled kids together for fields trips. An association. It could be a really good adjunct to what parents are already doing for their kids. I don't want to do day care. This would be more like teaching." The more she'd talked about it, the more Brett had encouraged her. Believed in her. She could turn it into a business, with his help and support.

"That sounds fantastic, Ivy." Gloria's smile brimmed with enthusiasm.

"Totally exciting news. You'll do great." Hannah gave her

blessing. It was wonderful to be surrounded by people who believed in you. Even when you believed in yourself.

"I think it's great." Then Jordana pouted. "But I thought we'd keep on working together."

Ivy laughed, patting Jordana's hand. "Of course we will. It's going to be a couple of years before I get there."

"I hate to rain on your parade." Jordana frowned. "But since it's not in the same line, the company won't pay for your expenses."

"I know. But there are scholarships for working moms." Brett had been checking the Internet for her.

Jordana smacked her forehead. "I can help with that. There's all sorts of resources I can turn you onto."

"Thank you." Friends were fabulous. She'd gone so long without any that she'd forgotten how good they could be.

Hannah circled her finger in the air. "So, now, a little bird whispered something else in my ear recently." She cocked one eyebrow at Ivy.

She knew about Hannah's gossipy little birds. "What did they tell you?" Ivy felt the smile rising in her, but she kept it off her lips for now.

"Something, something." Hannah looked at the ceiling, then back at Ivy. "Something about the CEO."

Ivy tutted, then couldn't stop the smile. "Where do you hear this stuff?"

Hannah shrugged. "Around. Ears to the ground and all that. So spill."

She glanced at Gloria. Then Jordana. They both already knew. Ivy had been bursting, but she'd sworn them to secrecy. That confidential tidbit had been dropped this morning in the staff meeting.

So Ivy could say it out loud. "The CEO and I are getting married."

Hannah smiled like the cat that ate the cream. Then started on the next saucer. "I knew it."

"Who told you?"

None of her friends would have gossiped, and certainly not Rhonda, who was still on probation as far as Brett was concerned. When he'd disclosed to his staff that he was dating an employee, Rhonda hadn't even freaked. So it had to be someone else in that meeting. Someone on the executive team.

But Hannah didn't say a thing, zipping her lips with a smile.

Not that it really mattered. Ivy had wanted it to come out. She didn't want to hide. Not from her friends. And not from the rest of the company either.

"We're so happy for you." Jordana's eyes were shining with tears.

Gloria toasted. "You two are perfect for each other." Then she rolled her eyes and snickered. "Especially after the way Brett shows around those pictures of his granddaughter. He's going to be a fabulous father to your little girl."

"Joy loves him. And he loves her." She sighed. "And I love him, too."

Hannah leaned in. "So dish. We want to hear everything. How it all happened." She made a gesture over her head. "Cone of silence. Whatever you say won't leave this table. I listen. But I don't talk."

Ivy told them everything.

Well, everything except the deliciously kinky X-rated parts.

10/06/2020

10/07/2022

ABOUT THE AUTHOR

NY Times and USA Today Bestselling author Jasmine Haynes loves giving readers sexy, classy stories about real issues like growing older, facing divorce, starting over. Her books have passion, heart, humor, and happy endings, even if they aren't always traditional. She also writes gritty, paranormal mysteries in the Max Starr series. As Jennifer Skully, she writes laugh-out-loud romantic comedies laced with a heavy dose of mystery. Look for Jennifer's new series written with Bella Andre, starting with *Breathless in Love*, The Maverick Billionaires Book 1. Having penned stories since the moment she learned to write, Jasmine now lives in the Redwoods of Northern California with her husband and their adorable nuisance of a cat who totally runs the household. Join her newsletter for updates on contests, new releases, and freebies by going to jasminehaynes.com.

Connect with Jennifer Skully & Jasmine Haynes

Newsletter signup: http://bit.ly/SkullyNews

Jennifer's Website: www.jenniferskully.com

Blog: www.jasminehaynes.blogspot.com

Facebook: www.facebook.com/jasminehaynesauthor

Twitter: https://twitter.com/jasminehaynes1

Goodreads Jasmine:
www.goodreads.com/author/show/130583.Jasmine_Haynes
Goodreads Jennifer:
www.goodreads.com/author/show/332472.Jennifer_Skully
Bookbub Jennifer:
www.bookbub.com/authors/jennifer-skully
Bookbub Jasmine:
www.bookbub.com/authors/jasmine-haynes

Made in the USA
Monee, IL
07 September 2020

41613029R00163